"I've brought your daughter."

Amber eyes set in a tiny heart-shaped face peered around the man's leg. "Yasmin?" Linnea whispered, crouching and holding out her arms. "Yasmin!"

Talal urged the child toward her, and Linnea reached and gathered the girl into her arms, tears forming in her eyes. "I'll never tire of looking at her sweet face," Linnea said. "I've missed her so." Tears gleamed in her eyes, and she blinked them away before she started frowning. "No," she whispered. "Oh, please, God, no. She can't be—she isn't—she's not my Yasmin. She's not my birth daughter. I can tell by her eyes."

Talal stared at her with frank disbelief. "On such flimsy evidence do you expect me to return her and produce another Yasmin for you to inspect?"

"No," she said in a quiet tone. "I'll never give up searching for the daughter I birthed, but this Yasmin is also mine—my gift daughter."

Dear Reader,

At long last, summertime has arrived! Romance is in full bloom this month with first-time fathers, fun-filled adventure—and scandalous love.

In commemoration of Father's Day, award-winning Cheryl Reavis delivers this month's THAT'S MY BABY! *Little Darlin'* is a warm, uplifting tale about a cynical sergeant who suddenly takes on the unexpected roles of husband—and father!—when he discovers an abandoned tyke who couldn't possibly be his...or could she?

In these next three books, love defies all odds. First, a mysterious loner drifts back into town in *A Hero's Homecoming* by Laurie Paige—book four in the unforgettable MONTANA MAVERICKS: RETURN TO WHITEHORN series. Then fate passionately unites star-crossed lovers in *The Cougar*—Lindsay McKenna's dramatic finish to her mesmerizing COWBOYS OF THE SOUTHWEST series. And a reticent rancher vows to melt his pregnant bride's wounded heart in *For the Love of Sam* by Jackie Merritt—book one in THE BENNING LEGACY, a new crossline series with Silhouette Desire.

And you won't want to miss the thrilling conclusion to Andrea Edwards's engaging duet, DOUBLE WEDDING. When a small-town country vet switches places with his jet-setting twin, he discovers that appearances can be *very* deceiving in *Who Will She Wed?* Finally this month, *Baby of Mine* by Jane Toombs is an intense, emotional story about a devoted mother who will do *anything* to retrieve her beloved baby girl, including marry a handsome—dangerous!—stranger!

I hope you enjoy these books, and each and every story to come!

Sincerely,

Tara Gavin
Senior Editor & Editorial Coordinator

Please address questions and book requests to:
Silhouette Reader Service
U.S.: 3010 Walden Ave., P.O. Box 1325, Buffalo, NY 14269
Canadian: P.O. Box 609, Fort Erie, Ont. L2A 5X3

JANE TOOMBS
BABY OF MINE

Silhouette®

SPECIAL EDITION®

Published by Silhouette Books

America's Publisher of Contemporary Romance

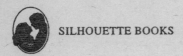

SILHOUETTE BOOKS

RECYCLED PAPER

ISBN 0-373-24182-8

BABY OF MINE

Printed in U.S.A.

Books by Jane Toombs

Silhouette Special Edition

Nobody's Baby #1081
Baby of Mine #1182

Silhouette Shadows

Return to Bloodstone House #5
Dark Enchantment #12
What Waits Below #16
The Volan Curse #35
The Woman in White #50
*The Abandoned Bride #56

*Always a Bridesmaid

Previously published under the pseudonym Diana Stuart

Silhouette Special Edition

Out of a Dream #353
The Moon Pool #671

Silhouette Desire

Prime Specimen #172
Leader of the Pack #238
The Shadow Between #257

JANE TOOMBS

was born in California, raised in the upper peninsula of Michigan and has moved from New York to Nevada as a result of falling in love with the state and a Nevadan. Jane has five children, two stepchildren and seven grandchildren. Her interests include gardening, reading and knitting.

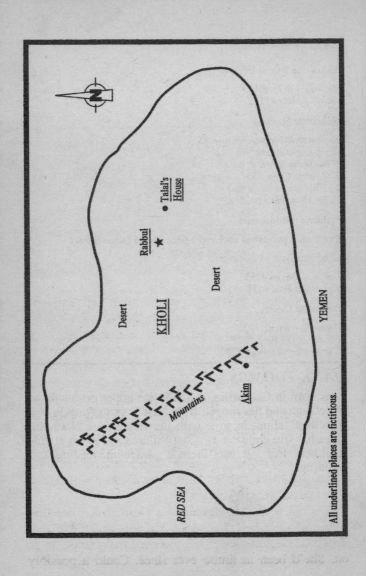

All underlined places are fictitious.

Chapter One

Why didn't it rain? The clouds, dark and ominous, obscured the hot July sun, and thunder muttered in the distance. Not a leaf stirred in the humid, oppressive air. Standing on her small patio at the rear of her condo, Linnea Swanson breathed in earthy dampness along with the sharp scent of geraniums seeping through the wooden wall screening the neighboring patio.

The few flowers she'd planted had been eaten by deer. The only blooms they didn't seem to relish were the spring daffodils, long gone by now. She minded, but she didn't blame the deer. The condo where she'd chosen to live had been built, after all, in a woods, and the deer had been here first.

She'd left the city for upstate New York more than two years ago, and the woods had appealed to her then as a place to hide while she gathered the strength to go on. She'd been in limbo ever since. Could it possibly be true the agony of waiting and wondering was coming to an end? Linnea glanced at the brooding sky and sighed. How much longer?

Looking at her watch, she saw it was after five. Before she thought about dinner, she ought to go in and put the finishing touches on the final illustration she was doing for the book on ancient Greek medicine. There was something not quite right about the way she'd drawn Galen's hands as the old Greek physician pointed out the sections of the brain. The contract for the illustrations was the most lucrative yet and she could use the final payment money. Thank God she'd found a way to make her minor artistic talent pay, because the money in the Manhattan bank was for another purpose and she refused to touch it to live on.

No matter how much she'd spent from that special account, though, she hadn't been successful in her search. Every agency she'd contacted came to the same dead end. And heaven only knows how many letters she'd written to no avail to various politicians in Washington. If the senator from her district hadn't suddenly needed a weapon to use against the president's policy concerning the Middle East, especially Kholi, she'd be no further ahead.

But was she really ahead? True, there'd been the encouraging phone call from the senator's office with a follow-up letter. That had been a month ago. Since then, nothing.

A streak of lightning split the clouds. Seconds later, thunder rolled, closer now. Linnea put out her hand, palm up, hoping to feel drops of rain. When none fell, she shook her head, opened the screen door to the kitchen and went inside. Dear God, she was tired of waiting.

* * *

As Talal Zohir turned his red sports car off the highway onto a local road, thunder growled a warning. Eyeing the ever-darker clouds, he pulled over to the shoulder.

Speaking in Arabic, he said, "Time to put up the top if we don't want to get wet."

The tiny girl seat-belted in next to him looked confused until he activated the mechanism, then shrank into herself, gazing upward with fearful fascination as the top slid into place. He took her hand in his and she gripped his forefinger tightly.

"It's all right," he said, smiling as reassuringly as he could. "I'm here, nothing will hurt you." She didn't offer a smile in return—he had yet to see her smile—but she did relax her grip on his finger.

As he pulled back onto the road, Talal began looking for a phone. He hadn't called from Washington because he wasn't certain whether he'd arrive at a reasonable hour today, in which case he'd planned to spend the night somewhere in the area and delay until tomorrow before calling the woman. But they'd gotten an early start, traffic had been remarkably light, the various state highway patrols hadn't spotted him and here they were.

He grinned, remembering his brother's prediction that red cars driven by speeding drivers were certain ticket getters. So far, on this present visit to the U.S., at least, he'd proven Zeid wrong.

The girl tugged at his sleeve. He turned to her, raising his eyebrows. "What is it, Yasmin?" he asked in Arabic.

"Mama?" she said.

"Soon," he told her.

She lowered her head, bringing the bent knuckle of her forefinger to her mouth.

"Don't be afraid," he said, knowing she was. Poor little thing, her world had changed so drastically in the past month that it was a wonder she'd been able to adapt at all. He admired her courage. Despite being surrounded by strangers in what was for her increasingly alien surroundings, never once had she cried. In the short time they'd been together, he'd grown attached to Yasmin.

Not that he relished the assignment his great-uncle had given him. But, as they said in Kholi, "A narrow house can accommodate a hundred friends and a wide palace cannot accommodate two enemies." It doesn't pay to anger your king, even if he is a relative. Or, perhaps, especially if he is. When he commands, you don't argue.

Of course, there was always a bonus waiting for him in America—in Nevada, to be specific. He intended to finish his mission here in New York as quickly as possible and fly west immediately.

Catching sight of a street name, Talal braked and swerved to the left. Almost immediately the address he sought turned up on his right. He shook his head. Not a phone anywhere in sight. He slowed and pulled to the curb, debating whether or not to go in search of a phone before arriving on the woman's doorstep. No, he was here, best to complete the mission. Obviously she would have been notified by someone in Washington that he'd be coming.

He drove into the parking lot, found the slot that matched the woman's condo number and noted a car occupied it. Good, she was home. He parked in an empty slot and coaxed a reluctant Yasmin from the car.

"You're tired, I'll carry you," he told her still speaking in Arabic.

She put her arms around his neck, nestling against him trustingly, and he realized how much he was going to miss her. His time with Yasmin had taught him how different little girls were from little boys. Even at eight months of age, Danny had never seemed fragile to him, but in his arms, three-year-old Yasmin felt as frail as the baby bird he'd once rescued when he was a child and carried home in his hands. He'd raised it despite his grandmother's objections and tried not to cry when the bird finally flew away for good.

But Yasmin didn't need him to raise her.

A few drops of rain fell as he carried her toward the door marked with the proper number. Though his watch told him it was only six, the lowering sky darkened the waning day to twilight. The rumble of thunder sounded farther off now; perhaps the storm would pass them by.

He paused on the mat outside the door, noting light shining from the tiny windows on either side before he pushed the bell. He heard it ring faintly inside, then footsteps approached the door. Yasmin squirmed in his arms, so he eased her down onto her feet. She promptly took refuge behind him.

Linnea flicked on the outside light, glancing through one of the windows before unlocking the door. The neighborhood was safe enough, but you never knew. She drew in her breath at the sight of the dark-haired man standing there. Though he wore an open-necked shirt and casual pants rather than the Muslim robe and headdress, she knew he was an Arab. Good-looking, of course—like Malik, they always were. Could he be an emissary of Malik's?

Wary, she put the chain on, unlocked the door, eased

it ajar and peered through the opening. "What do you want?" she demanded.

"Are you Linnea Khaldun?" he asked, instead of replying.

How well she knew that Middle Eastern arrogance. "My name is no longer Khaldun," she said coolly. "I am Linnea Swanson. Who are *you?*"

"Talal Zohir. Please, don't be frightened. I regret I was unable to call ahead, but I'm the one you must be expecting."

Linnea's heart began to pound. Was it possible...? She'd thought he was alone, but now she strained to see if anyone else was there. Glimpsing something move down low behind him, she caught her breath. A child! Undoing the chain, she flung the door open, crying, "Did you bring her?"

"Yes," he said. "I've brought your daughter."

Amber eyes set in a tiny heart-shaped face peered around the man's leg. "Yasmin?" Linnea whispered, crouching and holding out her arms. "Yasmin!"

He urged the child toward her, and Linnea reached and gathered the girl into her arms, tears forming in her eyes. She felt the child stiffly resisting her embrace and murmured brokenly, "I'm your mother, darling. Your mama."

"Mama?" Yasmin spoke so softly Linnea almost didn't hear her.

"She doesn't understand English," the man said. "Only Arabic. But the word *mama* is the same in nearly all languages."

An almost forgotten Arabic word for *yes* slid into Linnea's mind. "*Aiwa,*" she said. "*Aiwa,* Mama."

Yasmin melted against her and clung fiercely. Lifting her, blinking back tears, Linnea rose and carried the little girl inside, only half aware of the man following her and closing the door behind them.

Dropping onto the couch, Linnea cuddled Yasmin, crooning to her wordlessly, her heart too full to speak. The long and fruitless search was over, the miracle she'd prayed for had arrived. At last her daughter was back in her arms where she belonged. She'd never let her go again.

Brilliant light flashed through the windows, and the lamps flickered and went out as a rattling clap of thunder shook the house. Yasmin cried out in alarm, and in the dark, Linnea stroked her hair, trying to calm her as rain pelted against the windows.

The man spoke soothingly in Arabic, and Linnea remembered from her meager store of the language that one of the words meant *safe*. The child's frantic grip eased slightly. Apparently she trusted the man. What was his name? Talal something.

"Candles?" he asked.

"On the fireplace mantel in holders," Linnea said. "The matches are in the silver box at one end."

Talal found the matches and lit first one candle, then the other. He carried the second over to the couch and set it on the coffee table. In the flickering light the woman's face looked soft and luminous, her amber eyes reflecting the candle flame. Eyes like her daughter's.

He extracted a tiny, worn silver ring from his pocket and offered it to her on his palm. "Yasmin's baby ring," he said. "I thought it best to keep it safe until I brought her to you."

She stared at the ring for long moments before she reached to take it. For some reason the brief brush of her fingers against his palm tingled through him. He watched her try to slip the ring on Yasmin's finger and saw it fit only the smallest one.

"My grandmother's baby ring," she said softly. "My mother's and then mine. Yasmin was wearing it when she was—was taken. Thank you for returning the ring. And for—" Her voice broke and she shook her head, unable to go on.

He bowed slightly. "My duty and my pleasure to bring her to her mother. Yasmin is a beautiful child, a daughter to be proud of. I regret—" He spread his hands in lieu of words, recalling his great-uncle's bluntness.

"Never trust a Khaldun. Leave it to them to endanger our country's position with America. If that trouble-maker Malik wasn't dead I swear I'd have him beheaded. Thanks to Allah we've found the missing child and so can return her to show our good faith."

Talal pulled out Yasmin's American birth certificate, given to him with the ring, and placed it on the table. Yasmin, who'd been examining the ring on her finger, looked up at him and reached out a hand, patting the couch cushion, asking without words for him to sit beside her mother.

He hesitated, despite the pleading in Yasmin's eyes. The woman's attitude toward him had been distinctly hostile until she'd realized her daughter was with him.

"Do sit down," Linnea said, apparently understanding what Yasmin wanted.

He wondered how much Arabic she knew. Surely some. Malik Khaldun would have insisted his wife learn his language.

As if reading his mind, she said, "I don't recall very many Arabic words, but it's obvious Yasmin feels more secure with you near her."

He eased down, leaving a gap between the two of them, finding, to his surprise, that he wished he could be close enough to feel her warmth against him.

Bad idea. The Kholi phrase for American girls translated as *play-pretties*. Linnea was pretty enough, but any fool could see she was no plaything. Even Malik, the great seducer, had had to marry her to accomplish his goal. Talal didn't plan to marry again. Ever.

"She *is* beautiful, isn't she?" Linnea said, positioning Yasmin slightly away from her while, in the candlelight, she gazed at the little girl with such love that Talal's throat constricted. Taken back to his troubled childhood, he wondered if his own mother had ever looked at him like that. "I'll never tire of looking at her sweet face," Linnea said. "I've missed her so." Tears gleamed in her eyes and she blinked them away.

Still immersed in the past, Talal was asking himself if his mother could have missed him so acutely, when the lights came back on. As his vision adjusted to the sudden brightness, he watched, perplexed, while Linnea's expression as she gazed at Yasmin changed to frowning confusion, then stark disbelief. "No," she whispered. "Oh, please God, no."

He leaned toward her, concerned, and she looked away from the child, shot him an accusing glance and gasped hoarsely, "She can't be—she isn't—she's not my Yasmin, she's not my daughter."

As if understanding every word, Yasmin stared fearfully from one to the other of them. She opened her mouth and screamed, a cry of terrified anguish. Biting her lip, Linnea clasped the girl against her breast once more.

"See what you've done!" she snapped at him, then turned her attention to the child, rocking back and forth, holding Yasmin close while she murmured, "There, there, sweetheart. Nothing's your fault. I won't let anything happen to you, you're safe with me, you'll always be safe with me. Always. No matter what."

Apparently understanding her meaning, if not the words, Yasmin nestled against her.

Was this woman crazy? Talal asked himself. What had he done other than act as the king's emissary and bring the child to her? She'd said herself the ring came from her family, and he'd delivered Yasmin's birth certificate, issued by New York State, clearly stating Linnea Swanson was the baby's mother and Malik Khaldun the father. This child was exactly the right age, and his great-uncle had assured him the girl was Yasmin Khaldun. The king's word could be trusted implicitly; beyond any doubt he believed the child was Linnea's daughter. Had the king been fooled by the man who'd brought the child to him? Talal shook his head—it would be suicidal for any Kholi to hoodwink the king.

He'd seen for himself that mother and child had similar and unusual tawny eyes. Though Linnea's hair was several shades lighter than Yasmin's chestnut brown, mother and child both had slightly curly hair. What had led Linnea to suddenly reject the daughter she'd welcomed so lovingly? A child she hadn't set eyes on since the girl was a three-month-old baby.

"Babies grow and change," he said, thinking of going-on-two-year-old Danny. "My son—"

Linnea, her cheek pressed against Yasmin's hair, said, "Shut up. Please just shut up. I don't want you to upset her again."

Couldn't the idiot see that any discussion now might set Yasmin off again? Linnea asked herself. Whatever plot those miserable Kholis had devised, the little girl was innocent. A sweet, lovable innocent. Her warmth and weight felt so good, so right in Linnea's arms. The child may not be—wasn't—her Yasmin, but she'd never allow anyone to hurt the poor little thing. Cuddling her protectively, Linnea vowed she wouldn't give up Yasmin. If she did, the child would undoubtedly be taken back to Kholi—an unthinkable fate for a girl.

Besides, how could she ever part with this waif who needed her so desperately?

Her attention focused on Yasmin, Linnea barely noticed Talal pacing back and forth in her living room, but she sensed his annoyance and impatience disturbing the air around her. At least he had the sense to keep his mouth shut. Other than that, she found nothing in his favor. Kholi men were all alike—domineering, selfish and not to be trusted.

Yasmin relaxed against her, eyes closing, until at last she slept. Rising carefully from the couch, Linnea carried her to the master bedroom, only a few steps down the hall. She eased Yasmin onto the bed and covered her with a quilt. One edge of the bed was against the wall, and she barricaded the open side with bolsters and pillows to prevent the girl from rolling off in her sleep.

For a long moment she stood looking down at the sleeping child in the dim light filtering in from the hall. Rain still pattered against the windows, but gently now. Soothingly. Though the old, familiar ache had returned to her heart, the pain of loss was lessened by the sight of Yasmin asleep in her bed.

I'll never give up searching for the daughter I gave birth to, she told herself, *but this Yasmin is also mine— my gift daughter.*

At the door she hesitated, deciding to leave it open. If the girl roused from hearing them talk it would be more reassuring than waking to find herself shut into an unknown room alone.

"She sleeps?" Talal asked in a low voice when she returned to the living room.

Linnea nodded and squared off to confront him. He'd giving up pacing and was now leaning against the mantel as though he hadn't a care in the world. The scowl on his face, though, belied the casual pose.

"Why did you bring me the wrong child?" she asked bluntly.

"Why do you insist she is?" he countered. "You have the birth certificate and the ring. She exactly matches your description of your daughter."

A frisson of fear shot through her at his words. The ring had been her baby's. Where had this man acquired it? And the birth certificate?

As if anticipating her question, Talal said, "The king of Kholi himself gave me the ring and birth certificate. They, with the child, came from someone who swore on his life that the girl was Yasmin Khaldun, an orphan. As the king, my great-uncle's word is above question."

Orphan. "Malik is dead?" she asked in surprise, forgetting for the moment that the orphan in question wasn't the daughter he'd fathered.

"Malik Khaldun was accidentally shot and killed over a year ago," Talal said. Something in his voice made her doubt the shooting had been an accident, but in her relief at knowing her ex-husband would never menace her again she didn't question what had been said.

Belatedly she realized what Talal had said—the king was his great-uncle. That would make him a member of the royal family, one of those Zohirs Malik had hated. "You're a Zohir?" she asked.

He nodded curtly.

A Kholi prince. Which didn't change the situation in the slightest. If Malik was dead, their child truly was an orphan as far as having a father was concerned. Still, he had family, and knowing Kholi customs, she was sure the Khalduns would never willingly give up any child related to them by blood. Is that why this little orphan had been substituted?

"Someone in or from Kholi is not telling the truth," she said, keeping the anger from her voice as best she could.

He smiled thinly. "Then you believe one or all of us is lying. A strong accusation. Yet at first you accepted Yasmin as your daughter. What changed your mind?"

"She isn't the Yasmin born to me—I could tell by her eyes once I got a good look at them."

"Eyes so very like your own."

Linnea shook her head. "Different from mine and from my baby's."

His expression showed frank disbelief. "On such flimsy evidence do you expect me to return her to my country and produce another Yasmin for you to inspect?"

"No!" Belatedly aware she'd raised her voice, she glanced over her shoulder, but no sound came from the bedroom. "No," she repeated in a quieter tone. "Yasmin will never go back to Kholi. You gave her to me and she stays here. I intend to raise her as a daughter. But you can inform your king I still want my own daughter returned to me."

Talal shook his head, muttering, an Arabic word that sounded vaguely familiar to her. She couldn't recall what it meant, but she was sure it was an insult.

"Have the courtesy to speak English," she snapped.

He dipped his head in silent apology. When he met her gaze again, though, she saw the anger simmering in his dark eyes and forced herself not to take a step backward. When Malik grew angry, violence had followed. She had no reason to believe Talal would be any different—wasn't he also a Kholi?

"You don't accept Yasmin as your child, yet you refuse to give her up, is that your position?" Talal's even voice gave no hint of the rage she knew must be smoldering inside him. Rage at her, a mere woman, who'd dared to question not only his judgment but the king's.

"I prefer to put it slightly differently," she said coolly. "She's not the baby I bore, but I accept her as mine, though not in place of my birth daughter. In addition to. Yasmin needs a mother, she needs *me* as her mother."

His hands shot out. Before she could recoil, they'd fastened onto her shoulders, holding her where she stood. "I won't have that little girl hurt." He spoke between his teeth.

Linnea blinked in surprise. Was his anger at her actually based on concern about Yasmin's welfare? Hard to believe he cared that much about a child he scarcely knew. "Yasmin is my gift daughter," she said. "How can you think I'd harm her in any way?"

He echoed her words. "Gift daughter." His expression lightened, the dark scowl fading. His tight grip on her shoulders eased, and when he let her go, his hands slipped down along her bare upper arms to her elbows in what was almost a caress before he stepped back.

Annoyingly, his touch tingled through her. She eyed him warily. He smiled, white teeth against his dark skin, a charming smile. Kholi men could be charming when they wished—she knew that. Then why was she reacting to it? Recalling his mention of a son, she reminded herself that a son usually meant a wife.

"We'll call a truce for tonight," he announced. "I'll bring in Yasmin's belongings, leave her with you and return in the morning for further discussion."

She was about to agree when a howl from the bedroom froze them both. Recovering first, Linnea dashed down the hall, ran into the bedroom and picked up the sobbing Yasmin. Turning with the child in her arms, she found Talal behind her.

Yasmin reached for him, grasping the hand he held out to her, but when he would have taken her into his arms, she shook her head. "Mama," she sobbed, still clinging to Linnea. "Talal," she added, gripping his hand fiercely. Yasmin jabbered other words in Arabic, hanging on to both of them for dear life.

"She's afraid I'm going to leave her," he said to Linnea. "But she also wants to stay with you."

"Hadn't we decided she would?"

He half smiled. "It's more complicated than that. Yasmin doesn't want me to go. She insists on me staying here, too."

Chapter Two

Standing in her bedroom holding Yasmin, Linnea stared unhappily at Talal. The last thing she wanted was to have him sleep overnight at her place. If she could go by the expression on his face, he seemed to feel the same way. Yet how could they disappoint Yasmin? From the child's point of view, Talal must be the only familiar person in a world full of strangers whose talk she didn't understand.

"I do have a guest room down the hall," Linnea said reluctantly. "You could sleep there."

He shrugged. "It appears we don't have a choice."

By the tone of his voice he'd apparently noticed she hadn't exactly welcomed him to spend the night. Well, it was true she didn't want him to stay. The sooner he was out of her house—and her life—the better. She didn't trust any Kholi male.

To be fair, he hadn't actually done anything to offend

her. Not yet, anyway. And Yasmin obviously trusted him—a point in his favor.

"Please tell Yasmin you're not leaving," she said.

He spoke to the child and Yasmin answered with a spurt of Arabic, at the same time releasing Talal's hand.

"She wants a drink of milk," he said. "Chocolate, if you have any." He smiled one-sidedly. "I'm afraid that's my fault—I introduced her to chocolate milk, one of my vices."

"I've got milk and I think there's some chocolate syrup left. I'm sort of a chocolate freak myself." Still carrying Yasmin, Linnea started for the door and he stepped aside to let her pass.

As she entered the kitchen, with Talal behind her, she smiled to herself. Some vice, chocolate milk. What, she wondered, were his others? Undoubtedly she was better off not knowing.

"Let me take Yasmin," he said, plucking the girl from her arms and perching on one of the counter stools with Yasmin on his lap.

"I never thought to ask if you two were hungry," Linnea said, chagrined it hadn't occurred to her earlier. The unexpectedness of Yasmin's arrival, the shock of believing she'd recovered her long-lost baby only to find she was wrong, still had her off balance.

Anger at Talal no longer seemed appropriate. In ancient times emperors tended to kill the messenger who brought bad news—isn't that sort of what she irrationally had wanted to do to Talal? To be fair, it was entirely possible, wasn't it, that he could be innocent of any deviousness?

She shouldn't assume he was guilty simply because he'd been chosen to bring the little girl to her. Maybe he wasn't a part of the conspiracy, maybe he actually believed the child was her birth daughter. Glancing at Yasmin, Linnea smiled at the solemn expression on the child's face as she watched every move "Mama" made. There was no question in her mind—or her heart—that a bond had formed between them when she first took Yasmin into her arms.

I'll be your mama, she vowed. *I am your mama. None of this is your fault, and I won't let you suffer because of those uncaring, cruel villains back in Kholi.*

"We stopped to eat at several fast-food places on the way," Talal said. "Yasmin's fascinated with their children's play equipment. She's never seen anything like that before."

Since the child couldn't understand and therefore wouldn't be upset by her questions, Linnea decided to ask him if he knew where Yasmin had been living before she'd been produced for the king. She didn't recall seeing any orphanages when she'd been in Kholi.

"Was Yasmin in a foster home?" she asked.

"Sorry. I know nothing of how or where she lived before we were introduced. It didn't occur to me to ask."

Yasmin twisted in his arms, pointing to the banana hanger on the counter. "*Mooz,*" she said.

"Bananas," Talal said. "*Mooz*—banana."

"Do give her one."

Yasmin did her best to pronounce the unfamiliar syllables, and as Talal broke a banana free of the bunch and began to peel it for the little girl, it dawned on Linnea that this wasn't the first time he'd tried to teach the child English equivalents for Arabic words. His thoughtfulness in looking ahead for Yasmin impressed her against her will.

"I wonder if all kids like bananas," he said. "My

son, Danny the Tiger, would eat his weight in them if allowed to.''

Linnea stirred chocolate syrup into the milk she'd poured into a small glass, thinking this was the second time he'd mentioned the boy. It occurred to her that Danny wasn't the usual Kholi name. "How old is your son?" she asked.

He smiled. "Almost two. I can't wait to see him."

Something about his last few words puzzled her. Hadn't he just come from Kholi? From home? Therefore, he must have last seen his son no more than a week ago. Well, it was none of her business—what did she care about Talal?

Yasmin, having taken several bites from the banana, held it up to Talal's mouth and he obligingly bit off a chunk. Yasmin then offered the banana to Linnea. She hesitated, not so much from fear of germs as from the intimacy of putting her lips where his had just been. As if reading her mind, he grinned challengingly at her.

She couldn't refuse without hurting Yasmin's feelings. Stepping closer, she took a bite of the banana, murmured her thanks and was rewarded by the girl's shy smile.

''You're the lucky recipient of her first smile,'' Talal told Linnea.

Yasmin finished the banana and handed the empty peel to Talal. Then she drank the chocolate milk Linnea had mixed for her. When she was through, Talal spoke to her in Arabic, got up from the stool and set her on her feet. Yasmin trailed him from the kitchen to the front door, where he said one word to her in a firm, no-nonsense tone.

Yasmin stopped by the door, sliding the knuckle of her right forefinger into her mouth. Linnea came up beside her and put a hand on her shoulder. Together they watched from the open door while he crossed to the parking lot and disappeared around a corner. The rain, now no more than a fine mist, must be distorting her vision, Linnea decided, because he appeared to have a slight limp she hadn't noticed earlier.

"He'll be back," she said, hoping the girl would be reassured by the tone of her voice. "He's gone to get your things."

When he came into sight again, Yasmin took her finger from her mouth and murmured, "Talal," as though his name was a talisman.

After he set a large suitcase and a little traveling case in the master bedroom, Linnea showed him where the guest room was, just down the hall. He carried a small case with him into the guest room, Yasmin pattering at his heels.

When he set the case onto the floor, Yasmin stared from him to the bed, grasping his hand and pulling until he followed her.

She led him into the master bedroom, jabbering away as she pointed to the bed and then to herself, lastly to Linnea. Though Linnea didn't understand the words, the meaning was very clear. Yasmin wanted all three of them to sleep together.

"We've been sharing rooms on the trip, though not beds," he explained. "I suppose that's confused her."

"She's afraid to let you out of her sight. And no wonder. You're the only one who understands what she's saying."

"Your Arabic will come back to you," he said. "And Yasmin's already learning English."

Linnea shook her head ruefully. "She'll be chattering away in English long before I recall enough Arabic to form a coherent sentence. Meanwhile, we have a more immediate problem to solve.''

He slanted her a look that made her catch her breath, a look that suggested he wouldn't mind the three of them sleeping in one bed.

''No way,'' she muttered.

He raised his eyebrows inquiringly, but she didn't explain, instead saying, ''I'll put Yasmin to bed here and we'll both stay with her until she falls asleep. Then you can retire to the guest room.''

Talal hadn't expected anything else, but that didn't stop him from imagining Linnea in bed with him. Minus Yasmin, that is. He wondered what she wore to sleep in. American girls were fond of sleep-Ts, but perhaps she preferred sheer gowns. Or nothing at all. She had such pale, lustrous skin, he could imagine its smoothness under his fingers....

Enough! This was not the time. Or the woman. Definitely not the woman. They would do as she suggested, remain with the child until sleep claimed her. But then, he and Linnea must settle this nonsensical notion of hers. Of course Yasmin was her daughter. It must be the suddenness of his arrival that had, as they said here, rattled her cage, jarring her mind somewhat askew. He really should have called ahead. That wasn't why she was wary of him, though.

After telling Yasmin from now on it was Mama's duty to see that she bathed and changed into nightclothes, he retreated to the living room while Linnea readied the child for bed and tucked her in. Prowling about, he noticed some drawings on a desk in the corner and paused to study them. The nearby artist's gear led him to believe they were hers. Well executed, certainly, though the subject matter wasn't to his taste. He preferred brains to be covered by skulls, scalps and hair.

He heard Yasmin call for him plaintively from the master bedroom, reminding him once again of the imperious squeaks of the baby bird he'd raised as a child. *Come at once, I need you.*

"Both the mother and the father bird feed their fledglings," his grandfather had told him when he'd asked permission to keep the helpless little thing. "Your grandmother has already told you she doesn't care to have this bird around, so she won't help. You'll have to be mother and father in order to raise it."

Which he'd done. Now, with Yasmin, there was someone to share in her raising. He blinked and shook his head. What was he thinking? He'd done his part, he was no longer involved. Linnea was capable of caring for her daughter without any help from him.

He entered the bedroom to find Yasmin sitting up in the bed. She immediately demanded a story. "Not until you lie down," he told her in Arabic.

She squirmed around until she lay flat and let Linnea cover her with a sheet. "About that boy named Saud and the Ghoul," Yasmin said. "And the little sister."

The tale was one he had been told as a child, about the Ghoul who haunts the great desert. At first, despite the fact it was no more than a cautionary child's story, a fairy tale, he'd thought it might scare Yasmin so he hadn't told it until he'd run out of all the others he could remember. He'd been wrong to worry—Saud's escapade was her favorite.

He'd learned to draw it out, speaking slowly and repeating words and phrases to give Yasmin a chance to grow drowsy before he finished. He hadn't quite gotten to Saud's meeting with the Ghoul when he saw Yasmin's eyes droop shut. He lowered his voice, slowing to a singsong as he continued. As always, he went on to the end before stopping.

He nodded at Linnea, inclining his head toward the door. They both went out and he followed her into the kitchen.

"She fell asleep long before you finished," Linnea said over her shoulder.

"As a child I was taught never to leave a tale half told."

"Would you like coffee?" she asked. "There's still some in the pot, though it may be a trifle bitter by now. And maybe a sandwich?"

"Coffee, yes, please," he said. "What's in the pot will be fine."

"I have some homemade blueberry cobbler left."

Ah, a woman who cooked. Yasmin was fortunate. "You've tempted me," he said, smiling. "I can't resist your temptation."

Before she turned away, he saw with amusement that her cheeks had grown remarkably pink. He preferred to think she blushed because she was attracted to him, though he knew the likelihood was greater of her being angry with him.

The cobbler was excellent. So was the coffee, strong and aromatic, exactly as he enjoyed it. She fixed herself a glass of chocolate milk and sat one stool away from him, sipping at the milk while he ate.

"You are talented at more than art," he told her when he'd finished.

"Thanks," she said.

He decided to begin bluntly. "You don't like me being in your house," he said.

She bit her lip. "It's not you, not exactly."

"Because I am Kholi?"

Taking a deep breath, she let it out slowly. "I don't want you to think I'm prejudiced but..." Her words trailed off.

"But you were married to Malik Khaldun," he said, finishing for her. "Since you divorced him, it was, I assume, a negative experience. Be assured all Kholi men are not like him."

"You knew Malik?"

He nodded. "I did. We were not friends."

"Then you can understand why I divorced him."

"Yes. Malik was—difficult."

"When I started divorce proceedings, he was furious. He—he kidnapped my baby when she was scarcely three months old." Linnea's voice quivered. "He took her to Kholi, knowing I wouldn't be able to find her or have her returned to me. He was her father, but I never believed he abducted her because he really wanted Yasmin. He meant to get back at me."

She was probably right. Malik had always been vindictive, a Khaldun trait. "I am not Malik," he pointed out.

Linnea sighed. "I'm aware of that. It's obvious you've taken good care of Yasmin on the trip here. She adores you."

"While you continue to have reservations. Both about me and about Yasmin being your daughter."

Linnea slid off the stool, collected the dirty dishes and brought them to the sink. She stood with her back to him, rinsing them off while she said, "She's not my birth daughter, she's not the little girl Malik took from me."

Talal rose and crossed to her. Leaning against the

refrigerator, he said, "Despite your claim, you intend to raise her. Am I correct?"

"In that sense she is my daughter." Linnea swung around to face him. "You'll never take her away from me."

"I have no intention of doing such a thing. Still, it's difficult for me to understand how you can be so certain she's a changeling based merely on the color of her eyes."

For a moment he thought Linnea was about to defend her position, then she frowned at him and said, "I refuse to discuss it any further. But I do expect when you return to Kholi that you'll tell your great-uncle, the king, he must find the baby Malik Khaldun kidnapped, his child and mine. I'll never be satisfied until she's returned to me."

Seeing the futility of arguing, Talal straightened and shrugged. "If you insist. I'm not returning immediately, though."

"Good. Because I don't think Yasmin is ready to let you go. She needs to be weaned away from you. While you're working on doing that, I need to dig out my Arabic phrase books and study them so I can try to understand her after you do leave."

About to tell her he hadn't planned on remaining in New York any longer than absolutely necessary, that he'd intended to fly to Nevada by the end of the week, Talal held back. Much as he longed to fly west, he found he wasn't quite ready to desert Yasmin. Nor was he, for some reason he couldn't fathom, ready to leave Linnea just yet. To this there'd been added yet another problem.

Apparently taking his silence for agreement, she said, "Now that we've settled things, let's go to bed." She flushed and added, "What I mean is, I suggest we turn in."

He couldn't resist. "Together or separately?"

"You know perfectly well what I mean!" She turned her indignant face from him and would have stalked off if he hadn't grasped her wrist.

"I was taught never to go to bed until I wished my hostess a peaceful good-night," he said, raising her right hand to his lips and bowing over it. "*Maddamti,*" he murmured.

Instead of touching his mouth to the back of her hand, on impulse he turned it over and brushed her palm with his lips before releasing her. Without waiting for her reaction, he left the kitchen and walked along the hall to the guest bedroom.

Linnea stood staring at the spot where he'd been, her right hand pressed to her breast. She wanted to be upset, to be irked and annoyed with him; instead, she was suffused with a feeling of warmth. "This won't do," she muttered. "This won't do at all."

The warmth stayed with her while she loaded the dishwasher, checked the doors and turned out the lights. If Yasmin likes him, she told herself as she slipped into bed beside the girl, he can't be all bad. Even if he didn't believe her. That was okay, because she wasn't entirely certain she completely believed him—he could be in on this changeling business. She had no proof he wasn't.

In her sleep, Yasmin turned and cuddled next to her. Linnea stroked her soft hair, feeling peace settle over her, the peace Talal had wished her before he went to his room. She'd never give up her search for the child she'd borne, but this little girl Talal had brought her soothed her grieving heart.

* * *

Linnea had no idea how long she'd been asleep when she was jolted awake by Yasmin's voice calling "Mama!"

"Toilet?" she asked the child. "Bathroom? Potty? Drink? Water? Do you hurt?"

Her only response was Yasmin's spate of Arabic. In desperation, Linnea rose, picked up the girl and trotted down the hall to Talal. His light was on, and he was sitting up in bed. She plopped onto the edge of the bed, still holding Yasmin, and demanded, "Tell me what she wants. Is something wrong with her?"

Yasmin squirmed away from her and crawled to Talal, repeating the same words. He chuckled, turned Yasmin over onto her stomach and began rubbing her back.

"When we shared hotel and motel rooms and she woke at night," he said, "I'd get her to go to sleep again by rubbing her back. That's what she wanted you to do." He reached over, took her hand and brought it to Yasmin. "Take over, Mama."

Relieved, Linnea rubbed the girl's back. Finding the position awkward, she shifted so she was lying next to Yasmin. She continued to stroke her back gently, hardly realizing when she began to croon the same bye-lo lullaby she'd sung to her baby.

After a time Talal turned out the bedside lamp and Linnea stopped crooning, ready to take Yasmin back to her own bed. But when she tried to lift her, Yasmin resisted, whispering in Arabic.

"She wants you to go on singing." Talal's voice sounded drowsy.

Resuming the song and the stroking, Linnea told herself she'd wait until Yasmin fell asleep before trying again to move her. With the child between her and Talal, no part of him touched her, but she was very much aware of him being there. His scent seeped into her consciousness, a clean, male smell that surrounded her, triggering enticing thoughts of how erotic his skin would feel against hers.

An Arab proverb she'd heard quoted popped into her head. "Only a fool gets a snakebite from the same snake hole twice."

Malik had been a Kholi male. Maybe they weren't all like him, but she had no proof Talal wasn't. And she didn't intend to find out.

Yasmin wriggled closer to her, putting a hand to her cheek and patting it. "Mama," she murmured. Before Linnea could take the child into her arms, Yasmin turned away and said, "Talal."

He spoke to her in Arabic, soft, soothing words. Though she didn't know their meaning, Linnea knew they were words of affection. He seemed to be as fond of Yasmin as she was of him.

"She doesn't seem inclined to sleep," Talal said. "Maybe another story will do the trick. Why don't you tell her one and I'll translate."

Childhood tales flitted through Linnea's mind and she realized, like Talal's story of the desert ghoul, most of them had scary parts. "How about Goldilocks and the Three Bears?"

"Yasmin has never seen a bear or even a picture of one," he said. "Isn't there a tale about three goats? Goats she knows."

"How about trolls? There's a troll in that story."

"I'll change the troll to a ghoul when I translate. Don't tell all the story at once. Pause now and then to let me catch up."

Linnea propped a pillow under her head before beginning. If anyone had told her yesterday that she'd be lying in bed with a Kholi man—a sexy one, at that—telling bedtime stories, she'd have had a good laugh. Nothing was less likely. Yet here she was.

"Once upon a time," she began, "there were three billy goats...."

As she listened to Talal's slow, singsong translation, aimed at sending Yasmin to sleep, she yawned. When he paused, it took her a moment or two to recall where she'd left off. "Trip-trap, across the bridge," she said.

When she finished, he took up the story in Arabic. How soft his voice was, low and soft, a lover's voice. Linnea relaxed as she listened, her eyes drifting shut. Since she didn't understand what he said, she found herself providing her own meaning to the words, words Malik had never said to her.

My love, my only love...

Talal, supporting himself on one elbow, ended the story. Yasmin, next to him, didn't move, and he smiled in satisfaction. Asleep at last. Expecting Linnea to scoop up the girl and carry her off, he peered across Yasmin at her when she didn't. A streetlight slanting through the slatted blind at the window provided scant illumination but enough to tell him that she also slept.

His lips quirked in amusement as he pictured her dismay when she roused and discovered she's been sleeping in the bed of a man she mistrusted, a Kholi man, at that. The worst kind, as far as she was concerned.

He lay back on his pillow, closing his eyes and anticipating the awakening. An hour later, he was far from amusement. True, the child separated them so that there was no contact between their bodies, but that didn't prevent her subtle scent from invading his territory. Though he could identify most expensive perfumes, hers evaded him. Light and floral, mixing with her own scent, it was a sensual combination that would tempt any man.

Even if Yasmin had not been in the bed, he wouldn't so much as lay a finger on Linnea. Never mind how he longed to taste her soft lips, to hold her close and feel her respond to him. In the unlikely event she would respond, that is. But even if she would, he'd already decided she was, for him, forbidden. Taboo.

They were already at odds. He might not believe she knew what she was talking about when she claimed Yasmin was not the daughter she'd borne to Malik Khaldun, but he was aware she believed it. This strange conviction of hers had the potential to cause trouble. Perhaps an international incident if she decided to go public.

"I can count on you," his great-uncle had said. "You're the diplomat I was never able to be. Deliver the child quietly, give the woman the time she needs to recover, then notify the media. After all, in uniting mother and child, we've righted a wrong, we've proven our humanity, which, of course, strengthens our position with the Americans. A bit of publicity, therefore, will not be amiss."

Yes, it would make a great story, one the media would pounce on with glee. Unfortunately, unless he could convince Linnea not to share her doubt with anyone besides him, at this point publicity was to be avoided at all costs. So was any intimacy between him and Linnea.

Strange, she was anything but the usual carefree, frankly sexy type of American woman he was usually attracted to. She was what he thought of as a keeper, reminding him of Karen, his brother's wife. Not her looks so much as her tenderness toward Yasmin, the daughter she claimed wasn't hers and yet would not give up. Keepers were the kind of women men married.

Damn. He couldn't recall ever being so aware of a woman as he was at this moment. As he'd suspected, she'd been wearing a sleep-T. He could imagine how the soft cotton garment had crept up her thighs as she turned in her sleep, revealing enticing flesh waiting for his caress. Cursing his stupidity for landing himself in this predicament—wanting her and unable to touch her—he considered claiming the bed in the master bedroom as his.

No, the only pleasure he was going to get from the situation would be her reaction when she woke to find herself in bed with him. He didn't intend to miss that, so he'd stay where he was, frustration and all.

What a story it would make for his friends. Except, he realized, because Linnea was involved, this was one story he would never tell them. Hadn't he already called her *maddamti,* my lady? In any culture, in Kholi or America, anyone who was truly a man didn't speak idly of a lady.

He heard her sigh and felt her shift position in the bed. Her toes came in contact with his foot, flesh against flesh. Not on purpose, he was certain, but that didn't stop the tingle that rose from his foot to his groin.

Talal groaned and reluctantly moved his foot away from hers. He'd be surprised if he slept at all. Never again would he share the bed of a woman he couldn't make love to. Linnea may be the one to have the last laugh.

Chapter Three

Unsure whether she was awake or asleep, Linnea felt her cheek being stroked lightly. Caressingly. A pleasant, loving touch. If she opened her eyes she'd know whether or not it was a dream, but if it was, the dream would dissolve, so she tried to stay suspended between sleeping and waking.

"*Ya*, Mama," a child's voice whispered in her ear.

Linnea started, her eyes popping open. Sunlight filtering through the blinds showed her Yasmin's heart-shaped face. The little girl put a finger to her lips and pointed. Linnea glanced to her right and gasped.

A man lay sprawled on the other side of Yasmin. As she was still sleep-dazed, it took her a moment to understand who he was. Talal Zohir. She was in bed with Talal! As she stared at him, his eyes opened and he grinned wickedly before murmuring something in Arabic.

The words were vaguely familiar. She thought they meant something like "good morning." He didn't seem in the slightest surprised at her presence.

Linnea eased from the bed, pulling down her sleep-T as far as it would go as she stood up. "I don't find a morning that begins like this particularly good," she snapped. "Come, Yasmin, let's get dressed."

The child looked at her with a puzzled frowned. Before the obviously amused Talal could jump in with the correct Arabic phrase, Linnea beckoned to Yasmin, using what was apparently the universal gesture for "come with me," because the girl immediately slid off the bed and followed her from the room.

How had Talal managed once they arrived in America? Linnea wondered as she took Yasmin into the bathroom.

After dressing herself and Yasmin, she led the girl into the kitchen, where Yasmin immediately climbed onto one of the counter stools and pointed, saying "Bana-na."

Handing her a partially peeled banana, Linnea wondered what else to feed her. She'd have to ask Talal what Yasmin was accustomed to having for breakfast. Stupid, but in all her fantasies of recovering her daughter it hadn't occurred to her that there'd be this language barrier.

Her old Arabic phrase books would help, but even better, she'd get Talal to write down the English words she'd be using in everyday interaction with Yasmin and their Arabic equivalents. That way they could communicate and at the same time she could teach her new daughter English.

How long did he plan to stay?

"*Ya*, Mama," Yasmin said. Her next words were not

only in Arabic but almost unintelligible because her mouth was full of banana.

"Talal," Linnea said to her. "We'll ask Talal."

He spoke from the entrance to the kitchen, "*Maddamti*, I am at your service."

She turned to him. "I don't know what to feed Yasmin or what she's trying to tell me. She really shouldn't talk with her mouth full—she might choke."

"It's also impolite. Like everyone else, Yasmin must learn her manners." He rattled off a string of Arabic and Yasmin lowered her head, looking up at him from under her lashes.

"Already a coquette," he said, then spoke more Arabic to Yasmin.

She brightened, swallowed and began chattering, evidently telling him what she wanted to eat because he turned to Linnea and said, "Chocolate milk, bread and jam."

"How about you?" Linnea asked.

"I smell coffee brewing. I hope it's leaded, as my brother would say."

"I'm trying to switch to decaf, but caffeine in the morning's hard to give up," she said, pouring him a mugful of coffee. "By the way, why does Yasmin call me '*Ya*, Mama'? What's it mean?"

"In Kholi, when you're speaking to someone, it's considered polite to preface their name with *ya*. The closest English equivalent would be *oh*. When I awoke this morning and saw you in bed with me I might well have said, 'Oh, Mama!'" The inflection he gave the two words was very different from the way Yasmin said them. "Or, perhaps, *Allah kareem* because I felt God *was* generous. But I had a feeling you might not be."

She wished she'd poured the coffee in his lap. Choosing not to reply, she busied herself fixing Yasmin's breakfast.

"Would you be generous enough to allow me to make the coffee after this?" he asked. "Presuming I haven't already outstayed my welcome."

Now he was telling her he didn't like the way she made coffee. Evidently he'd preferred last night's dregs of the pot. But, as annoying as she found him, she was relieved to know he didn't plan to desert her immediately. Only because she needed to pick his brain for the right words to say to Yasmin, of course.

"We need to talk," she said.

"I agree. After we eat. I'm not reasonable before breakfast."

Nor necessarily after, either, she was tempted to say but held her tongue.

Later in the living room, she sat on the couch with Yasmin while he prowled about the room, stopping to examine her Galen sketches again.

Yasmin watched him for a few moments, then slid off the couch, ran into the master bedroom and returned, hauling the little case. She dumped its contents on the living room floor. Plastic blocks, rings, squares and triangles tumbled out. Nodding in satisfaction, Yasmin plopped down beside the toys and began fitting them together.

Talal strolled over to the couch and sat down on the opposite end from Linnea. Still too close as far as she was concerned. Her former husband had insisted on wearing a cloying cologne as, she'd noticed in Kholi, many Arab men did. Talal did not. Why, then, was she so conscious of the faint scent of what must be his aftershave? Because it mixed with his own intriguing male smell, one she responded to against her wish?

Defensively, she began talking, telling him about the list of words she needed from him.

"I'd planned to do something of the sort," he said, somewhat impatiently, she thought. "We have another, not so easily solved problem ahead of us." He gestured toward Yasmin, absorbed in her play. "Your daughter."

Linnea sat straighter. "Why is she a problem?"

"When the media show up, and they will sooner or later whether I notify them or not, what do you intend to tell the reporters? That she's not your kidnapped daughter?"

"Media!"

"Didn't it occur to you that a long-lost daughter returned to her American mother by a Kholi king is a newsworthy event?"

"Well, yes, I suppose so," she said slowly, "but—"

"What will you tell them?" he repeated.

"I—I hadn't considered the possibility of reporters."

"Do so."

She stared at him. "I suppose you expect me to lie."

"I don't know what to expect from you. What I'm sure of is if you insist she's not the child your husband abducted from America, you risk losing her."

"No!"

Yasmin looked up from her blocks. Talal spoke soothingly to her and she resumed playing.

Doing her best to keep her voice even so as not to upset Yasmin again, Linnea said, "I've already told you I won't give her up."

"You'll have to if the king insists she be returned to Kholi, and chances are he will. That American birth certificate is for the child your husband kidnapped. Once you announce she's not that child, you label her as Kholi-born."

Linnea clutched her hands together. She hadn't gotten that far in her thinking. In fact, beyond knowing she'd never give up Yasmin, she hadn't planned ahead at all. "You said she's an orphan. If she has no relatives in Kholi, why wouldn't the king let me raise her?"

"I've told you. If she's not your abducted daughter, she's Kholi, not American. The king wouldn't permit an American woman to raise a Kholi child who was not her own."

"How cruel!"

He shrugged. "We're protective of our own."

"*Protective* is not the word I'd choose. You Kholis are all as selfish and mean-spirited as Malik." Despite herself, her voice rose. Yasmin sprang up from the floor and laid her head on Linnea's lap.

Linnea stroked her soft hair, murmuring, "It's all right, sweetheart. Everything's all right." Apparently reassured by the tone of her voice, Yasmin raised her head and glanced at Talal, who smiled at her and gestured at the toys she'd been playing with.

When Yasmin was seated again on the floor, Linnea said, "I can't give her up. I won't. But you're telling me I must lie to keep her."

He glared at her. "I'm doing no such thing. You're the one who insists she's a changeling, not me."

"You believe I'm wrong, then."

"Everything I know and see points to the fact that I've brought you the right child."

Linnea turned an anguished gaze on him. "You're putting me in a no-win position. If I don't lie, I'll lose her. If I lie, I'll lose any chance of ever recovering my birth daughter. You can't be so cruel as to sic the media on us."

He reached over and touched her hand momentarily.

"I don't intend to, not under these circumstances. But that doesn't mean some enterprising reporter won't smoke you out. If I'm still here, the problem will be compounded."

"Because you'll be saying one thing and I'll be saying another." Linnea covered her face with her hands. "What am I to do? If I tell the truth I may have to fight the king in the courts and drag Yasmin through miserable publicity."

"With a good chance of losing." Sliding closer, he took her hands from her face and held them in his. "I don't want any of this to happen to you, Linnea. Or to her."

Looking into his dark eyes she recognized genuine concern. "Do you understand that my great-uncle would not knowingly send you a changeling?" he asked. "If she is one, then someone has deliberately lied to the king of Kholi, someone who's aware the penalty for that is certain death."

She took a deep breath and pulled her hands free. "I don't doubt what you say is true. But it doesn't change my truth. God knows, I loved her from the moment I held her in my arms yesterday. But she's not—" Her voice broke.

This time Yasmin climbed into her lap and put her arms around Linnea's neck, hugging her.

Talal gazed at the two of them, mother and daughter, and cursed Linnea's stubbornness. If ever he saw a matched pair, these two were it. He felt responsible not only for the child but for Linnea as well. He had to protect them both from the media, at least until Linnea came to realize she was wrong. If ever she did.

A temporary solution sprang to mind. The problem wasn't going to go away but he could buy them time.

"How would you and Yasmin like to take a trip?" he asked.

Linnea turned to look at him. "A trip?"

"To Nevada. I'm going there. You two fly with me."

Her brow furrowed. "To Nevada?"

"Yes. As soon as possible. If you're not here, how will anyone know where you've gone? Or whether the child ever got here?"

"I don't know—"

"Don't stop to think. There isn't time, and thinking hasn't helped and won't help. Pack."

"But—Nevada?"

"My brother, Zeid, has a ranch in the Carson Valley. We'll stay with him."

"Zeid," Yasmin said, unwinding her arms from Linnea's neck to look at him.

"Zeid and Karen and Danny," he told the child.

"Karen. Danny," she repeated. He smiled at her, proud of the way she remembered what he'd told her. A bright little girl as well as pretty. A daughter anyone would love.

Danny? Wasn't that his son's name? Linnea asked herself. And who was Karen? But the questions could wait until she no longer had to worry about a reporter showing up. Meanwhile she needed to share a new worry. "There's a possibility someone in the complex saw you arrive with Yasmin," she said.

"With luck the rain prevented that. We'll split up to leave and hope no one makes the connection. Or finds out where we're going."

"I don't like the idea of running away, but I guess there's nothing else to do," she said doubtfully.

"Then pack. What's the closest major airport near here? Newark?"

She shook her head. "Stewart, in Newburgh. About thirty miles from here. My grandmother—" She broke off. Now was not the time to talk about her family. But she was momentarily distracted by the memory of bringing her baby up from the city so her grandmother in Newburgh could see her. Grandma had died six months later and baby Yasmin...

Caught up in the past, she was aware of Talal phoning but didn't listen.

"No available flights until tomorrow morning," he told her as he hung up. "We'll check into a motel near the airport until then."

Linnea took a deep breath and brought herself back to the present. Fixing her gaze on Talal, she said, "About the motel—I certainly don't intend to share a room with you."

He chuckled. "Not even after last night?"

"I wasn't—we didn't—" she sputtered.

"We'll get adjoining rooms, ostensibly for the child, since we'll be registering as man and wife. Under false names, so we won't leave a trail. Are there rental units nearby where we can store both our cars? I don't want either of them left here or parked at the airport."

"You mean like those storage spaces? I guess some of them are big enough to park a car in—I never thought about it before. We do have several around the area."

He nodded, lifted Yasmin off her lap onto his and began murmuring to her. When he finished in Arabic, he said to her in English, "We go."

She looked up at him. "Yasmin go?" When he nodded, she asked, "Talal go? Mama go?" Again he nodded and then set her on her feet. Apparently satisfied, she began picking up her playthings and putting them back into the little case.

"Yasmin's getting ready," he said to Linnea. "How about you?"

A thousand and one details flashed into her mind. Send the Galen drawings off. Have the mail held. Cancel the newspaper. What clothes to pack. As far as she was concerned, Nevada was almost a foreign country. She knew about Las Vegas and Reno, though she'd never been to either, but Carson Valley?

Talal rose from the couch. "I'll call about the storage units while you pack."

Linnea asked him to call to have the newspaper held as well. Then, feeling she'd been rushed into a decision she wasn't ready to make, she walked slowly into her bedroom, trailed by Yasmin.

"*Ya*, Mama go?" Yasmin asked her.

Linnea dropped to her knees and hugged the little girl, murmuring, "We go together. Always together."

She packed in a daze, uncertain she was doing the right thing but not finding any viable alternative. Above all, Yasmin must be protected.

When finally Talal announced they were ready, the unreality of what she was about to do kept Linnea off balance. Yasmin was going with Talal, and she looked uncertainly back at Linnea as he urged the girl through the kitchen door and across the patio in a roundabout way to the parking lot. Linnea watched them, Talal burdened with her suitcase as well as the three bags he'd brought with him. Yes, he did favor his left leg a trifle.

After waiting the fifteen minutes that Talal had specified, feeling more and more like a character in some spy drama, Linnea picked up her package of drawings. At the last minute something occurred to her and she hurried into the bedroom, where, standing on tiptoe, she pulled a plastic bag from the shelf and brought it with her. As she was leaving by way of the front door, her phone rang. She hesitated, then decided to let the answering machine take care of the call, just in case.

She met no one on her way to her car and made an uneventful trip to the post office, where she sent off the Galen package and had her mail held. Unsure how long she'd be gone, she told them a month.

At the storage unit, she arranged for the rental, drove her car into the metal cubbyhole, closed the door and padlocked it. She'd seen Talal and Yasmin parked along the road in a red sports car on her way in and hurried through the open gate to join them. Yasmin, buckled into the cramped back seat, greeted her with a big smile.

"I'm not accustomed to skulking," she told Talal.

"We're not skulking. We're a happy, three-unit nuclear family on our way to Nevada."

She slanted a frown his way. "Happy?"

He shrugged. "How about content?"

"Mama," Yasmin said from in back. "Talal." Linnea had to admit the little girl sounded content with them both in her sight again. "Go Ne-va-da," Yasmin added.

"That's another thing," Linnea said. "My conception of Nevada is of glitter and gambling in Las Vegas and Reno, or else desert and mountains."

"It's beautiful country as you will see. There's also Lake Tahoe, where my sister Jaida lives. Part of the lake is in Nevada."

This Kholi prince had a sister in Nevada as well as a brother? "So your brother and sister live in Nevada," she said. "Permanently?"

"Yes. They're Americans."

"How about your parents?"

"Dead." His tone warned her not to probe further.

"Mine are, too," she told him, and dropped the subject even though her curiosity was far from satisfied. Talal's command of English was excellent, far better than Malik's had been, but his slight accent was definitely Kholi.

She decided to risk one more comment. "You gave me the impression that you lived in Kholi."

He nodded curtly.

"Ice cream," Yasmin said clearly.

"I knew I'd regret teaching her that word," Talal muttered. "*Badayn*," he told Yasmin. "Later."

Linnea delved into the plastic bag she carried and noticing Yasmin's restlessness, unwrapped a bright pink stuffed kitten. Turning toward the girl, she offered her the toy, saying, "Kitty."

Yasmin took it from her, examining the cat gravely. "*Aziz*," she murmured finally, and hugged the toy to her.

"Does that mean *cat?*" Linnea asked Talal.

He shook his head. "The word means many things, like *dear* or *cherish*. It's also a name. I think she's decided to name her new friend Aziz." He said a few words to Yasmin, who replied in Arabic.

"Besides thank you, she's saying she loves the cat—and you," he said.

Touched, Linnea smiled at the child. The toy, bought almost three years ago for the other Yasmin, had been stored on the shelf, awaiting her daughter's return. Her heart was soothed to see how much it meant to her gift daughter. "I love you, too, Yasmin," she whispered under her breath. Or so she thought.

Talal glanced at her and spoke again to the child, who

smiled shyly at Linnea. "I translated your words," he said.

They rode in silence until they came to a five-corner intersection with traffic lights, where a direction sign showed the distance to the airport.

"Five miles," he said. "Close enough."

He chose a motel where each room was entered from the outside rather than from inside a lobby. Linnea remained in the car with Yasmin. "*Ya*, Mama," the girl said, "ice cream."

Recalling the word Talal had used, Linnea said, "*Badayn*. Later."

"La-ter," Yasmin repeated.

The adjoining rooms were clean and attractive enough in a generic motel mode. They settled in, Linnea and Yasmin in one room, Talal in the other. The open door between the two reassured Yasmin, resigning Linnea to the idea it would have to remain open.

"Yasmin has asked for ice cream," Linnea called to Talal. "Maybe we should go and find some for her."

"The less exposure of the three of us together, the better," Talal said, coming through the connecting doorway. "I'll go out and bring back some ice cream."

He returned in no time with a quart of chocolate, plastic spoons and plastic bowls. Yasmin started to eat hers with enthusiasm but had taken no more than a few spoonfuls when she pushed the bowl away, her face paling. Moments later she vomited onto the table and the floor and herself.

Linnea rushed her into the bathroom where she threw up again in the toilet. Her forehead felt unusually warm—feverish, in fact. Linnea tried to keep the fear from her voice as she called to Talal.

"We'd better take her to a doctor."

He appeared in the bathroom doorway. "Is she that ill?"

"I think so. I don't want to take any chances."

"Neither do I. Do you know a children's doctor in the area?"

About to say no, she remembered her long-ago visit to her grandmother. Her new baby had seemed to be developing a cold, and, worried, she'd taken her to a Newburgh pediatrician recommended by one of her grandmother's friends. He'd been kind, competent and reassuring.

"I might," she told Talal. "Find the phone book and see if a Dr. Collinsworth is listed. I took my baby to him once."

He was listed and Talal called him. Linnea listened to him explaining to the receptionist that they were in the area only temporarily, that they were, in fact, waiting for a flight and their child had taken ill. The doctor had happened to see their child, Yasmin Khaldun, as an infant three years ago, so, in a manner of speaking, she was his patient.

"We're to bring Yasmin in at twelve-thirty," he told Linnea after he hung up. "Dr. Collinsworth will see her before he leaves for lunch. That's an hour from now."

Yasmin had stopped vomiting so Linnea stripped off her soiled clothes, washed her quickly and put on clean ones. Talal, who'd been hovering in the doorway, lifted the girl into his arms, carried her to the bed, laid her gently down and sat beside her, speaking soft, soothing Arabic words.

Linnea noticed he'd made a few swipes at the mess Yasmin had made on the table and the floor. Though there was still cleaning up to do, she was surprised he'd made any effort. Malik certainly wouldn't have. Yet

Talal, who belonged to the Kholi royal family and had undoubtedly never had to clean up vomit in his life, had tried to help her with the unpleasant chore. As she glanced at Talal, crooning to Yasmin, a barrier in her mind went down. He might be a Kholi male, but he was different from Malik. Favorably so.

At the doctor's office, they were shown into an examining room immediately, and it wasn't long before Dr. Collinsworth came in, bringing a chart with him. On the ride to the office, Talal had prepared Yasmin for what to expect, so she made no fuss about being examined.

The doctor listened to her heart for what seemed to Linnea to be an inordinately long time, so long that the worried Linnea finally blurted, "Is there something wrong with her heart?"

He glanced up at her, a strange look on his face, and shook his head. Then, though he'd already looked into Yasmin's eyes, he picked up his ophthalmoscope and examined both of her eyes again.

"Will she be all right?" Talal asked.

The doctor straightened, looking first at Talal, then at Linnea. "Your little girl has a mild case of intestinal flu. It's a bug that's been going around, but none of my patients have been sick longer than a day or two at the most. There's no cause to worry about what's wrong with her." He glanced down at Yasmin. "My concern is more with what isn't wrong with her. Perhaps we'd best not discuss this in front of her."

"She doesn't understand English," Talal said. "Only Arabic."

Dr. Collinsworth nodded. "Then I feel free to ask why you're trying to pass this little girl off as the baby named Yasmin that I examined three years ago."

Chapter Four

Listening to Dr. Collinsworth, Linnea had tried to brace herself for what was coming, but despite this, Talal recovered before she did.

"Not the same child?" Talal challenged. "Please explain your statement."

The doctor drew himself up. "Certainly. Baby Yasmin had a serious congenital heart condition." He fixed his gaze on Linnea. "When I mentioned it to her mother—you...?" At Linnea's nod, he went on. "You told me you were aware of her heart problem and your New York City pediatric surgeon had told you he planned to operate when she was between six and nine months old. Her fragile condition, you said, was why you were concerned about her coming down with an upper respiratory infection. I duly recorded all this." He gestured toward the chart on the cabinet counter.

"The type of heart condition the baby had does not

repair itself. She would have required surgical intervention at an early age to have her heart be anywhere near normal. Yet this girl I've just examined has a perfectly normal heart, normal in every way. She has no surgical scars, as there would be if a congenital heart condition had been repaired. As a further corroboration, I noted on the baby's chart that she had a wedge-shaped brown coloration in her lighter colored right iris and two polka-dot-like spots of brown in her left.''

''Her eyes,'' Talal murmured. Linnea knew he was recalling what she'd said to him about Yasmin's eyes.

''Exactly,'' the doctor said. ''These iris spots are benign as far as sight goes, but permanent. A child is born with them and they don't go away. The individual retains them all her life. As I'm sure you're both aware, the little girl here has no such spots in either of her irises. My statement is based on these irrefutable findings—this Yasmin is not the baby named Yasmin I examined three years ago.''

Before Linnea could decide what to say, Talal spoke. ''You're right, of course. When Yasmin became ill, my wife remembered you'd seen her daughter in the past. I'm afraid I lied a little when I said this was the same girl. I'm sure you know it's difficult to get a doctor's appointment on short notice, especially if the doctor has never seen the patient before.

''We were worried about Yasmin's illness and wanted to be sure you'd examine her, so I said she was your patient. Actually, she's my daughter, not my wife's. Coincidentally, both girls are almost the same age and both are named Yasmin.''

He played the part of the concerned but abashed father so well that Linnea wasn't surprised to see that Dr.

Collinsworth seemed to be swallowing what was to her a preposterous story.

The doctor frowned at Talal and shook his head. "Not a good idea."

"I realize that now. It was stupid of me. I should have known your records would show me up."

The doctor smiled faintly. "It's possible I kept more detailed records three years ago when I was beginning my practice than I do now. When we get too busy, we tend to omit details."

"I apologize," Talal said, holding out his hand. As the doctor shook it, he added, "Thank you for examining my Yasmin. It's a relief to know she's not seriously ill."

"Yes," Linnea chimed in. "Thank you very much."

The doctor glanced at his watch and said, "The nurse will give you my standard sheet of instructions for dealing with stomach flu."

He was obviously eager to be off to lunch and to rid himself of the people who'd tried to fool him. He probably didn't realize that she and Talal were in just as much of a hurry to get away as he was.

After the doctor left, Linnea dressed Yasmin while Talal took care of the bill at the front desk. He returned, gathered the little girl into his arms and carried her out to the car.

"I've acquired two aliases in one day," he said as they drove away. "We're registered as the Youngbloods at the motel, and since the doctor's receptionist assumed I was the husband of Linnea Khaldun, with an address in New York City, I didn't correct her." He grimaced. "Not a last name I'd choose."

Apparently he didn't intend to discuss Yasmin at the

moment. Deciding not to bring up the subject until he did, Linnea said, "Why Youngblood?"

He shrugged. "It sounded like a real name, not one somebody would make up."

Neither spoke again until they were inside their motel rooms with Yasmin settled into bed. She immediately fell asleep. Linnea rose from the side of the bed and looked at Talal. "Well?" she said.

"Why didn't you explain what you meant about the eyes?" he asked.

"I thought it wouldn't be any use, that you'd refuse to believe me, no matter what I said."

"I didn't want to believe you, that much is true. Now we have even more reason to avoid the press. The doctor has no reason at present to open his mouth, but if there's a leak in Washington to the media and they find us, it's possible patient confidentiality won't hold."

Linnea shuddered, imagining Yasmin's name and face on TV and splashed across newspapers all over the country.

"I'm going to the airport and I'll call my great-uncle from there," Talal said. "He needs to—"

She caught his arm. "No, don't tell him anything! He'll take Yasmin away from me."

Talal put a hand over hers. "I have to let him know he can't release any information about Yasmin. I intend to tell him she's ill and nothing can be done until she improves. A partial truth, at least. I dislike lies."

"That story you told the doctor was unreal."

"But effective. Once you admit you're wrong and the other guy's right, it spikes his guns." He crossed to the bed and leaned over Yasmin.

"I think she's better," Linnea said. "I assume you'll bring back what's on the doctor's list, though."

He nodded. "And some food for us. Any suggestions?"

"There's a good Mexican restaurant, Los Amigos, just before you get to the airport."

She stood in the doorway watching him slide into the car and drive away. As she closed the door she muttered to herself, "I'm getting as bad as Yasmin—can't let him out of my sight. That won't do, not at all."

She determinedly put him from her mind as she closed the door. At the same time, she shut away the insidious niggle of fear that threatened to invade her mind. Her birth daughter was alive and well somewhere in Kholi. She had to be. Malik knew about the necessary heart surgery and, as the baby's father, surely would have arranged for it to be done in his country.

Yasmin was still sleeping when he returned a couple of hours later. "We leave tomorrow just before noon," he said. "In Chicago we'll change to a Nevada airline. One short hop and a somewhat longer one. If Yasmin isn't up to going on from Chicago, we can always stay there overnight."

She nodded a bit dubiously, hoping Yasmin would be well enough to get on the plane tomorrow. "What did your great-uncle say?" she asked.

"He's not happy with the situation but agrees we have to wait. So there'll be no official announcement out of Kholi. I can't do anything about Washington, though. Your capital city is notorious for leakage."

She couldn't deny that. "When we get to Nevada, then what?"

"Let's get there first, we'll discuss the what afterward." He began to open the various bags he'd brought back with him. "Mexican food, as ordered, *maddamti*."

"What's that word mean?" she asked, aware he'd used it several times before when referring to her.

He faced her and bowed slightly. "My lady." His gaze caught hers and she found she couldn't look away. "I apologize for doubting you."

His words took her aback. Malik had been so sure he was never wrong that it wouldn't have occurred to him he ever needed to apologize. Yet it wasn't Talal's words but the warmth in his dark eyes that held her. Did the fact he called her 'my lady' mean anything or was it merely a form of courtesy?

He took a step toward her, then another and another. Her breath caught, she couldn't move, didn't want to move. He laid the palm of his hand against her cheek, looking into her eyes. Fear mixed with anticipation jingled through her—did he see it in her eyes? See that she didn't know what she wanted?

His hand moved caressingly down her cheek and around to her chin, where he paused to tilt her face up toward his. Slowly his lips lowered to hers, so slowly that she had time to back away. She found it impossible. Every nerve in her body, every cell, it seemed, was aware of him, waiting for him. Involuntarily, her lips parted.

His kiss, soft and light as dandelion fluff, set up a resonance within her, transmitting a thrill to every part of her body. Without conscious will she inched closer to him, raising her arms to enfold him. When she touched him, his arms came around her, pulling her against him. His kiss deepened, no longer a mere brush of lips but an urgent, passionate melding.

An intense need exploded inside her, so strong and irresistible that she moaned and pressed herself closer to him. He responded by cupping the curves of her hips, holding her against his arousal. Some distant part of her knew they were plunging headlong down a steep hill she wasn't sure she wanted to risk, but she couldn't bring herself to call a halt to the delicious momentum.

And yet somehow she must. This was too soon. Too intense. She sensed she could lose herself with this man and that mustn't happen. Ever.

She was the one who must stop. At first his kiss had been tentative. Asking. She'd had to respond before he released his passion. Summoning all her will, she tore her mouth from his. "No," she whispered. "We can't."

For a long moment she thought he wasn't going to release her, then his arms fell away and he stepped back. "I've been trying not to do that," he told her hoarsely. "As the doctor said, not a good idea."

Right. Not a good idea. She absolutely refused to get involved with another Kholi. Talal was not Malik, true, but he came from that same culture, one that treated women far differently than she was accustomed to. Markedly different from how she expected to be treated.

He smiled wryly. "At least we can satisfy another appetite by enjoying the Mexican food."

As they sat at the table and began unwrapping containers, Linnea shook her head. She hadn't given a moment's thought to Yasmin, who was sleeping right here in the room with them. In fact, she hadn't thought at all; she'd deliberately allowed herself to be caught in a web of passion. What was the matter with her?

She knew the answer. Talal. She'd dated a few men after her divorce, but since none of them had triggered any desire on her part, it was easy to forestall any attempt at lovemaking. Not so with Talal. Unfortunately she couldn't immediately escape this enforced intimacy they had to share so she'd have to be on guard, as much against herself as him.

Biting into a guacamole tostada, she savored its smooth tang, realizing she really was hungry. "Good," she said to Talal.

"*Muy bueno,*" he agreed. "Very good. Still, it leaves something to be desired." He shot her a wicked grin before taking a bite of tamale.

Ignoring his insidious reference to their interrupted lovemaking, she fastened on the Spanish words he'd used. "How many languages do you speak?"

"Five. But only Arabic, French and English at all well."

"I'm impressed."

He shrugged. "The direction my education was to take was laid out by my great-uncle while I was in the lower grades. He intended from the first that I should become his American liaison."

"Did he raise you?" she asked, remembering that he'd told her his parents were dead.

"No. My grandparents did."

He didn't elaborate, and his tone of voice warned her off the subject of his upbringing. She took a tangent.

"As I recall, the Kholi royal family is quite large."

Evidently mentioning this wasn't taboo because he chuckled. "Too large. I'm not even sure how many cousins and half cousins I have. Quite possibly there may be some I've yet to meet."

For a moment she envied him. Her family consisted of one aunt on her mother's side and one uncle on her father's. The aunt lived in New Mexico and the uncle in Alaska. She hadn't seen either of them in years and they corresponded only at Christmas. Neither had ever married, so she had no cousins.

She glanced over at the bed. Now she wasn't alone, she had Yasmin to love and cherish. And someday, as soon as she could find a way, Yasmin would be joined by her birth daughter.

With this in mind, she said, "We still haven't discussed what's at the heart of the problem—where my other daughter, my birth daughter, is. I know Malik took her to Kholi, so she's somewhere in your country." She stared challengingly at Talal.

"Give me time to decide what to do. I'm not ignoring the situation, but, remember, I didn't realize the problem existed until a few hours ago in the doctor's office. When I make my plans you'll hear about them."

Linnea's mouth tightened. There it was again, that flash of Kholi arrogance, shutting her out because she was a woman. Only the fear they'd wake Yasmin if they got into an argument kept her from expressing herself in no uncertain terms. She did fire off one shot. "Well, I'm sure we won't find her in Nevada."

He scowled, seemed about to retort, then didn't. Instead, he finished his meal in silence and rose. "I'll retire to my room and leave you in peace," he said.

Linnea watched him stride through the connecting doorway and muttered, "Good riddance."

She collected the remnants of food and disposed of them, cleaned the table and then checked on Yasmin, who still slept. She was relieved to find the girl's forehead cool to her touch. Now what? Too early to go to bed, and if she turned on the TV, Yasmin might wake. Recalling she'd tucked a book in her suitcase for the plane ride, she unearthed it and tried to curl up in a motel chair. Impossible. In any case, she didn't feel like reading.

What was Talal doing? Tiptoeing to the connecting

doorway, she listened. Was he watching his TV? If so, he'd turned it so low she couldn't hear a sound. Peeking into his room, she saw he was slumped in one of the straight-back chairs, his feet propped on the table, his back to her. Reading? Brooding? Dozing? She couldn't tell, but he looked perfectly relaxed, which annoyed her.

On impulse, she dug into her suitcase again and brought out a sketch pad—she never traveled without one—and a charcoal pencil. Carrying a chair to the doorway, she eased it down quietly, sat on it and began to sketch Talal.

Talal contemplated his shoes. One of the great things America had come up with was the various types of running and walking shoes—all comfortable. His were an expensive name brand, white with black bands. He'd found Yasmin a pair almost like them, but when he showed them to her, she shook her head. She wanted a pair with little animals on them.

Girls were not always easy to satisfy. Women, either, for that matter. There were flitting butterfly types like Danny's mother, who were easy to take and easy to leave. And there were types like his wife who, though seemingly submissive, rebelled in secret.

Then there were women like Linnea. Keepers. Women best left alone unless a man had honorable intentions. Even if he did have, he'd think twice before linking himself to such a stubborn one—she'd be nothing but trouble.

But he wanted her, his need for her ran deep and hot, even though every instinct told him to leave her alone. Her response to his kiss had heightened his desire until he could feel it simmer even thinking about her.

Once he'd made certain she was safe with his brother, he'd have to return to Kholi. Confronting his great-uncle with the unpleasant truth, telling him that the child he'd brought to America and delivered was a changeling, was something he didn't look forward to. Then, of course, he'd be honorbound to find Linnea's real child whom Malik had kidnapped, no doubt well hidden by the Khalduns, who obviously would have arranged for the required heart surgery. Even if it wasn't a matter of honor to him, he knew the king would order him to find the child.

And what about little Yasmin there in the other room? If he didn't bring her back to Kholi with him, his great-uncle would have his hide. He could plead illness on Yasmin's side, but that would only postpone the inevitable and make it all the more difficult for Linnea to part with Yasmin.

He could adopt Yasmin once they'd returned to Kholi, but though that would ensure her future, it wouldn't cure Linnea's broken heart. He had the feeling she'd never forgive him for taking Yasmin away from her even if he found her birth daughter for her.

Linnea had correctly labeled it a no-win situation. In any way, shape or form. There was an Arab proverb his grandmother was fond of quoting: *Patience is the key to solutions.* Not this time.

He wondered what Grandmother would think of Linnea. Not that she'd ever meet her.

Sighing, he straightened and rose from the chair. When he turned, he saw Linnea sitting in the doorway with something in her lap and realized after a moment that she was sketching him.

"Are you that bored?" he asked, denying his pleasure that she found him interesting enough to draw.

"Actually, yes," she admitted, rising and holding her sketch close to her so that he couldn't see it.

They stood facing each other in the no man's land of the connecting doorway. For some reason he couldn't seem to find any words, and apparently, neither could she. But the silence pulsed with emotion.

Finally they both started to talk at once. "Ladies first," he said.

"Yasmin's fever is gone," she told him.

"Good. That means we'll be in Nevada by tomorrow night." He didn't add it couldn't be soon enough for him. He'd never realized what torture it was to be forced to stay this close to a woman he wanted but knew better than to touch.

"I'm glad," she said. "Being cooped up..." She didn't finish, instead turned to prop her sketch pad on the seat of the chair, the drawing of him facing the chair back so he was unable to see it.

"Plenty of space in Carson Valley," he said inanely.

"I imagine there is."

Her words weren't any more intelligent than his, telling him she shared his frustration at this awkward position they'd been thrust into—by him, he realized. They were in this motel at his suggestion.

As though she'd been reading his mind, she said, "I forgot to tell you the phone rang when I was leaving the house. I was afraid to answer it and I didn't wait for the answering machine to pick up so I don't know what the call might have been."

Should he ask her to call and check the message? Most answering machines let you do that.

"I thought of calling to check," she said, following his train of thought, "but then I decided I'd rather not know."

"The message might be innocuous."

"Or not. Whatever it is, I'm in no position at the

moment to do anything other than get on that plane for Nevada, so why call?''

"Nothing important you could be missing?"

She shook her head, glancing behind her toward the bed where Yasmin slept, telling him clearer than words what was most important to her.

"I know you don't understand why I have to keep Yasmin as my daughter," she said.

"Perhaps it's because of those few minutes when you believed she was the child you'd borne.''

"More than that. There's a bond between us. I can't explain it, but I feel the bond and I think she does, too." She looked up at him, her tawny eyes wide with appeal. "It's as though we've chosen each other, Yasmin and I.''

Her plea for understanding struck his heart and lodged there. Which would make it all the more difficult to do what must be done.

She gripped his arm. "You do see, don't you, Talal?''

Didn't she remember how dangerous it was for them to touch? It took all his willpower not to take her into his arms and hold her close. His immediate motive might be comfort, but he didn't trust himself to keep it that way once he held her.

He lifted her hand from his arm, held it briefly between his hands and let her go. Any words he could find seemed like lies. The only phrase that came to him was his grandmother's adage, so he offered it to her. "In Kholi we say, 'Patience is the key to solutions.'''

She stared at him. "Patience? During this miserable time of waiting I've run out of patience. I have my gift daughter. I love her and will fight to keep her, but I want my baby, too. My poor little baby with her congenital heart condition. I've so worried that Malik didn't have the surgery done, though he knew she needed it. Still, he must have, don't you think?'' Tears brightened her eyes.

Those tears snapped his control. He reached for her, wrapping his arms around her, soothing her as he would Yasmin, murmuring in Arabic.

Linnea leaned against him, finding the comfort she needed so desperately in his warmth and strength. For the moment, she caved in to her need for strong arms around her, giving her the feeling she wasn't alone. She didn't know the words he said but that didn't matter, she understood his soothing tone.

After a time, much too soon as far as she was concerned, he held her away, saying, ''Did I hear Yasmin?''

Snapping back to reality, she turned and hurried to the bed, Talal following her. Yasmin's eyes were open. ''Ice cream?'' she said hopefully.

Linnea and Talal looked at each other and laughed. If she could ask for what she'd been eating when she threw up, Yasmin was definitely better.

Talal said, ''Later.''

Yasmin's mouth drooped. ''Aziz?'' she murmured. Linnea plucked the pink kitten from the dresser and handed it to the little girl, who cuddled the stuffed animal to her and began whispering to it.

''Telling the cat how mean we are,'' Talal said. ''What does the doctor say we can give her?''

A few minutes later, Yasmin sat propped up against pillows sipping a lemon-lime soft drink, Aziz in her lap. ''Go Nevada?'' she asked.

By early evening of the following day, Linnea found herself staring at the red-gold reflection of the setting sun shimmering in the windows of tall buildings in Reno as the plane slanted down between the mountains toward the landing strip.

Soon, with Talal carrying Yasmin, they were on their way to claim their baggage, passing slot machines pulsating with colored lights and making electronic noises. Distracted momentarily, Linnea listened to the occasional rattle of coins on metal, hinting of wins, though it seemed to her that, overall, people were putting more money in than was coming out.

Forcing her attention away from the exotic, seductive machines, she asked, "Are you going to rent a car?"

He shook his head. "I made other arrangements."

She gave him a speaking look, which he ignored. His tendency to keep important details to himself infuriated her. When they reached the baggage claim area, instead of watching the carousel for their luggage, he kept looking around.

From her vantage point near his shoulder, Yasmin looked, too. Suddenly she pointed, saying, "*Ya*, Talal."

He turned toward where she pointed and a grin spread over his face. Linnea craned her neck and saw a tall, dark man striding toward them. As he neared and she got a better view of him through the crowd, she drew in her breath in surprise.

She noticed Yasmin staring at the man. The girl bent down to look into Talal's face, then fixed her gaze on the man again. He was now nearly to them, a man in jeans and cowboy boots who seemed to be a carbon copy of Talal.

"Zeid!" Yasmin crowed. "Zeid, Zeid!"

"That's Zeid, all right," Talal said. "That's my brother."

His other arrangements, Linnea thought with some asperity. He'd also neglected to mention that Zeid was his identical twin, though he'd evidently told Yasmin.

Zeid belonged to the royal family. She'd wondered before, and the incongruity of it struck her again. Why was a Kholi prince living on a ranch in Carson Valley, Nevada?

Talal thrust Yasmin at her and embraced his brother, kissing him on both cheeks in the fashion of Kholi men. They both turned to Linnea at the same time, and Talal introduced her to his brother.

"Hello, Zeid," she said, still marveling at their close resemblance.

"Zeid is Talal's Arabic pronunciation, Linnea," he said in a voice as American as her own, with no trace of a Kholi accent. "Call me Zed, that's my name."

Chapter Five

On the drive back to Zed's Carson Valley ranch, Yasmin was clearly fascinated with the man Talal told her to call Uncle Zeid. Buckled into the rear of the extended cab of Zed's pickup with Linnea, she watched every move he made.

For that matter, he interested Linnea as well. His speech and gestures were so typically American as opposed to Talal's that it blew her mind.

"*Ya,* Uncle Zeid," Yasmin said finally. A string of Arabic followed.

He turned to glance over his shoulder at her, saying, "Sorry, honey, I don't understand. I don't speak Arabic."

"She wants to know if you have a little horse," Talal put in. "I told her about Windy."

"Oh, the pony. Yes, Yasmin, Windy's waiting for you to try him out."

While Talal translated, Linnea tried to come to terms with the reality of his having an identical twin brother who didn't know Arabic.

Her confusion grew after they arrived at the ranch. As they piled out of the pickup, she hardly had time to take in the backdrop of the mountains or the tree-shaded rambling house before a toddler came running from the house, followed by a blond woman. The little boy flung himself at Talal, shouting, "Daddy T!"

Talal scooped him up and raised the boy over his head, holding him there momentarily before embracing him. "Yo, Nimr," he said. "How are you, my son the tiger?"

Watching, Yasmin clutched Linnea's hand hard. "Nimr?" she whispered.

Apparently *nimr* meant tiger and the word upset Yasmin. "Danny," Linnea told her reassuringly, fairly sure she was right. "That's Danny."

"Danny?" Yasmin echoed, keeping her gaze fixed on Talal and the boy, her grip relaxing slightly.

The blond woman came up to them. "I'm Karen," she said, smiling. "You're Linnea, I know, and—" she crouched down to Yasmin's level "—you must be Yasmin. Welcome to Nevada."

Yasmin shrank bashfully against Linnea. Reaching down, Linnea lifted her into her arms. "Hello, Karen," she said, desperately trying to make sense of the relationships.

"Karen," Yasmin murmured, peeking at the blond woman.

"She says my name like Talal," Karen said, chuckling. "He must have taught it to her. But why are we standing out here? Come on in where it's cool and relax.

Hey!'' she called to the men, ''that goes for you guys, too. Inside!''

A beautifully carved wooden cradle sat on the floor of the living room, its occupant waving tiny arms and legs. Yasmin wriggled from Linnea's arms and walked to the cradle to peer down at the dark-haired, tawny-eyed baby who stared solemnly back at her.

''Baby,'' Linnea said, joining her.

''Her name's Erin,'' Karen told them.

''Danny's sister?'' Linnea asked, hazarding a guess.

Karen hesitated, then finally said, ''I guess Talal hasn't explained. We call her that, but actually Erin and Danny are cousins. She's named after Danny's mother.''

Her explanation left Linnea more confused than ever. Apparently it showed because Karen smiled ruefully. ''It's sort of complicated. I'll start at the beginning when we have a chance to be alone. To be brief, Zed and I are raising Danny even though he's Talal's son. Danny's almost two. Erin is our child and she's three months old.''

Danny bounded into the room, stopping momentarily when he saw Yasmin standing by the cradle. Marching over to her, he looked from her to the baby and back. ''Mine,'' he announced.

Karen shook her head. ''He's usually friendly, but he's also at the possessive stage.''

Yasmin's only reaction was to stare at him. ''Danny,'' she said finally.

He smiled at her and grabbed her hand. ''Choo-choo,'' he said, pulling her toward the far end of the room where toys lay scattered around an unlidded chest. Danny was slightly taller and had a sturdier build than Yasmin.

To Linnea's surprise, Yasmin trotted after him without a backward glance.

"Talal said she was three—she's a tiny little thing, isn't she? She must be small-boned. But she's exquisite." Karen gestured toward a chair. "Please make yourself comfortable."

Warmed by Karen's friendliness, Linnea began to relax, feeling safe for the first time since Talal had warned her about the media.

"I don't know how they'll get along," she told Karen. "Yasmin doesn't understand English."

"Don't worry. Kids find ways to communicate even when they speak different languages. I noticed it when I was teaching." She glanced around. "Zed must have taken Talal to the barn to see Najla's colt. She's the Arabian mare Talal sent us for a wedding present—a gorgeous creature."

Linnea's curiosity got the better of her. "Danny's mother—" she began.

She got no further before Karen spoke. "Erin was my cousin. She died when Danny was born and I became his guardian."

Though aware that couldn't be the entire story, Linnea decided not to probe any further at the moment. The back door opened and a female voice called from the kitchen, "Anybody home?"

"In the living room, Jade," Karen answered.

A slim woman with chestnut hair and green eyes strode into the room, her entrance charging the air with vitality. "Hi," she said to Linnea. "I'm Jade, the twins' sister." Tilting her head to one side, she examined Linnea. "Hmm, I can see why you might get to Talal. Can't you, Karen?"

"Don't embarrass Linnea," Karen chided.

"Well, she has and you know it." Focusing her attention on Linnea again, she added, "Don't mind me, I'm harmless."

Karen rolled her eyes, but all she said was, "I think the guys are out in the barn if you want to say hello."

"Much as I like horses, I can wait. Though it might be a long one. Once those two get together..." She broke off, walked to the cradle and knelt next to it, touching Erin's tiny fingers. A moment later Danny was beside her.

"Mine," he said, as he had to Yasmin.

"Yes, I know she's your sister, but can't I be Auntie Jade to her like I am to you?"

While Danny appeared to think this over, Yasmin started to walk past the cradle on her way back to Linnea. Jade reached out an arm and stopped her. "Hello, Yasmin," she said. "I'm Jade."

Yasmin looked at her. "Jaida?" she said uncertainly.

"I can see we'll have to do some retraining," Jade told her. "Talal and his Jaida." She smiled at Yasmin and stroked her hair. "Jade, honey," she murmured. "Just plain Jade."

Linnea thought "plain Jade" was a gross understatement. Jade was as attractive a woman as the twins were men. She started to call to Yasmin, then held back as Danny reached for Yasmin's hand. "Mine," he said, frowning at his aunt.

As Linnea and Karen tried not to laugh, Jade scowled back at Danny, and in that moment, the two looked so much alike they could have been mother and son.

Jade reached and tousled Danny's hair, saying, "Kid, sooner or later, you're going to have to learn to share."

"Why don't we feed Yasmin and Danny now," Karen suggested. "Then maybe we can eat in peace later." As she rose from her chair, the baby started to fuss.

"You go ahead and take care of Erin," Jade said. "Linnea and I will handle the other kids." So saying, Jade herded the children ahead of her toward the kitchen.

Linnea joined her, thinking about Jade's initial remark to her. What had led Jade to believe Talal might be "taken" with her?

Unsure what to feed Yasmin, Linnea settled for the chocolate milk she found in the refrigerator and some bread and jam.

"Ice cream?" Yasmin asked.

"So she does speak some English," Jade said.

"Very little. About as many words as I remember in Arabic."

"Ice cream," Danny repeated.

"Ice cream later," Jade said. "After you eat my wonderful omelette."

"Later," Yasmin echoed. *"Badayn."*

Evidently liking the sound of the word, Danny repeated it. *"Badayn, badayn."*

Yasmin giggled, joined by Danny.

"Good grief, is she already teaching him Arabic?" Jade looked to Linnea for confirmation.

"Sounds like it. This is the first I've heard her laugh. I'm glad she and Danny are getting along so well. At first she wouldn't let me or Talal out of her sight. It made for some awkward moments."

Jade grinned at her. "I can imagine."

"Talal?" Yasmin asked, looking at Linnea.

While she was struggling for a way to make Yasmin understand he'd be coming soon, Danny offered the carrot stick he was eating to Yasmin. She looked from the carrot to Danny and back at the carrot, finally taking a small bite before handing the stick back to him.

"I think our little Arab charmer has discovered a new taste treat," Jade observed.

Talal and Zed came in the back door as Linnea was placing carrot sticks on Yasmin's plate. "That's Yasmin," Danny informed them. "My fwend."

The adults ate later, after Danny and Yasmin were through and once more playing with his toys. By then Erin had been put to bed in the nursery and Karen joined them. The conversation remained general, no one asking any questions about why Talal had brought Linnea and Yasmin to Carson Valley with him.

Over coffee, Jade yawned, apologized and added, "It's not the company, that blasted well over near Dayton had me up at five and I was on the site half the day. One problem after another on what should have been a routine drilling. The only good thing was that Wyatt finally got to work on a bad drill. Can't have the kid thinking well drilling's a breeze. Anyway, I'm going to make my excuses and run or I'll risk falling asleep going up Kingsbury Grade."

"I enjoyed meeting you," Linnea told her as she prepared to leave.

"You're really not what I expected," Jade said. "But then I've always liked pleasant surprises." She slanted a look at Talal. "Watch out for my Arab brother." She gave him a hug as she went past. "These macho foreign types are *mucho* dangerous."

"Don't mind Jaida," Talal said when she was gone. "My little sister is outspoken but she has a good heart. This boy she's teaching to drill is one labeled 'incorrigible' by the authorities. She refuses to believe in labels."

"Nothing fazes our little sister," Zed put in. "I keep telling her one day she'll meet a man who's her match, but she claims no man *is* her match. I can hardly wait until the guy, whoever he is, shows up. There'll be some fallout."

"Zohir women are notoriously hard to handle," Talal added.

"I didn't understand about the well drilling," Linnea admitted.

"Jade owns and actively runs the Adams well-drilling business," Zed told her. "I got the ranch, so we're both happy."

"Zed," Karen said, "there's something I need to show you. Will you excuse us?"

"My tactful sister-in-law is leaving us alone," Talal said after they left the kitchen. "I'm not sure whether her motives are practical or romantic."

"I'm rooting for practical," Linnea said warily.

"I agree that two children crashing block towers in the next room isn't particularly romantic. Yasmin seems to have made a complete recovery. *Inshallah.*" He added the last word almost under his breath. She recognized it as meaning God willing and was touched that Yasmin meant so much to him.

"How much have you told them?" she asked.

"Very little over the phone before we arrived. One learns to be careful about phone calls. The truth to my brother while we were in the barn. He'll tell Karen. Are you comfortable here?"

"This place feels almost like home. I like your family. But we can't stay here forever. We need to discuss—"

He held up his hand. "Yes, but not tonight. Not until we consult with Zeid and Karen. Tonight we will sleep.'' He rose, smiling, and held out his hand. ''Once more under the same roof. It's getting to be a habit.''

She took his hand and let him pull her to her feet. ''While we're still alone,'' he murmured, ''permit me, my lady.'' He raised her hand and brushed his lips across the palm again rather than the back of the hand in what was, for her, far from a courtesy kiss. More like an imprint of ownership, like Danny saying ''Mine!''

But that was being fanciful. Talal had kissed her hand because they both realized it was the closest to a good-night kiss they dared to exchange. As it was, the feel of his lips on her palm tingled through her.

Yasmin slept on a trundle bed right next to Linnea's bed. Either the little girl was too tired to worry about where Talal was or she was getting accustomed to not having Talal within sight all the time.

When Linnea awoke in the morning, to her surprise, Yasmin wasn't in the trundle bed. Opening the bedroom door, she heard Karen's voice, then childish laughter, and she relaxed. It was mutual. Danny had become Yasmin's ''fwend,'' as well as the other way round.

Though she regretted just a little not having Yasmin depend on her so completely, she knew it meant her daughter was taking a step forward. Once dressed in jeans and a T-shirt, she made her way to the kitchen where Karen, holding Erin, sat with a coffee mug on the table in front of her.

Apparently noticing her looking around, Karen said, ''Zed and Talal have taken the kids to the corral to meet Windy the pony.'' She started to rise.

''Stay put,'' Linnea urged. ''Tell me where things are and I'll feed myself.''

''Decaf's on the stove, leaded in the pot.''

Linnea smiled. "I assume Zed, like Talal, prefers leaded. I'm trying to wean myself from the stuff." She took a mug from the tree and poured herself decaf before joining Karen at the table.

Baby Erin stared at her, then suddenly grinned. Linnea tried to respond, doing her best to ignore the pang in her heart.

"Zed says your little girl was the same age as Erin when she was taken from you." Karen spoke matter-of-factly, but sympathy shone in her eyes.

"My Yasmin, yes she was."

"And now Talal, all unknowingly, has brought you another Yasmin, a little girl that isn't the baby you lost." Karen's even tone of voice made it easier for Linnea to respond.

"I love her just the same," she said. "I'll never give her up. But I want my—" She paused, struggling to keep control as tears threatened.

Karen leaned toward her. "Of course you do! What mother wouldn't? I know Talal will find her for you."

"You do?" Despite herself, bleakness threaded through Linnea's words.

"Even if he didn't care about you, it would be a matter of Arab honor." As she spoke, Karen rose and crossed to the cradle, now in the kitchen. After arranging Erin comfortably in the cradle, she stood looking at Linnea. "I understand your ex-husband was Kholi."

"Yes."

"Then you must know something about Kholi honor. Talal feels he must right the wrong even though he isn't the one who made it wrong." Karen smiled. "Besides, once he met you…" She let the words trail off. "Let's just say I've seen my brother-in-law come on to attractive women before, but I've never seen him behave the way he does with you. *Gallant* is the word that occurs to me."

Made uncomfortable by Karen's words and at the same time wanting to hear more about how Talal might feel about her, Linnea veered off at an angle. "Was your cousin—that is, did Talal—?" She broke off, not wanting to offend by being too blunt.

"They weren't married. They had only a brief affair and my cousin never told him she was pregnant. She died having Danny without telling me or anyone else who the father was, though I had a snapshot of her with a man on a boat. Through a mix-up, I identified Zed as that man and accused him of fathering Danny. It became a real mess because he didn't even know he had a twin."

Linnea raised her eyebrows. "Zed didn't know about Talal?"

"Believe it or not. The story's a strange one. Talal can tell you about it better than I since he was the one who straightened things out. But you'll have to catch him before the plane leaves. He's taking off for Kholi tomorrow."

Setting her mug down with a thump, Linnea muttered, "Just like him not to let me in on his plans. Those damn arrogant Kholis." She stood. "Which way to the corral?"

She found Talal holding Yasmin on a gray pony's back while Zed sat on the top rail of the corral fence with Danny on his knee. She climbed up beside him.

"What time tomorrow does Talal's plane leave?" she asked.

Zed gave her a wary glance, apparently alerted by her grim tone. "Seven in the morning."

"From Reno?"

He nodded. "Don't worry. You and Yasmin will be safe with us, I guarantee it." He nodded toward the pony. "Look how she's fitting in already—we'll make a real Nevadan out of her."

"Me ride," Danny said loudly.

"I hear you," Talal responded, lifting Yasmin off the pony. She ran to the fence.

Linnea slid off and hugged her.

"*Ya*, Mama," Yasmin said excitedly, "pony, ride pony!" She looked up at Danny. "Danny ride pony."

"He's had his turn," Zed said. He jumped down and set Danny on his feet. "How about showing Yasmin the barn kittens?" Without waiting for an answer, he shepherded the two children from the corral, offering them a hand apiece. Yasmin took his hand without any hesitation.

"She's adjusting even better than I hoped," Talal said, joining Linnea.

"I agree." Evidently something in her voice warned him because his smile, that oh-so-charming Kholi smile, faded.

"You're not pleased?" he asked.

"I'm definitely pleased. It won't be so hard for me to leave her when I know she'll not only be well taken care of but happy."

Talal scowled. "Leave her? What in the name of a thousand demons do you mean?"

"I think you can come up with the answer."

At that moment, Windy, looking for a handout, butted his head against Talal. "Not now, old hoss," he muttered to the pony. "You've had your share."

"Hoss?" she echoed.

"This is 'Bonanza' country," he said. "It's become a habit to take on the protective coloring of the area

I'm in.'' He eased the gate open and they left the pony behind in the corral.

Pausing outside, he turned her to face him, letting his hands rest on her shoulders. ''You're not traveling to Kholi with me, if that's what you're planning to do.''

She shrugged free. ''You're not in your country. At the moment you're still in mine. Women may have a ways to go here yet, but at least we're treated as thinking human beings. I have the right to share in any plans you make about finding my birth daughter. Why didn't you tell me you were leaving for Kholi tomorrow?''

''I was going to.''

''When? By calling from the Reno airport? Or did you plan to leave a note on my pillow?''

He shook his head. ''A note on your pillow? Linnea, you're being unreasonable.''

She glared at him. ''I am not! I merely refuse to be treated like some helpless creature. That seems to be the way you Kholis view women.''

His hands fastened on her shoulders again. ''I warned you not to confuse me with Malik. I believe you to be a very capable woman, if stubborn.''

''Then you must realize you stand a far better chance of finding my birth daughter if I'm with you in Kholi. Think about it. I'm the only one who can be sure whether or not any child you come up with is, in fact, mine. I'd be able to identify her positively as no one else could.''

His grip loosened and he turned from her, walking with a slight but definite limp to where an empty hay wagon sat in the shade of a thick-trunked cottonwood. She followed on his heels. He leaned against the wagon and she stopped, confronting him. ''Well?'' she demanded.

"You'll stay here," he said with finality. "Because of your prejudice against my country, it's no place for you. Our customs are not yours, and I doubt, with your attitude, if you could even try to conform to them. Therefore, you'd be nothing but trouble. I don't want to spend my time rescuing you from awkward situations."

Taken aback, she could only gape at him until her anger surpassed her surprise. "How do you know what I could and couldn't do?" she cried. "I can do anything in the world that's necessary to regain my child."

He lifted one eyebrow. "I understand you've never been to Kholi."

He was right. Malik had urged her to visit his country with him but she'd known almost from the first that their marriage had been a mistake, and once she became pregnant she was afraid if he ever got her to Kholi he might hold their child hostage to keep her from leaving.

"No, I've never been there," she said bitterly. "After Yasmin was kidnapped by Malik, I tried to get a visa to fly to Kholi and search for her but my request was repeatedly denied. Your country obviously didn't intend to have me interfere."

"Then why do you think you'll be able to obtain a visa now?"

She shrugged. "You belong to the royal family. I'm sure Prince Talal can arrange pretty much what he wishes."

Talal took a deep breath and released it slowly. He started to speak but apparently was distracted by childish voices coming from the direction of the barn. Grasping her arm, he propelled her away from the wagon and around the corner of the house to where a red sports car almost identical to the one he'd stored in New York was parked. He opened the passenger door.

"Get in," he ordered.

"Why should I?" she challenged.

"Because we're not going to argue in front of Yasmin."

He had a point. Linnea slid into the car. Moments later he roared out of the drive.

"Do you have one of these waiting for you in every state in the union?" she asked snidely.

He slanted her a sharp look and jammed his foot onto the accelerator. The car shot recklessly ahead, its speed effectively distracting her. She clamped her mouth shut, refusing to beg him to slow down and forcing herself to resist the urge to hang on to something. He was, she told herself, just waiting for her to show fear. She might be scared silly, but she was damned if she'd let him know it.

They squealed around a corner, gravel from the shoulder spurting out from under the wheels. How she'd love to see him pulled over. Where were all the sheriff's patrol cars? Not on this road, certainly.

"Where are we headed?" she asked finally. "Other than the hospital or the morgue, that is."

He shot her another glance, more assessing than the last, and eased up slightly on the accelerator. "J.J.'s," he said.

Wherever and whatever that was.

J.J.'s turned out to be a small casino called Lucky Joe's off to the side of another road not far from a little town. Talal ushered her into the dark, smoky, noisy interior and led her past the brightly lit, musically muttering slot machines to the far end of the building where a small bar was tucked into a corner. They were the only two customers. He pulled out a chair and she reluctantly sat at the small table. At least the circulation system worked efficiently in this part of the casino because the tiny room seemed almost smoke-free.

He bellied up to the bar and came back with two glasses of foaming beer. She could take beer or leave it alone. For the sake of not bringing up trivia, though it wasn't her favorite drink, she said nothing.

"I like it here," Talal said. "My brother and I first came to an understanding at this very table."

Fine, but what did that have to do with her?

"Here, where there will be no interruptions, is where we will also come to an agreement," he added.

The darkness and the alien jingle of the slots in the background made Linnea feel this wasn't quite real, almost like a dream. She took a sip of the beer, more to keep oriented than because she wanted a drink.

When she set the glass down, Talal reached over and ran his finger along her upper lip. "Foam," he said, licking his finger. "The best taste of all."

A frisson ran along her spine, almost as if he'd licked the foam from her lip instead of touching her with his finger. She shook her head to rid herself of the sensation.

"I admit you've made one valid point," he said. "You alone can make a positive identification of your child. I'm not sure that's enough reason to risk bringing you along because, based on the time I've spent with you, I don't believe you'll do as I say and not cause problems in Kholi."

His words had the sound of compromise in them. Linnea cautiously let go of her anger and sat back in her chair, getting ready to negotiate. "I didn't realize you found me so hard to get along with,'' she said sweetly.

He swallowed half his beer before replying. ''One thing I can't bear is deception. So far, unlike most women, you haven't been guilty of deceit. If you try to deceive or betray my trust in any way while we're here, I'll see that you never get a Kholi visa. Betray me in Kholi and you'll put yourself at such risk even I may not be able to save you from the consequences.''

Betray him? Linnea bristled. What was he talking about? How could she possibly do that? ''I don't believe women are any more deceitful than men,'' she said. ''Malik, for one, was a master of deception.''

Talal waved a hand, dismissing Malik. ''We'll stick to us, to you and me. Perhaps you're naturally honest, as you appear to be, perhaps not. I warn you, we must always be open with each other.''

''Ha! You're about as open as a frozen clam. You may not consider it deception and maybe it actually isn't, but you don't discuss what you intend to do ahead of time, you just expect me to go along with whatever your plan is. That won't wash. As long as we're forced to be in each other's company, I want to be consulted before you make decisions.''

''You find my company distasteful?''

I wish I did, she thought. Everything would be so much simpler. ''No more distasteful than you find mine,'' she countered.

He grinned. ''In that case, we've reached an agreement, *maddamti*.''

She hoped she wouldn't come to regret it.

Chapter Six

Talal couldn't sleep. He rose from his bed in the annex his brother had added to the ranch house and pulled a pair of khaki shorts over his nakedness. Pushing open the sliding door leading to the rose garden flourishing to one side of the pond, he padded out onto the cool brick path, where he paused and glanced upward. The same familiar constellations as in his home sky blinked down at him. He thought of going back to get Zeid's telescope but shook his head. Not tonight. The moon, a crescent sliver, seemed to follow as he ambled on toward the pond, the delightful scent of roses beckoning him.

From somewhere in the direction of the barn, one of the ranch dogs, evidently sensing his presence, woofed twice and subsided. The night air, soft and warm as the hand of a woman, caressed his skin. Which reminded him of Linnea.

Why had he, against his better judgment, postponed flying to Kholi until he could arrange for her to come with him? He suspected his own motives. While it was true she was the key identification person where her daughter was concerned, he'd also been influenced by his desire to have her with him—even though he knew he'd be better off leaving her in Nevada.

Perhaps, for Yasmin's sake, he still should do exactly that. With both of them gone, she might be frightened. Yet, she seemed to be adjusting here. Danny was already her friend. And while she didn't confuse Zeid with him, it was clear she trusted his twin. Karen, of course, mothered every child.

At the pond, he saw the outline of the gazebo at its far end silhouetted against the night sky. The two white ducks had retired for the night to the small island at the pond center. How still it was, the quiet unbroken by any sound of civilization. Like his desert home in Kholi. He wouldn't take Linnea there, she'd be better off staying in the city with his grandmother, who'd keep an eye on her during the times he was away.

Linnea might be honest, but American women were accustomed to making their own decisions rather than being guided by the men in their lives. In Kholi that wouldn't, as she put it, wash.

Yes, Linnea would be a problem. Was a problem, right here and now. No matter how many times he banished her from his thoughts, she reappeared. Perhaps if he allowed himself to bed her, his ever-increasing desire for her would vanish like raindrops in the desert sand. After all, no woman had ever held his interest for long once he'd made love to her. How could it be any different with Linnea?

Talal tensed, sensing someone moving inside the gazebo. The dogs should have created an uproar if a stranger had entered the grounds, but they might have missed the intrusion. After all, he'd only rated two woofs. He moved warily toward the small open structure. He'd almost reached the gazebo when a woman spoke his name.

"Talal?"

Linnea. How, in this darkness, had she known it was him? "So I'm not the only one unable to sleep," he said, advancing to climb the three steps to join her inside the gazebo.

"Jet lag," she suggested, moving away from him and seating herself on one of the benches lining the interior walls.

"Perhaps." He remained standing, unsure whether to stay or leave. Act on his impulses or be prudent and retreat?

When had a Zohir ever retreated?

"Smell the roses," she said softly.

There was an American saying about stopping to smell the roses, one he was tempted to respond to. He eased down beside her and stretched out his left leg. "How did you know it was me?" he asked.

"By your walk."

So she'd noticed the limp his doctors had assured him would lessen with time. What had he expected her to say—something romantic from an Arab poem about being able to sense his nearness?

"A boat accident," he muttered, trying to dispel his unreasonable disappointment. "Never try to outguess ocean weather."

"Sailboat?" she asked.

"Yes, a beauty. I miss her."

"I haven't sailed in ages. When I was a child we

used to summer on Cape Cod and we practically lived on a sailboat. I miss those days.''

He pictured her on his sailboat, the new one he hadn't yet bought. She'd be wearing a one-piece suit that both revealed and teased. Or, if the weather was warm and they lay at anchor in some secluded cove—nothing. Something Zeid had told him came to mind and he smiled, shifting position to lay his arm along the ledge behind her.

"My brother moors his sailboat at Lake Tahoe," he said. "Just a few miles up the mountain. While we're waiting for your visa, we might sail his boat to Emerald Bay. Zeid tells me it's the most beautiful spot in the world.''

"I'm sure Yasmin would love sailing," she enthused.

He had no intention of taking the child along. "I think she prefers being with Danny and Erin," he said firmly. "Which is good. The more she bonds with those here before we leave, the better. To tell the truth, I was beginning to worry that she depended too much on me.''

The nape of her neck lay only inches from his fingers. If he moved them, he'd be caressing the silk of her hair, feeling the enticing warmth of her nape underneath. He'd turn her face toward him and cover the soft sweetness of her mouth with his...

No. Talal clamped down on his imaginings. Not tonight. Here, alone in this romantic gazebo, surrounded by the scent of roses, with only a small slice of moon lighting the sky, she expects you to kiss her and she may very well resist. Don't be predictable. Surprise her.

He shook his head. His strategy was beginning to take on the outline of a battle campaign. Never before had he planned how he'd make love to a woman. It hadn't been necessary—they usually fell into his arms. But then, none of those women had been Linnea.

"It's so peaceful here by the pond," she said. "I had no idea Nevada would be like this."

"Your place in New York with the woods around it must have been peaceful."

"Not like this. Malik never lived in that condo, but the possibility was always there that he might return to America and find me."

"Where did you meet him?"

"At a friend's party in Manhattan." She sighed. "I wasn't very good at looking underneath a charming surface then."

"And now?"

"I've learned. You—" She paused.

Needing to touch her, he temporarily flung strategy aside. Taking her hand, he began playing with her fingers. "How many times do I have to insist I'm not Malik?"

"No, but you *are* Kholi."

"My marriage also failed," he said, surprising himself. He'd spoken to no one but his twin about that marriage. There was something about Linnea that invited his confidence.

"I understood you weren't married to Karen's cousin," she said.

"I wasn't. My wife was Kholi, a marriage arranged by our two families—not uncommon in my country." The pretty dark-haired girl who'd been his bride had faded to a dim memory. He could no longer recall how she'd felt in his arms.

"You divorced her?" Linnea asked.

"She died, a victim of her own deception." Bitterness laced his voice.

Linnea closed her fingers around his. "I know how painful it is to be betrayed by someone you thought you could trust."

Talal took a deep breath. Malik had taught her that. But Malik had been a master of deceit while his wife had seemed so submissive and dutiful, obeying his every wish. He eased his breath out and said, "But merciful Allah granted me a son, Danny, thus freeing me from any reason to marry again."

Linnea withdrew her hand abruptly. "Are you saying you married in the first place only to father a son?"

"In Kholi, it's every man's duty to father sons."

He could sense her anger before she spoke. "What do you do with daughters—drown them?"

"Again, you speak nonsense. We cherish our daughters."

"For themselves or because they will one day bear sons?" Her words quivered with hostility.

"Linnea, this discussion goes nowhere."

She sprang to her feet and he rose to face her. "Malik made it very clear how furious he was with me because I didn't bear him a son. That's why I didn't—" her voice broke but she went on "—why I didn't realize my baby, my Yasmin, was in danger. He didn't want a daughter, he took her from me for spite." She began to sob. "For revenge."

Talal pulled her to him, holding her loosely against him as he stroked her back, murmuring in Arabic because the words of comfort seemed more potent in his language. What a dog Malik had been. He'd died like one, too, shot down by an unknown assassin.

Actually, not quite so unknown as the king gave out. Talal suspected one of his Zohir cousins had a hand in it. Rumor was Malik had been trifling with a Zohir daughter, one too young to beware of honeyed words.

"I'll find your Yasmin." He put his heart into his words. "I swear I will." He didn't add *if she still lives*, though in his mind he acknowledged the possibility he knew Linnea might not. He didn't want to believe her daughter might not be alive and reassured himself by deciding Malik must have gone ahead with the baby's surgery.

Linnea pulled away from him. "I believe you," she told him. "I know you won't disappoint me."

Hearing the trust in her voice, he decided he'd rather die than fail to live up to his promise to her. More than his honor was involved. Much more. So much it frightened him.

In an effort to lighten the immediate situation, he said, "When I do, we'll have two Yasmins on our hands." Belatedly he realized he'd said *we* instead of *you,* but since her only response was a strained laugh, he decided she hadn't noticed. Best to leave well enough alone, though he certainly hadn't meant the *we.*

Before he understood what was happening, Linnea put her hands to his face, rose on her toes and kissed him. Even as he told himself it was a kiss of gratitude, he gathered her close, unable to help himself, and deepened the kiss. She sighed and snuggled closer, her response triggering a rush of desire he struggled to control.

His hands slipped down to cup her against him, inhaling her faint feminine scent mixed with the perfume of the roses. She was so soft, so enticing, and she fit in his arms as though meant for him alone. He wanted, he needed...

"Talal," she murmured against his lips, saying his name like a prayer.

He had to have her, he couldn't wait, the need throbbed through him hot and urgent. But here? On the wooden floor of his brother's gazebo? No, it would be wrong, not right for Linnea and an insult to his brother's hospitality since she was a guest in Zeid's home. Besides, he might well be taking advantage of her emotional state.

Summoning strength he didn't know he possessed, he unwrapped her arms from his neck and stepped back, still holding her hands in his. He bent and kissed each palm before releasing her entirely.

He murmured an endearment, swung on his heel and strode toward the sliding door to his room.

Linnea stared after him, feeling both bereft and annoyed at herself. Part of her wished to be back in his arms, it had felt so right to be held next to him. So right that she'd come within an ace of letting go, of giving herself up to the passion surging through her. Of becoming another of what she suspected were his many conquests. And she couldn't blame it on the sexiness of Kholi men this time. Malik hadn't even come close to making her feel so utterly abandoned.

Why hadn't she had the sense to pull away? She'd been wary enough of being alone with him when he first entered the gazebo, but the moment he took her hands in his, her wariness had vanished like smoke in the breeze. How galling that he'd been able to stop instead of her calling the halt.

Maybe he didn't find her sexy enough. Linnea shook her head furiously. Now she was blaming herself for not being appealing. Damn the man. Never again, she vowed.

* * *

Late the next morning Karen took Linnea aside to share her plans for a barbecue on the following day. "Just family," she said. "We want you and Yasmin to keep a low profile at present. Jade will be here and, surprise, surprise, my brother, Steve. Zed called him yesterday because he thought Steve could be of help in quashing any story about Yasmin that might leak out of Washington. Steve responded by telling us he was coming to meet you and Yasmin."

Not sure how to take this, Linnea asked, "What does your brother do?"

Karen shrugged. "Something secret for the government—he tends to be fuzzy about what it is. If anyone can stop a leak, I'm sure he can. Zed did consult Talal before he called Steve."

Reassured, Linnea said, "I'm sorry Yasmin and I are cluttering up your life."

"Nonsense. Yasmin has totally enthralled Danny, while you—" She paused and smiled at Linnea. "I won't tease you, but it's clear you've shaken Talal to the soles of his feet." She lowered her voice. "One minute he was telling Zed under no condition would he let you go with him to Kholi, and not two hours later he's calling to get you a Kholi visa. This from a man who takes orders from no one—especially a woman. Jade and I are enjoying every minute of it."

"The truth is he finally realized I was the only one who could positively identify my daughter."

Karen shook her head. "Part of the truth, maybe." She eyed Linnea assessingly. "I doubt he knows what's hit him. I'm sure you're able to handle things but—" She paused and gnawed on a fingernail, at last adding, "I keep remembering my cousin Erin. Even though I realize there were no deep feelings on either her side or Talal's, her death haunts me. I've come to love my brother-in-law, but don't let him hurt you.''

Danny and Yasmin interrupted with demands that Linnea come with them to see the barn kittens. "I'll show you our darling Najla at the same time,'' Karen said. "We're still trying to pick a name for her colt.''

"Aziz,'' Yasmin said, picking up her pink toy kitten.

"Do you know what that means?'' Karen asked Linnea.

"*Cherished* or *beloved* in Arabic, as I recall. It's Yasmin's name for her toy.''

"And not a bad name for our colt. Aziz. I like the sound of it as well as the meaning.'' Karen ruffled Yasmin's hair. "Thank you, sweetheart.''

Yasmin favored her with a smile, and the four of them set off for the barn, Danny in the lead.

After lunch, both children settled in for a nap on Yasmin's trundle bed because Danny refused to be parted from her. It eased Linnea's worry over leaving the girl when she saw how attached the two children had become.

"Tell me what I can do to help prepare for the barbecue,'' she asked Karen.

"Jade's already organized everything,'' Karen told her. "The guys will be bringing the supplies and doing the real work—at least Zed will. Talal has never had to do that kind of thing—in Kholi it would be considered menial work and the royal family is above all that. It's not snobbishness, it's simply a way of life that Talal absorbed as he grew up.''

Linnea was looking for a way to ask how it came about that the twins were brought up in different countries when Zed and Talal arrived.

"Everything's under control," Zed announced, "so Talal's going to run up to the lake with Linnea and take *Fancy Lady* for a sail."

"Great idea," Karen said. "It'd be a shame for Linnea to miss seeing Lake Tahoe." Before Linnea could think of any reason not to go, Karen was leading her down the hall to the master bedroom.

"The lake's too cold to swim except in the shallows," she said, "but a suit might come in handy. You didn't bring one, did you?" At Linnea's head shake, she pulled a gold-and-black one-piece from a drawer. "I've never worn this because after I bought it I realized the colors were wrong for me. But they'd suit you— take it along. There are cover-ups and towels and stuff like sunscreen on the boat."

"I'm not sure I should run out on you when you're planning a—"

"Hey, grab the moment. I used to be a cautious Connie, but I learned—from Zed actually—that you'll miss the boat if you hang too far back." Her smile was secret, a personal smile.

Linnea was none too sure she wanted any more moments alone with Talal, but the idea of the sail did appeal to her and she knew enough about boats to understand that if it was a good-sized sailboat, as she expected it must be, they'd both be kept too busy for fooling around.

They set off with a picnic basket and drove along the valley floor until they came to a turnoff marked Kingsbury Grade. As the red sports car climbed the steep rise of the mountain, Linnea watched the rocky walls with their sparse growth of evergreens become more and more heavily forested. The aromatic scent of pine and fir invaded the car, and she swallowed to clear her ears as the road rose up and up.

When they crested the summit and Lake Tahoe came into view, she drew in her breath. The pictures she'd seen of the lake didn't begin to do justice to its sparkling magnificence.

"I'm glad I came," she said impulsively.

"So am I." Talal's words were ambiguous. Did he mean he was glad he'd come or that he was glad she had?

Linnea smiled. Maybe both. And what did it matter? Perhaps the high altitude made her euphoric, but why not? They were heading for the most beautiful lake she'd ever seen, the water so blue as to be unbelievable. The sun was shining and there wasn't a cloud in the sky. As a bonus, she loved to sail.

Fancy Lady was a fourteen-foot clipper, large enough to keep two people occupied until they got her away from shore. The wind caught the sails, and she scudded along briskly until at last they'd passed all the noisy powerboats and silence reigned.

"Take the rudder," Talal suggested—at least she chose to interpret it as a suggestion and not an order. Mellow was the order of the day.

She slipped into his place and grinned with exhilaration when she felt the response of the boat under her hand. "This is the life," she said. "Sailing's like nothing else."

He nodded agreeably, then pointed in the direction he wanted her to take. "We're heading for Emerald Bay."

She couldn't imagine how the bay could possibly be more gorgeous than the lake itself. The surrounding mountains with their green canopy of evergreens were

very different from the Cape Cod sand banks of her
youth. Away from the shores there were far fewer boats
on the lake than she'd expected. At times theirs seemed
to be the only one.

Caught up in the magic of sailing, she said little and
Talal also remained quiet. It took forever, and yet no
time at all seemed to have passed when he retook the
tiller and began to tack toward what appeared to be a
passage into a bay. Beyond, the water appeared more
green than blue. Emerald Bay. "Is that an island?" she
asked, pointing toward a rocky upthrust. "There's some
kind of building on top."

"I'm told it once was a teahouse, something like
what the English call a folly, now in ruins. No one lives
on the island. Getting hungry?"

Until he asked she hadn't realized that she was rav-
enous. "Definitely."

"I'll drop anchor before we eat. Makes it easier." He
angled toward shore and tossed in the anchor as the
water grew shallower.

Once the boat lay at rest, without the wind blowing
past, Linnea felt the power of the sun. Since she'd worn
the suit underneath, she pulled off her T-shirt and began
applying sunscreen to the skin areas that had been covered up.

Talal plucked the container from her hand, saying,
"You can't reach your back properly," and proceeded
to rub the lotion over her shoulders, along her spine and
to either side. Wary, she expected him to linger over
the application, but when he did not she missed the
sensual feel of his hands on her back.

At the ranch, when she donned the suit, she'd
checked out the fit in a mirror and found that Karen was
right—the colors became her. Deciding to take a dip in

the cool water before she ate—after all, they were in the shallows—she shucked off her shorts, pleasantly aware of Talal's interested gaze.

"The water's cold," he warned.

"So is the Atlantic," she countered, and slid over the side of the boat.

"Cold" was inadequate to describe the Arctic chill of Tahoe's water. One quick dunking was all she could take. Clambering back over the side she grabbed a towel and wrapped it around her, then climbed up to lie flat atop the cabin, soaking up the welcome warmth of the sun.

After she stopped shivering, she sat up to see what Talal was doing. He'd stripped down to a very brief pair of black trunks that didn't leave a whole lot to the imagination. He had a magnificent body, wide shoulders, tapering to a narrow waist and then down to... With an effort, she dragged her gaze upward and noticed a ridged scar over his left rib cage.

"Another result of your boat accident?" she asked, aware he must know she saw the scar. Among other things.

He nodded.

The picnic basket, she noted, sat open on the seat beside him. Jumping down to the deck she looked inside, her stomach rumbling with anticipation of the wrapped sandwiches on the top. She glanced into the neatly furnished cabin and decided that, though there was a table with benches inside, she'd rather eat on deck.

"After all, this is a picnic," she said aloud.

"And picnics are for the outdoors," he said, finishing her sentence as he reached into the basket.

Without thinking, she slapped at his hand and he

drew it back, blinking at her. "That's not the right way," she told him. "You put down a cloth and lay everything out before eating. There must be a cloth in the cabin."

She waited for him to move but he remained where he was, watching her expectantly. "If you look, you might be able to find that cloth," she said, determined that he was going to lift at least one finger to help.

He finally rose and hunkered down through the hatch, returning with a large towel. She hadn't meant a towel, but she kept her mouth shut. Without comment, she spread the towel on the deck and, kneeling, began to remove the food from the basket. At the bottom was a thermos full of chocolate milk. "Ready," she told him, and sat next to the towel, her legs curved to one side.

He arranged himself tailor-fashion opposite her, straining the black fabric of his suit in a most interesting fashion. She pretended not to notice. Though she was hungry, she was hardly aware of what she ate because her senses were overloaded with Talal's near nakedness. His maleness was a potent lure—all he'd have to do was reel her in.

If she were a fish, that is. She wasn't. And she didn't intend to become his latest catch. She watched him pour more chocolate milk into his cup, admiring his grace of movement. Like a large, sleek animal, he was worth watching. And like such an animal, he was dangerous.

Without warning, he looked at her, his dark eyes catching her gaze and holding her trapped. "How beautiful you are, *maddamti*," he said softly. "That was the name of my lost boat, *Maddamti*. She, too, was a beauty and I miss her. Perhaps, though, I have lost one lovely lady only to find another."

Linnea forced herself to look away, breaking the spell

he was casting, and realized she'd stopped breathing while she listened to him. Irritated with herself, she snapped, "What number have you assigned to me?"

"Number?"

"Sailboats have registration numbers. I can't help but wonder if you don't also assign a number to each of your new women."

He chuckled. "You make me sound like an old-time sheikh with a hundred wives."

"Can't Kholi men have more than one wife if they choose?"

"Four is the limit, but only if the man can support them all equally, both financially and timewise. The custom is dying out. Today, no Zohir has more than one wife. I'm perfectly satisfied with none."

She could understand his satisfaction. After all, she had no desire to marry again. So why did his words annoy her?

Deliberately changing the subject, she said, "Have you met Karen's brother Steve? I understand Zed called him."

"Steve's the best insurance I can think of against anyone bothering Yasmin while we're in Kholi. He has Washington contacts in all the right places. He'll assure Yasmin's safety until our return." Talal half smiled. "You'll like him. Like us, Steve has survived a marriage of deceit."

"Zed and Karen are fortunate."

Talal nodded. "Karen's an unusual woman, one of the few I'd trust under any circumstances." His gaze roamed over her. "But I have to admit that suit looks better on you than it would have on her."

To her distress, Linnea felt herself reddening. But it wasn't entirely because of what he'd said. Something else troubled her—her flush had elements of anger as well as embarrassment, though she wasn't sure why. "Isn't it about time we started back?" she said, turning away in the hope he wouldn't notice.

Talal put his forefinger under her chin and turned her face toward him again. "I think it's charming that my admiration can make you blush. I mean what I say. You're the most desirable woman I've ever met."

He started to lean toward her, their lips almost touching, when she suddenly sprang to her feet. "No!" she cried, realizing what was bothering her: the picture Karen had showed her of Talal standing on a sailboat— no doubt his lost *Maddamti*—with his arm around the pretty redhead who'd been Danny's mother.

"As far as I'm concerned," she said coldly, "a boat's for sailing, not seduction."

Chapter Seven

Linnea and Talal pulled into the ranch drive before sunset, barely speaking. The sail across Lake Tahoe back to the mooring had been fast and flawless, enjoyable despite the fact the only words they exchanged related to the boat. Once in the car, he'd played CDs on the drive down the mountain and she'd given her full attention to the gorgeous scenery and the music— or pretended to.

As he parked and shut off the ignition, she decided she'd had enough of the coolness between them. "Thanks for taking me sailing and showing me Emerald Bay," she said. "The lake and the bay are both spectacular and you're a class-A captain."

"The captain's only as capable as his first mate," he told her. "We make a good team." His raised eyebrow dared her to make something of his words.

She smiled, relieved to be back on semireasonable

terms with him once more. If they were going to be allies they needed to be civil to each other.

Though Zed's pickup was parked at the back of the house, nobody was home. Zed's note on the kitchen table explained why: "Took everyone out for pizza. Back by eight at the latest."

Evidently they'd gone in Karen's car, Linnea decided. She glanced at the clock. Six. She and Talal must have just missed the others.

"What is my lady's pleasure?" he asked. "Shall we scrounge for food here or dine out?"

"Actually, we had our picnic so late I'm not very hungry," she said. "How about a snack for now?"

"Excellent choice. Crackers and cheese, grapes and wine in air-conditioned comfort. We'll have it in Zeid's game room in the annex."

"After I shower," she agreed. "I'll fix, you carry."

He nodded. "An equitable arrangement."

She started across the kitchen and suddenly stumbled, finding it difficult for a moment to find her balance. "That wasn't me," she gasped, holding on to the door frame. "I swear the floor moved."

"A small tremor, nothing to worry about."

Linnea's eyes widened. "You mean an earthquake? Nevada has earthquakes?"

"Minor quakes only in this area of the state, I'm told."

"I've never actually felt an earthquake before," she said, "and I'm none too sure I care to again."

Talal shrugged. "I've been in others. There was no danger in this one."

Easy for an earthquake veteran to say, she thought as she headed for the shower. What a strange sensation to have the very ground under your feet shift unexpectedly. One moment rock solid, the next quivering.

As she rinsed off in the warm flowing water, it occurred to her that ever since she'd met Talal, the ground under her feet had been none too stable, something she couldn't blame on an earthquake. Deliberate or not, he kept her off balance.

She chose a bright pink cotton shift and slipped into sandals, padding into the kitchen where she found Talal, clad only in leather thongs and white shorts, frowning at the wines in the rack. She did her best to ignore the fascinating male flesh exposed to her view.

"You may have to choose," he said. "At home, I don't drink any form of alcohol, so my experience has been limited."

Focusing on his words, not his body, she said, "But you do drink in America."

"I go by the customs of the country I'm in as much as possible," he said. "As an unofficial diplomat for my great-uncle, I find it best not to call attention to differences, to fit in. Besides, I learned to enjoy beer at Princeton." He grinned at her.

His hair, still damp from the shower, curled in dark ringlets over his head, giving him a boyish look that appealed to her. The rest of him was anything but boyish, though—he was a thoroughly adult male. A sexy adult male.

"Your dress is the color of Yasmin's kitten," he said. "Aziz."

His voice lingered caressingly on the Arabic word and her breath caught, wondering how it would be to hear him murmur that she was his beloved—in whatever language.

Careful, she warned herself. Watch it, lady.

After fixing a platter of cheese, crackers, the requisite grapes and other nibbles, Linnea handed the plate to Talal. She chose a white wine at random and, carrying the bottle with two stemmed glasses, followed him along the corridor to the annex. She was aware his bedroom led off the game room, but she had no intention of setting foot inside his room, not on any pretext.

Deciding to take charge of the conversation and stay clear of anything remotely romantic, once they were settled—she in a chair, Talal on the nearby couch—Linnea said, "I'm intrigued by the fact you were raised in Kholi and Zed in Nevada. Karen said it was a complicated story and she'd rather you told me about it."

Talal paused in pouring the wine to look at her. "Circumstances separated us when we were three, too young to remember or understand. Although, since I was the one left behind, I never forgot there had once been another half of me named Zeid, he had no clue he was a twin." He paused, filled her glass and passed it to her.

She sipped the wine, waiting.

He tasted his and shrugged. "I can't judge whether it's good or bad, but I trust my brother's taste. As I trust him. Implicitly."

"Why were you two separated?" she asked.

"Our Kholi father was dead, our pregnant American mother wished to return to her parents—the Adamses—in California to have her baby—Jaida—there. Our Kholi grandparents refused to allow her to take us with her. She escaped secretly but was able to bring only one of us. Zeid."

"So Jade was born in this country while you two were born in Kholi?"

He shook his head. "We were born in California, prematurely, and brought home to Kholi when we were infants. After our mother fled from my country, she feared pursuit, feared she might lose Zeid, and so she begged her parents to adopt him and the baby about to be born and to change their names. This was done. After our mother's death, the Adamses moved to Nevada to make it more difficult to be found.''

Linnea, fascinated, asked, ''Did your Kholi grandparents search for Zed?''

''My grandmother says not. Apparently they were equally afraid that our mother would try to retrieve me by legal means, since I was actually an American citizen. They sought help from my great-uncle, who issued a birth certificate showing I was born in Kholi and therefore a citizen of that country. I grew up believing this.

''It wasn't until Zeid was accused of being Danny's father and began to search for the boy's real father that we found each other. By this time my grandfather was dead and so were both of the Adamses. With my grandmother's reluctant help, I managed to fill in the gaps.''

''What a story! And what a shame.''

''But now we're together. Grandmother Noorah can't wait for me to bring Danny to Kholi, and though she doesn't admit it, I know she's eager to see Zeid once more and become acquainted with Jaida, the granddaughter she's never met. You'll be staying with her.''

Taken aback, she stared at him. ''With your grandmother?''

''It wouldn't be appropriate for you to stay in my home since I have no women's quarters at present. Besides, Grandmother Noorah will be company for you. She understands English quite well though she doesn't speak it fluently.''

Company for her? "Why will I need company?" she asked. "Where will you be?"

"I can't easily take you anywhere in Kholi with me since we aren't related. My great-uncle is fairly liberal about such things, but lately, for political reasons, he's had to placate the *muttawa,* the religious police, and so, at the present time, we're all expected to strictly obey their prohibitions."

Linnea remembered Malik telling her about them. "You mean I'll have to wear a black cover-up when I'm not inside a house?"

"Probably not. Just modest clothes. But it wouldn't be wise for you to walk alone in the city, because unattended women, even foreigners, are sometimes targeted by the religious police. If my grandmother goes with you there'll be no problem—any male relative of hers can accompany the two of you. I may be too busy much of the time to be that escort."

"Sounds like great fun," she muttered.

"You insisted on coming along. When in Rome, you know."

Did he sound slightly smug? Linnea swallowed the rest of her wine to keep from saying so. Anything to help to find her daughter. She'd even be willing to don a black veil if necessary—but she didn't have to like doing it.

They finished the snacks and the wine, then strolled out to the pond where she scattered cracker crumbs to the ducks. The sun had dropped behind the western mountains, creating what seemed to her to be an early twilight, accustomed as she was to the long summer evenings of New York. Talal, she noticed, was staring up at the sky. She'd rather expected him to try to kiss her here in the dimming light, but he hadn't so much as touched her since she'd cut him short on the boat. Denying any disappointment, she told herself it was all to the good—maybe he'd learned his lesson.

"We're supposed to be able to see the new comet this month," he said. "When it gets a bit darker I'll try out my brother's telescope." Glancing around, he added, "The viewing would be better if we drove to where the ranch property ends. There's no light pollution whatsoever there."

"I take it you're into astronomy."

"One of our great Arab poets was an astronomer. Omar Khayyám. Remember how he mentions rising through the Seventh Gate to sit on the Throne of Saturn?"

"I'm afraid my knowledge of Omar begins and ends with that jug-of-wine quatrain."

"Mythologically, Saturn was Lord of Seventh Heaven."

"Seventh Heaven, I've heard of," she admitted, "though not in connection with astronomy."

"The comet is supposed to be passing through that area. Shall we go searching for it?"

She knew he must be referring to a search for the comet, but her disobedient mind presented her with a vision of joining Talal in their own personal seventh heaven. She pictured a lavishly furnished tent somewhere in a desert, she swathed in varicolored transparent veils, reclining on soft rugs. He stood over her, opening his robe, ready to cast it aside....

Linnea brought herself up short. What was the matter with her? She'd already decided she didn't want to make love with him, so why did she keep conjuring up erotic scenes from old sheikh movies? It must be the wine.

"We'll take the truck," he went on. "The telescope won't fit in my car."

"The truck's fine," she said absently, concentrating on banishing her seventh heaven imagery once and for all.

The next she knew, they were jouncing away from the ranch in the pickup, along a back road in increasing darkness, the telescope in the back, swathed in a blanket and strapped down securely to protect it. For some obscure reason it pleased her to find Talal was interested in astronomy. Not to mention poetry, of all things. Well, Arab poetry, anyway.

She recalled looking through a small telescope at the moon when she was a teenager, but her knowledge of the heavens was limited to the Big Dipper and the North Star. She might be able to pick out Venus and maybe Mars, but that about covered her range.

"I'm an astronomy illiterate," she admitted.

"When I was very young," he said, "I would lie on a blanket under the stars in the courtyard and look up at them, holding Zeid's red ball in my hand and wondering if my other half had somehow ascended into the heavens. Even then I knew better than to mention his name aloud."

Impulsively, she reached over and covered his hand with hers for a moment. "I've heard identical twins share a special bond."

"I never found him in the sky, even when I acquired my first telescope. As I grew older, my fascination was transferred to the stars and planets themselves. But now I have the stars and Zeid, too." He turned toward her, the flash of his smile revealed by the dim light from the dash. "First sailing, then poetry, now astronomy. I've reached overload. There's something about you that tempts me to reveal all my secrets.''

"I'm sure you still have a few tucked away where no one can get at them,'' she said lightly.

"I hope so.'' He spoke as casually as she had. "Still, it's only fair you tell me one of your secrets in return.''

An image of Glinda, the Good Witch of Oz, sprang unbidden into her mind and she blurted, "When I was a little girl, more than anything I wanted to be a beautiful golden-haired princess. But after my best friend laughed at me, pointing out my dark hair and general scrawniness, I never did act out my fantasy, not even when I dressed up in costumes for Halloween.''

Talal didn't comment right away, and she'd begun to feel foolish for revealing so trivial a childish secret when he said, "Wishes have a strange way of being granted, though often so disguised one misses the truth.''

Ambiguous but tactful. He really could be rather sweet. For a Kholi, anyway.

He braked, pulling to the side, and stopped the truck. "We've arrived at the perfect spot.'' He switched off the headlights. "Don't get out until your vision adjusts to the dark.''

Night had settled over the valley. Not the pitch black of midnight, but darkness, none the less. A crescent moon was just rising. Through the open window of the truck she heard a faraway half bark, half howl, soon echoed by another, then another. Her first thought was of a dog, but then something else occurred to her.

"Those can't be coyotes!'' she cried.

"Why not?''

"I've never heard a real, live coyote howl before.''

"Jaida says the Paiutes believe Coyote is laughing at

humans. This boy she's taken under her wing is a Paiute, and she seems to be studying to become an honorary one. Not that I belittle her accomplishments. She's a sister to be proud of.''

"A beautiful mountain lake, an earthquake and coyotes all in one day," she marveled. "What more does Nevada have to offer?"

"Perhaps a comet," he said, easing from the truck. She opened her door and jumped out before he could come around to do the honors, then watched him untie and unwrap the telescope. "Bring the blanket," he said. "I may need to put it underneath to level the telescope."

Carrying the folded blanket, she followed him into an empty, unfenced field. He put down the telescope and fiddled with the legs. She offered him the blanket.

"No, I've got things under control," he said, and proceeded to adjust the eyepiece. Standing back, he scanned the sky and then turned the lens toward the left. Her sense of direction was so completely skewed by now that she had no idea which quadrant of the sky he was aiming at.

He peered skyward through the eyepiece, continuing to focus it. Time passed. She unfolded the blanket, spread it on the ground and sat down, giving herself up to enjoying the brush of the wind through her hair from a breeze that carried the tang of sage.

"Ah!" Talal cried. "Come, look, Linnea."

"I thought you were supposed to shout 'Eureka!'" she commented as she rose. "Or is that just for inventors?" Obediently she put her eye to the telescope and magnified stars came into view.

"Near the top of the viewer," he told her.

She focused there, saw what appeared to be a fuzzy blob and said so.

"That's the comet you're looking at. It's not yet close enough to be more distinct."

Despite the vagueness of the image, a thrill shot through her. A comet, she was actually staring at a comet, something she'd never seen before in the flesh, so to speak.

Afterward, he showed her Orion and other constellations, but the high point for her was the hazy blob of the comet and she eventually sat on the blanket again. Not long afterward he turned from the telescope, saw her on the ground and stretched out beside her on the blanket, staring up at the sky.

"What do you hope to find up there now that you're reunited with your brother?" she asked.

"Perhaps I hope something will find me," he said. "Tell me what you see in this Nevada sky."

She craned her neck, trying to look up from a sitting position, found it uncomfortable and lay back next to him. Above her, stars glimmered and glittered. The moon had risen higher. Searching, she located Orion and was about to try to find the Big Dipper when a shooting star flashed across her vision.

"Look!" she cried. "My aunt always said if you make a wish and then see a shooting star your wish will come true."

He chuckled. "If that's true and you viewed the night sky with any regularity, you'd have to be careful what you wished for because meteors are common. As it is, you're stuck with becoming a golden-haired princess."

She laughed. "Fat chance. What about you?"

"That was your shooting star, you saw it first, so my wish will have to wait."

"You know, if you look long enough you get the illusion the stars are falling toward you," she said. "Or maybe that you're falling up into the stars."

He rose onto one elbow and gazed down at her. "Climbing into Omar's Seventh Heaven, maybe?"

Talal lay beside her. His nearness commanded all her senses, blotting out the moon and the stars. His scent mingled with the sage, making the Nevada night his. Wise or not, she yearned to touch him. To have him touch her.

He leaned toward her, not completely closing the gap between them, leaving it up to her to decide what came next. Heart pounding, unable to stop herself, she raised her hand until her fingers traced the curve of his lips, caressed his cheek and then slipped around to his nape, urging him gently toward her until his mouth met hers.

She savored his kisses as his lips teased and explored hers in a prelude to the passion she knew must be simmering inside him as it was within her. Her desire for him had been with her all day, had plagued her almost since the moment they met. She'd resisted as best she could.

Why? Distracted by the overwhelming pleasure of his caresses, she couldn't recall a single reason to resist her own desires any longer. He was Talal, the man she wanted, and he was here beside her, making her heart sing.

His tongue urged her lips apart and she opened to him, tingling with anticipation and need.

Talal burned with need, fighting his impulse to rush into completion. He'd allowed her to make the first move, to show him she wanted to be kissed. Even though her tiny moans of pleasure kept fueling what was already a close-to-explosive desire, he forced himself to a slow pace, enjoying the sweetness of her mouth and the silken feel of her soft curves.

He was granting her what he'd offered no other woman before—this first time was hers to control. But Linnea was different from any other woman. He'd planned to seduce her on the boat but had temporarily given up after her caustic remark about numbers. So much for planning ahead. He hadn't counted on so much as a kiss during this jaunt to see the comet. Then she'd spread out the blanket and sat on it, and she'd brought his lips to hers. Unplanned and all the more precious.

If she wanted him to stop, she'd have to say so soon because she was driving him up so fast he felt like a comet flaming in the heat of her atmosphere. When she pressed herself tightly against him, he groaned. He needed her beneath him, flesh next to flesh, opening her velvet warmth to him, welcoming him, enclosing him.

He eased away far enough to remove her dress, then her bikini panties. He stripped off his shorts and she touched him.

Losing all sense of time and place, he caught her close again, murmuring to her in his language, telling her she was more beautiful, more alluring, more desirable than any woman to be found in paradise.

She whispered his name, a plea in her voice. Not for him to stop, he knew, but to bring them both up through the Seventh Gate to what awaited them beyond.

His intimate caresses confirmed what he already knew, that her passionate need for him matched his for her. This was meant to be, she was meant for him this night under the Nevada sky.

Despite his eagerness, he forced himself to take her slowly, savoring every moment as she began to move with him, sending him deeper and deeper into her enticing warmth until he could hold back no longer. His thrusts grew harder, stronger. As in a dream he heard her cry of completion and sensed her convulsion of pleasure.

He gave himself up to his own pleasure, joining her on their journey together toward Saturn's Throne to a heaven neither could reach alone.

Afterward he was surprised to find himself reluctant to let her go. Even with his desire temporarily sated, he wanted to keep holding her, to continue gently stroking her skin. How had it come about that he'd allowed this woman so much power over him? True, they'd be together for the trip to Kholi, but then they'd part. This could be, would be no more than a short liaison. As his affairs always were. He wanted, he needed nothing more from any woman.

One marriage had taught him not to walk that path again; he had no intention of acquiring another wife. No woman could be trusted not to betray. But his conviction that this was the truth didn't help him to put Linnea aside. His arms still held her close, her scent surrounding him, her soft curves beginning to trigger another tickle of desire.

Linnea told herself she should move away from Talal, but his naked warmth held her in thrall. How wonderful to lie here without the urgency of need, to simply enjoy the feeling of being close to him, to savor the pleasure of his hand caressing her back. Not that she meant to allow this night to lead to anything permanent. The last thing in the world she intended to do was to become seriously involved with another Kholi male.

Apparently she needn't worry about another night like this one—at least not while she was staying with his grandmother in Kholi. And after Kholi... Linnea sighed. Once they found her birth daughter she'd probably never see him again.

The idea of going to Kholi frightened her, but she was determined. Though she hated to leave Yasmin, she knew as long as the girl remained here in Nevada with Zed and Karen she'd be safe. Zed was a prince of the ruling family, after all, so if any attempt was made to take Yasmin back to Kholi in her absence, he had the ability to thwart it. In addition, Steve was connected with the powers-that-be in Washington.

So she needn't worry about Yasmin. Or about herself, if she was to be protected by Talal while in Kholi. The idea of needing his protection unsettled her. She'd been on her own for enough years to be confident she could fend for herself—even in Kholi—if she were careful to obey their laws and customs. Which she meant to do. She was going there to find the daughter Malik had stolen from her and discover why another child had been substituted for that daughter. Whatever she must do to accomplish this, she would, even to wearing the black veil. Even to staying with his grandmother, whom she was certain wouldn't approve of her.

His grandmother had already lost one grandson because his mother was an American. Wouldn't she see Linnea as a threat? Wouldn't she worry that Talal might disappoint her by taking an American wife? He wouldn't, of course, any more than Linnea would marry him even if he asked her. His grandmother had nothing whatsoever to be apprehensive about where she was concerned.

There was no real reason to be frightened. Yet she shivered as the locked door in her mind cracked open.

Was her birth daughter still alive? She must be. She had to be!

"Cold?" Talal murmured, holding her closer.

She started to tell him no, but his lips caught the word as he kissed her. The heat of his mouth on hers called up an answering warmth from deep inside her, and before she understood exactly what was happening, a renewed need for him wiped her mind free of all else.

Their second trip to Omar's Seventh Heaven was slower, their initial driving urgency replaced by sensual exploration of each other, adding another dimension, an erotic sweetness to falling into the stars.

She clung to him in the afterglow, thrusting away the chilly thought that the law of gravity still held sway—what falls up must also fall down. If there was to be no future together for them she could still savor each glorious moment of the present. Here and now was enough.

It had to be enough because there would be no more.

Chapter Eight

When Talal and Linnea returned to the ranch, a drowsy Yasmin cuddled next to Linnea. "*Ya*, Mama," she murmured, "pizza good." After Linnea put her into the trundle bed, Yasmin clung to her. "Story," she begged.

Though amazed at the rapidity of the girl's acquisition of English, Linnea knew she wouldn't yet understand much of any story and tried to decide which one to choose.

"Goat," Yasmin said. "Trip-trap."

"You are one smart little girl," Linnea said, hugging her close. "You're mine, you're my darling daughter."

"Mama, mine."

Linnea's breath caught. If Yasmin truly understood the meaning of the word she'd obviously picked up from Danny, it meant that her little girl knew Linnea belonged to her as much as she belonged to Linnea. She hated to leave Yasmin behind. Yet she must.

Blinking back tears, she tucked Yasmin under the sheet and brushed a strand of hair from her forehead. "Once upon a time," she began, "there were three billy goats." Holding up three fingers, she repeated the number, then went on with the story.

Yasmin fell asleep even before the first and smallest goat trip-trapped over the troll's bridge.

When Linnea returned to the living room, Zed and Talal were nowhere in sight. "They've gone to view the comet," Karen said. "Isn't it amazing that they both have this fascination with astronomy?"

"And sailing, I gather," Linnea said.

Karen nodded. "At first I didn't think they were much alike, outside of their physical resemblance. But the more I see of Talal, the more I find other similarities to Zed."

"Talal..." Linnea began, intending to point out that he was raised in another culture. Instead, she found herself saying dreamily, "Talal certainly improves on acquaintance."

Karen eyed her assessingly. "If that secret smile means what I think it does, be careful. I speak from experience—with Zed. Those twins wield a fatal attraction where women are concerned."

"You and Zed seem happy together."

Karen smiled. "We are. Now. When we first met, would you believe I called him a conniving weasel, convinced I was speaking the truth. I fell in love with him despite myself. So, be warned."

Linnea didn't need to be warned, she already knew her relationship with Talal had led her into earthquake country, with her feet on shaky ground. "He likes Omar

Khayyám," she said, needing to talk about him but resisting the impulse to share her uncertain feelings with Karen.

Karen rolled her eyes. "Poetry, already. I see my warning comes too late."

"Omar was an Arab astronomer," Linnea protested. "Talal told me that while we were looking at the comet. And I assure you I have no intention of getting in over my head."

"Neither did I," Karen said dryly.

"In any case, Talal and I won't be seeing each other once we find my kidnapped daughter in Kholi and I bring her back to America with me. Apparently I won't be with him that much in Kholi, either, since I'll be staying with his grandmother." Linnea sighed. "I expected to be an active partner in the search for my daughter, but he's doing his best to discourage that. In a way, I understand because I know there are many places in Kholi where women aren't allowed. So I suppose it's true I might hamper his search, but he needn't think I'm going to spend all my time sitting around drinking tea with his grandmother."

"Do they? Drink a lot of tea, I mean?"

Linnea nodded. "Tea and coffee, both. Usually sweetened. I learned from my ex-husband that it would be an offense to the host or hostess to refuse any refreshments offered in Kholi. And he told me for the most part the women are segregated in separate quarters."

"You're not too fond of Kholi, I take it."

"Part of my dislike may have been because my husband and I didn't get along. But from what he told me, Kholi *is* a difficult country for an American woman to get used to. I'd never marry another Kholi."

"You sound like Talal." Karen said. "He's sworn never to marry again, not a Kholi woman or any other."

Linnea started to ask what had happened to his wife but broke off the question when she heard Talal's voice. A moment later the twins came in from the annex. Talal's dark gaze caught hers, making her pulse pound as he crossed to her.

"Is Yasmin sleeping?" he asked.

"I didn't even come close to finishing the goats and troll story before she dropped off," she told him.

"It's good she's grown confident enough not to need me with her all the time." His wistful tone belied his words. Maybe he was more attached to Yasmin than she realized. Or he realized.

"I'm getting sleepy myself," Linnea admitted.

"A day on the water'll do that to you," Zed commented, dropping onto the couch next to his wife and putting an arm around her shoulders.

Talal's glance at Linnea hinted that he knew of another reason for her sleepiness. He reached a hand to her, a silent offer to help her up from her chair. With no thought other than wanting to touch him, she placed her hand in his, vaguely aware of Zed and Karen exchanging a meaningful look.

"I'll see you safely to your room," he told her.

As though the hall to her bedroom was filled with myriad dangers. She smiled wryly at the thought, perfectly aware the only peril facing her was Talal himself.

At her ajar door he bent and brushed her lips with his, then murmured in Arabic. *Maddamti* was the only word she understood. My lady. His lady. Was she?

Shaking off her bemusement, she said, "Good night, Talal," and left him in the hall.

Sleep claimed her almost as soon as she laid her head on her pillow....

She walked in a green meadow beside a wide and fast-running stream that muttered and grumbled its way over the rocks. On the other side of the churning water a man she knew was Talal stood with his back to her, focusing a telescope upward instead of looking at her. Though it was imperative to attract his attention, danger lay in calling out to him. Her only choice was to reach him by crossing the turbulent stream over the dilapidated wooden bridge ahead of her.

The bridge gave her a strange feeling in the pit of her stomach, apprehension rather than fear, with another emotion akin to hate mixed with it. She wished she were nowhere near this spot, yet to reach Talal she must cross that bridge.

As she neared the span, she noticed that the grass in Talal's meadow grew more lush and green than in the fields on her side. She belonged in his meadow, not alone over here. Gritting her teeth, she set her foot on the wooden boards of the bridge. One foot, then the other, her boot heels clicking against the planks.

She longed to run across, but no matter how hard she tried, she couldn't quicken her slow pace. It took forever to reach the halfway mark. As she did, a dark form suddenly vaulted over the railing, coming from beneath the bridge. She stopped abruptly, anger mingling with fear. How dare anything block her way to Talal!

Though she'd expected to see a monster, she realized a man stood before her. A man she knew. A man she'd hoped never to see again. She spat out his name.

"Malik."

"No farther," he growled.

"You're dead, you can't stop me."

He laughed, laughter that changed to a howl as his face shifted and changed, becoming monstrous. She cringed back, trying desperately to call to Talal, but no sound emerged; she remained mute.

Forcing herself to stop retreating, she confronted the repulsive half man, half monster. "Where is she?" she cried. "What have you done with her?"

"She's mine," he growled. "Only mine. Mine!"

Linnea woke with a start, the word reverberating in her ears, the dream shards still holding her prisoner.

"Mama?" Yasmin's sleepy voice shattered the spell of the dream, returning Linnea to reality.

"I'm here," Linnea whispered to her. "Mama's right here. I'll always be here for you."

Though in a way, she wouldn't. For Yasmin's own safety, she was temporarily leaving her behind to go off searching for the daughter Malik had taken to Kholi. But what else could she do? She couldn't risk losing Yasmin.

Yasmin fell back to sleep quickly, but Linnea remained awake, her thoughts leading her back to the unpleasant dream, keeping her from relaxing. Caught again in the strands of that nightmare, she started at a sound from the hall. Footsteps. Karen or Zed checking on baby Erin or on Danny, she tried to tell herself. But somehow the noise seemed alien, not a normal household sound. A side effect of her bad dream, maybe, but she remained tense.

Disturbed, she slipped from her bed, aware she'd never sleep if she didn't identify what she'd heard. Easing open her door, she stared into the hall, lit only by a night-light. A strange man stared back at her.

Before she had time to do more than gasp, he said in a low tone, "I'm Steve. Sorry to startle you. I hoped not to wake anyone while I tried to discover where Karen wanted me to sleep. Apparently in the annex, since these bedrooms are all taken.''

Her relief rendered her temporarily speechless, and all she could manage to say at first was ''Oh.'' Deciding she ought to act as proxy for her hostess, she reached in back of the door, unhooked her robe and slid into it. Stepping into the hall, she motioned to him to follow her, whispering that they risked waking everyone if they talked where they were.

In the kitchen, Steve turned on the desk lamp that illuminated no more than the low counter with the shelves where Karen kept her cookbooks. Evidently he was completely familiar with the house.

''You're Linnea,'' he said, offering his hand. His shake was quick, firm and no-nonsense. ''I arrived earlier than I was expected. Since I knew where the hidden outdoor key was, I let myself in.''

''Karen did put you in the annex,'' she said. ''Talal's the only one sleeping there. He's in the room to the left as you go into the game room.''

''Thanks.'' His smile came and went as quickly as his handshake had, making her believe he meant to say good-night and head for the annex. Instead he gestured to a kitchen chair, saying, ''Mind spending a few more minutes with me?''

She shook her head and sat down, wondering what he wanted.

Steve lifted a chair and turned it around so that he sat facing the chair back, resting his arms on it as he gazed at her. ''Not a good idea for you to go to Kholi,'' he said.

Taken aback, she bristled. ''Why not?''

''The country's going through one of its periodic

shifts where the *ulema,* the religious extremists, are allowed enough power to make it seem they're in control. Actually, the Zohirs retain their tight grip on the government but, at the moment, find it politically expedient to throw a bone to the religious faction.''

"What does this have to do with me?'' she demanded.

"During these religious alignments with the *ulema,* the *muttawa* are allowed much more freedom. You've never tangled with the Kholi religious police.''

His statement meant he knew she'd never been to Kholi before. She eyed him narrowly. They probably had a dossier on her somewhere in Washington, and whatever he did there must give him access to things like that. "I think the fact that I'll be accompanied by a Zohir will offer sufficient protection,'' she said tartly. "And I'll be staying with Talal's grandmother.''

Steve's left eyebrow rose a fraction. "Good move. But you *are* an American woman. While ordinarily that would offer you some immunity from the *muttawa,* I wouldn't count on any during present conditions. Stay home.''

She gazed directly into his intent hazel eyes. "I can't. I'm the only one who can positively identify my lost daughter.''

"You already have the daughter Talal brought you,'' he said. "Be satisfied. The search for Malik Khaldun's child may dig up buried feuds. If it's expedient, a Kholi family can put revenge on a back burner for x number of years, but it keeps simmering there, never really cooling off completely.''

"She's my daughter, too!'' With effort Linnea kept herself from shouting the words at him. "I love little Yasmin and I'll never give her up, but my lost daughter is still somewhere in Kholi and I can't rest until she's found, until I can hold her in my arms again."

He shook his head without speaking.

A thought struck her. "Do you have any children?" she asked.

His "no" was clipped.

She nodded, her resentment at his unasked-for advice fading. If he'd never been a parent, how could she expect him to understand the way she felt? "I appreciate your willingness to help protect Yasmin," she said, changing the slant of the conversation. "While I'm gone, I need to know she's kept safe from harm—and the media—here in Nevada. Karen assures me that's within your power. So thank you in advance."

He gave her a wry smile. "In other words, shut up, Steve, and go to bed."

With that, she decided she might be able to like him, after all. "More or less," she admitted.

He rose. "I can see you're going to keep Talal on the edge more often than not in the next few weeks. In more ways than one. Do him good. But watch yourself in Kholi—be very, very careful."

"I intend to be," she said grimly.

"We'll see each other again tomorrow, but I'll say *Fi aman Allah* rather than good-night. You'll need it— and more." He turned on his heel and left the kitchen.

Linnea rose slowly, the meaning of the Arabic words filtering through to her. Godspeed, he'd wished her. As she made her way toward her bedroom she wondered how much Arabic he knew. She'd do well to study her phrase book and memorize vital words she might need to have readily available once she arrived in Kholi. With Talal.

She carried his name with her into bed, once more

reliving the intense pleasure of being in his arms. The mere thought of his kisses made her begin to tingle. She fell asleep in a warm flush of anticipatory desire.

The following day, Linnea had no chance to be alone with Talal for even a moment. Rather than directly helping with the barbecue, her assignment involved keeping track of Danny and Yasmin, corralling them when necessary, and that kept her busy. Jade arrived and took over Erin's care, leaving Karen free to coordinate operations. The men were responsible for the actual cooking.

When she came outside with the children, Linnea kept an eye on Talal. While he didn't actually lounge around watching Zed and Steve work, she noticed he had to be told what to do. It occurred to her that might be because he'd never in his life actually cooked a meal for himself, let alone for anyone else. Or even seen it done. The thought made her remember what she kept forgetting—he'd been raised as a prince of the royal family. He *was* royalty.

He wore blue shorts and a Nevada T-shirt Zed had given him. At the moment Talal looked every bit as American as Zed and Steve and certainly didn't fit her conception of a Kholi prince.

Steve was slightly taller than the twins, not dark, with auburn hair. He was attractive enough, but, for her, he paled next to Talal. Even Zed, she felt, wasn't quite as impressive as his twin brother. Perhaps it was because Talal had an air of command that Zed lacked. At least in her opinion.

What kind of musing was this for a woman who knew there'd be nothing permanent about her relationship with this man she found so impressive? A man she didn't even *want* a permanent relationship with.

Belatedly she realized that Jade had joined her and was saying something about guitars. "Sorry, I didn't quite catch that," she apologized.

"I said I wish I could have persuaded Wyatt to come with me so we could show off with a guitar duet later on," Jade said. "But he's shy about strangers. Or maybe *wary* is a better word."

Linnea had to search her mind for a clue as to who Wyatt could be. Oh, yes, the Paiute boy Jade was big-sistering. Before she could comment, Jade began talking again.

"Did you notice Yasmin is starting to call me "Tee" like Danny does? Comes from Auntie. She's a quick little thing."

Warmed by her words about Yasmin, Linnea smiled. "What do you think about Steve?" she asked.

"Likable despite his leanings toward being a control freak. I suspect his ex-wife may have bailed out of the marriage because of that tendency of his—though Karen has other ideas about what went wrong. If you mean will he keep Yasmin safe, not to worry. He'll handle any problems from back East—Zed and Karen will do the rest right here. With a little help from me." Jade paused for a moment, then added, "I hear you'll be staying with Grandma Zohir. Take notes, because we'll be picking your brains about her when you get back."

On her return from Kholi she would, of course, be coming back to Nevada to collect Yasmin. She realized she hadn't planned much beyond that, assuming the three of them—she and the two Yasmins—would live in New York. Now she wondered if that's what she really wanted to do. Somehow, though, she couldn't bring herself to plan further ahead than Kholi and finding her lost child.

Danny and Yasmin ran up. "Erin wants Tee," Danny said.

"*Ya*, Tee, Erin cry," Yasmin put in.

"I had a feeling she wouldn't nap long," Jade said. "I swear babies have a sixth sense about parties—they want to be part of the action. I'm off on my rescue mission."

Danny tugged at Linnea's hand. "Yasmin wants to see the kitties," he said.

"Kitties," Yasmin echoed. "See kitties."

Since the children weren't allowed to go in the barn without permission, Linnea offered a hand to each of them and set off in that direction. Before they reached the barn, Talal appeared.

"The kittens?" he asked.

She nodded, secretly pleased he'd been paying enough attention to notice what she was doing and take the chance to be with her, away from the other adults.

In the barn, once Danny and Yasmin were occupied with the kittens, he drew her off to one side. "Steve doesn't think you should risk Kholi," he said.

She'd been hoping Talal meant to say something a bit more intimate. "So he told me," she said shortly.

"He made a good point about the—"

She cut him off. "It takes more than a threat of the religious police to stop me from going. I've already told you I'd put on the entire Kholi head-to-toe black outfit if I have to. What more can anyone ask?"

Talal frowned. Linnea acted like a mother cat ready to attack. Why she'd gotten her back up over a few innocuous words puzzled him. For more reasons than one, he wished he'd never agreed to let her go with him to Kholi. Steve had correctly diagnosed the present situation in Kholi, not actually dangerous but touchy, with all having to toe the religious line. But that didn't worry him so much as his obsession with her did.

"Why not come right out and say you don't want me along?" she demanded. "It's perfectly clear that you don't."

"Steve—" he began.

Again she interrupted. "Why blame it on him? You're using his words as an excuse and you know it."

Beautiful. Desirable. Intelligent. And too sharp for her own good. Or his. Women could be such maddening creatures, Linnea in particular. Didn't she realize what he really wanted to do at this moment was carry her up into the loft, fling her down on the hay and make love to her for the rest of the day?

"Well?" she snapped. "Have you nothing to say?"

He wanted her with him in Kholi so much that it made him uneasy. They'd be better apart, with an ocean between them until he cooled off. Because he would in time, he always had. No woman intrigued him for long. She was a woman, how could she be that much different?

"What is there left to say?" he asked.

She stared at him, her amber eyes narrowing. "I'm going to Kholi, one way or another."

"You're going with me. Tomorrow. You will stay with my grandmother and will do as she advises at all times. End of discussion." Because he couldn't trust himself not to grab her and kiss her into submission, he turned and strode from the barn.

Once with the men again, he began to relax. How much easier men were to deal with than women. Easier companions, easier to understand, easier to get along with. He and Zed shared something more than most brothers; they usually knew exactly, without words, how the other felt. Steve was good to be with, too, a man to be trusted.

While women... He sighed. Unfortunately, men couldn't live without women—he certainly wouldn't want to.

The meal was perfect. Once the hot Nevada sun settled behind the mountains, the evening quickly cooled to a comfortable temperature, great for dining al fresco. Zeid's special barbecue sauce turned the beef into a rare delicacy and Karen's beans were the best he'd ever tasted.

After the unsurpassable homemade strawberry ice cream, Jade fetched her guitar from her truck and played American folk songs while they sang along. He remembered many of the songs from his days at Princeton and was able to join in, making him feel one with the group.

He was startled when his sister began playing a minor-key melody, one he recognized as a familiar old Kholi song. She evidently noticed his surprise because she chuckled.

"I learned the melody," she said, "but the words are beyond me. Do you know them, Talal?"

He did and, momentarily taken back to his childhood in Kholi, began to sing in Arabic. Yasmin rose from Linnea's side and trotted over to him, cuddling close. After a bit she sang with him, her small voice sweet and true.

There was silence when they finished, then the others applauded. Yasmin climbed into his lap and put her arms around his neck, whispering into his ear that she loved him. Tears pricked his eyes as he told her he loved her, too. Here was someone he would always regret leaving.

Much later, after Jade had left and everyone else was in bed, Talal stood outside by the gazebo, gazing up at the waxing moon. He couldn't see the comet with his naked eye, but he knew it was there, sailing along on its fixed course. Perhaps one day a meteor or some other cataclysmic cause would deflect the comet from its course and Earth would never see it again.

Last night he'd viewed the comet through a telescope, first with Linnea, then with Zeid. Much as he loved his brother, the second time had been a definite anticlimax. This comet he would always associate with Linnea. With the first time they'd made love. First and last time?

Talal shook his head. He was nowhere near ready to give her up. And that was the problem.

Linnea lay sleepless in her bed. If she didn't fear Talal might be looking at the stars, she'd get up and go outside. She didn't want to take the chance of encountering him, because he'd believe she was deliberately looking for him.

So Jade thought Steve had leanings toward being a control freak? She ought to take a good look at her Kholi brother. Talal was a you'll-do-as-I-say-or-else type if ever she met one, and she suspected he'd be even more so in Kholi. She was sure she'd eventually begin to hate him.

And yet she'd almost come undone when he began singing in Arabic and Yasmin had joined him. How tender he could be, how loving. As he'd been with her the night before.

Once and never again? She took a deep breath and

eased it out in a sigh. Maybe she'd better begin practicing to hate him right now, before she found herself wandering outside under that crescent moon, searching for him....

Chapter Nine

Linnea assumed they'd be boarding a commercial jet in Reno because that was how they'd flown from New York to Nevada.

Once inside the Reno terminal, Talal led the way, and she didn't pay enough attention to note they weren't going in the same direction as other travelers, not until she found herself outside, heading for a parked jet. Two uniformed men approached, saluted Talal, relieved the skycap of the luggage and took up positions to either side. Belatedly she realized the men weren't wearing any uniform she recognized and it dawned on her they were Kholi.

Talal must have seen her puzzled expression because he murmured, "Palace guards. My great-uncle honors us."

At that point she realized the plane waiting for them

must be a private jet. The size of it—as large as some of the commercial planes—boggled her mind.

As soon as they'd climbed the steps leading up to the boarding door, an attractive young woman wearing a soft flowing dress that only vaguely resembled a uniform showed her first to a fully equipped powder room, then to an upholstered seat that was more like a lounge chair than any airline seat Linnea had ever seen. Another young woman in a similar but different-colored dress hovered over her, asking, in English, if there was anything she could do to make Linnea more comfortable.

"I'm fine," Linnea said, unobtrusively glancing around for Talal. He was nowhere in sight. Her scan of the cabin made her compare it favorably to a luxurious hotel suite; she even glimpsed a bed through a partially ajar door.

Refusing to be put off balance by the obvious wealth a jet such as this represented, she decided to relax and enjoy being treated like a princess, even if she wasn't dressed like one. Her clothes were adequate for an international flight but nothing special. Actually she didn't own anything really special. These past three years she hadn't much cared what she wore—her wardrobe was far from trendy.

Without asking, one of the attendants brought her iced tea and a cloth napkin. She started to take a sip when a man wearing a *thobe*, the long white robe of Kholi, emerged from one of the inner cabin doors. A white *gutra* was wrapped, Arab fashion, around his head, and for an instant, she thought he was a stranger. When she finally understood she was looking at Talal, she choked on her tea.

Immediately both attendants rushed to her side, offering tissues and asking if she was all right. Sputtering, she waved them away, set down her tea glass and dabbed at her lips with the napkin, her actions slow and deliberate to give her time to adjust to this new version of Talal. When Zed drove them to the airport, Talal had been dressed much like his brother, in jeans and an open-necked knit shirt, dressed like a Nevadan. Now he looked like the Kholi he actually was. The plush surroundings reminded her he wasn't just any Kholi, either, he was royalty.

She'd thought he was impressive in western clothes; in his Arab garb he took her breath away. At the same time she felt distanced from him and could think of nothing to say.

"You're comfortable?" he asked, easing into the chair-like seat next to her.

She nodded, vexed with herself for being tongue-tied. "I hadn't realized we were going to fly in a private jet," she managed to say at last.

He shrugged. "I like to relax when I travel. That's impossible in most airliners. The reason we flew a commercial jet to Nevada was to keep a low profile because of Yasmin."

Linnea bit her lip. "I miss her already. I hope she'll be all right while we're—while I'm gone."

"With Danny for a companion, Steve as watchdog, Zeid and Karen as foster parents and Jaida standing by, she won't have time to miss you or me."

"You forgot baby Erin," she said, keeping her voice light to conceal her pang at the possibility he'd raised. She wanted Yasmin to be content and happy, but it hurt to think her new daughter might not miss her at all.

"And the pony," he added. "And the kittens. Not to mention pizza." He reached across the space separating them and took her hand in his, stroking the back of it with his thumb.

The sensuous caress tingled along her nerve ends. No matter how he dressed, Talal affected her strongly. Too strongly. Much more of this and she'd be unable to control her wayward impulse to sit in his lap. Reluctantly she removed her hand from his.

"Yasmin knows we're coming back," he said.

She knew he'd spoken to the little girl in Arabic before they left the ranch. "What did you tell her?"

"A story about a mother who'd searched a long time to find a perfect daughter. What she found was a little girl who was naughty at times, got her clothes dirty and didn't always obey. But the mother loved the little girl, anyway, loved her so much she decided that her new daughter was perfect for her in every way that mattered and she would never give her up."

"And they lived happily ever after?"

"Eventually. But there's more to the story. I told Yasmin she'd hear the rest when we came back to her."

His use of "we" was because he wanted to be certain she and Yasmin were reunited; there was no reason to make any more of it. Would he then accompany the three of them to New York to see them settled in her condo?

Linnea shook her head, unable to picture herself living in that condo with two little girls. But where else would she go?

As though in answer, Talal said, "I prefer Nevada above all the states in this country."

"Didn't you once tell me it reminded you of Kholi?"

"Some, yes. But more than that. Nevada welcomes me, the night sky—" He paused and smiled at her. "The Nevada night sky offers me new visions."

He meant through the telescope. Or did he?

A man's voice spoke in Arabic over a loudspeaker, derailing her train of thought.

"We've been cleared for takeoff," Talal translated. "Fasten your seat belt."

He relaxed into the chair as the jet roared down the runway, comfortable in the loose robe he always enjoyed getting back into. After about an hour he'd be accustomed to wearing the headdress again—it was so much a part of his life that he'd soon forget he had anything at all covering his head.

He glanced at Linnea, who was looking out the window. She counted on him to find Malik's daughter for her. And he would. If the child was in Kholi, as she must be, she couldn't remain hidden once he'd spoken to his great-uncle. The king didn't yet know Talal had delivered the wrong child, that was a matter best spoken of face-to-face. He wasn't looking forward to that task.

The king wouldn't relish discovering someone had duped him and, though he'd know Talal had no part in the wrongdoing, there'd be a backlash from his great-uncle's fury that would land on his shoulders. At the very least the king would demand Talal head the search for the culprit as well as locate the right child.

With the king's power behind him, he couldn't fail to be successful on both counts. He had never failed his king; he wouldn't this time. Nor would he fail Linnea.

But Linnea remained a problem. He must make sure she stayed with his grandmother at all times to prevent her from inadvertently violating any of the current stringent religious rules. He must impress upon his grandmother the necessity of seeing that Linnea didn't wander off by herself, as she might be tempted to do. He intended to strictly obey the rules himself, including his own rule of never being alone with her, even in the privacy of his grandmother's home. If they were alone together, he wouldn't be able to keep his hands off her and that would lead to Allah only knew what complications.

Right now his urge to unbuckle her from the chair, carry her across the cabin into one of the bedrooms and lock the door behind them was all but overwhelming. If he gave in to his need for her, the crew would spread the news all over Kholi the moment the jet landed. For himself the gossip didn't matter, but it would do Linnea no good to be labeled his play-pretty before she even stepped off the plane.

Why did he care so much what his countrymen thought of her? He'd never worried about any other foreign woman's reputation before.

Talal deliberately dismissed the reason behind his concern as being unimportant. Unfortunately, he couldn't dismiss the concern, which meant he'd have to forgo what would have been, at the very least, a diverting pasttime. And, worse, shut up in this jet for hours and hours he'd be tempted by her over and over again. This promised to be a very long, frustrating flight.

Despite being able to stretch out in a bed, Linnea didn't sleep well and she was exhausted by the time the plane finally set down at the Rabbul airport, Rabbul being Kholi's capital. She leaned on Talal as they disembarked in the hot evening dusk and found herself almost immediately climbing into a waiting helicopter along with Talal and the two palace guards.

"I've never been in a helicopter before," she said. "Where are we going?"

"Rabbul is in the desert and hot during the summer,"

Talal told her, "so at this time of the year the king chooses to live at Akrim, in the mountains where it's cooler. He has a copter pad outside his quarters there."

Dazed by her fatigue, it took her a few moments before her mind shifted gears. "Your grandmother is in Akrim as well?"

He nodded. "Everyone who can goes to the mountains in the summer. You'll spend the night with her and will be brought to meet the king sometime tomorrow."

At the moment she didn't care where she was to go as long as the accommodations included a bed. When the helicopter reached its destination, Talal led her to a waiting limo, whose driver opened a rear door. Talal helped her inside where a black-veiled woman already occupied a seat.

"This is Ailia, my grandmother's personal companion," he said. "She'll escort you to the house. "Ailia, this is Ms. Swanson."

Ailia murmured what Linnea presumed to be an Arabic greeting and she mumbled an English response. Only when Talal started to close the door did her sluggish mind understand he wasn't coming with them. Fear clogged her throat. She needed him with her.

"No!" she cried. "Wait. Where are you staying?"

He leaned into the car. "Calm yourself," he ordered. "I'll be with my great-uncle. A car will pick you up tomorrow and bring you to his quarters. I'll see you then. Good night, *maddamti.*"

He shut the door. Linnea sank back against the seat and closed her eyes. Despite the apprehension caused by what seemed to her to be Talal's desertion, she half dozed and had to be roused by Ailia when they reached their destination. In a daze she followed the woman to a bedroom, plucked off her outer clothes and would have fallen into the bed in her bra and panties if Ailia hadn't insisted on sliding a sheer white nightgown over her head.

Linnea woke completely disoriented in a warm, darkened room where sunlight sneaked along the edges of blinds covering the windows. Above the bed, a ceiling fan swung noiselessly. Groggy, she sat up and struggled to focus her mind on her surroundings. She was in Kholi. In Talal's grandmother's house. His grandmother's name, without the Arabic nuances of her lineage, was Noorah Zohir. Talal had said it would be all right to call her Mrs. Zohir.

While she was putting this together, someone tapped on her closed door. "Yes?" she said.

"Is Maha," a woman's voice said. "Maha help."

"Please come in," Linnea told her, deducing that Maha was one of the Zohir servants, temporarily assigned to her. She was grateful that the woman knew at least some English.

Maha pushed a large cart ahead of her into the room. She lifted off a tray and placed it on the low table next to the bed. The tempting aroma of coffee tickled Linnea's nostrils. Heaped neatly on the cart were clothes, most of which Linnea recognized as her own.

After slitting open the blinds to allow light into the room, Maha pushed the cart to a handsome teak wardrobe in a corner and began hanging the clothes inside. Between sips of the very strong, very sweet coffee she'd poured into a cup, Linnea investigated the contents of the tray.

Besides the embroidered napkin and a small, graceful Arabic coffeepot, she found a bowl with dates neatly centered in a circle of orange sections, a pot of honey and a small basket of warm brown bread. After looking in vain for a spreading knife or spoon, she decided that fingers must substitute for silverware in Kholi homes. She'd be expected to dip the bread into the honey.

Maha didn't talk or approach the bed until Linnea finished eating. Then she brought a dress over, a blue cotton with short sleeves and a skirt that went below the calf, holding it up for approval. "Today?" she asked.

Unused to being waited on, Linnea said, "You needn't bother, Maha. I'll do it myself."

Maha, a tall, thin woman who looked to be in her thirties, didn't move. "Madame say help Amreekee."

After mentally translating *Amreekee* to *American* and hoping she was right, Linnea gave in rather than upset the woman and maybe be thought to be meddling in household affairs. If Talal's grandmother wanted the servants to wait on her, she'd just have to accept being pampered while she stayed here.

"The dress is fine for today," she told Maha.

"I fill bath," the woman said.

Linnea watched her disappear through an inner door and then heard water running. "I draw the line at letting her wash me," she muttered, and slid from the bed. Padding across the cool tile floor to the windows, she opened one of the blinds fully. Bright sunlight dazzled her. When she could see clearly, she drew in her breath in appreciation. The window faced on a courtyard filled with colorful flowering plants. Several date palms grew in the center, and stone paths meandered through the foliage.

Turning back to the room, she noted that its sparseness allowed the occupant to admire the intricate fret-

work along the walls and the carved wooden cross-
pieces decorating the high, arched ceiling. The bed, low
and wide, the table beside it, a stool with a leather back,
the wardrobe and a matching teak chest furnished the
room. There were no ornaments on any of the pieces
and no pictures hung on the white walls. No rugs were
on the floor and no drapes were on the windows.

"Uncluttered," Linnea said aloud, just as Maha returned to the bedroom.

"Miss?" Maha asked.

"No matter." Deciding to make her position clear,
she added, pointing to the bathroom, then to herself,
"Alone. I take my bath alone. Me. Not you."

"Aiwa," Maha said. "Yes, miss."

Climbing into a tub large enough for at least two,
Linnea sank gratefully into warm, perfumed water. The
toilet, she'd been relieved to note, was modern, the
Western type of fixture she was accustomed to rather
than the ubiquitous Arabic drain holes she'd heard existed and feared having to use.

As far as the bathroom went, at least, Mrs. Zohir
appeared to have opted for the new rather than the old.
How would Talal's grandmother react to her?

By the time Linnea had donned the blue cotton dress
Maha had chosen, the sun was nearing its height. Past
time for her to seek out her hostess. Chin up to conceal
her trepidation, she emerged from the bedroom just as
Ailia was coming toward her door. Like Maha, she wore
no veil inside the house.

Ailia said something in Arabic, motioning for her to
follow.

For a moment Linnea thought she'd said Talal's
name, but then she remembered that a similar word
meant "come" in that language. As she trailed after

Ailia, she wished the Arab woman actually was leading her to Talal instead of, she suspected, his grandmother.

The large room Ailia led her to was furnished with several couches and a chair. A gorgeous Oriental rug covered the tiles in the room's center. The most striking object in the room, though, was the white-haired older woman who sat in one of the chairs. As she approached the chair, Linnea felt as though she was being presented to a queen.

"Miss Swanson," Ailia announced before leaving the room.

Linnea responded in Arabic, choosing the greeting she'd memorized that meant "peace be with you."

Mrs. Zohir answered in an even, giving-nothing-away tone. The greeting was the same, but for some reason, the words had to be reversed in answer.

Noorah Zohir wore a black dress that reached to her ankles, but there was nothing old-fashioned about the cut or the fit of the dress or the stylish black shoes on her feet. Though she wore no veil, a black silk scarf lay across her shoulders, ready to be pulled over her white hair if necessary. That hair, short and curly, framed a still-attractive round face dominated by assessing dark eyes.

Since Linnea didn't want to be confronted with words she couldn't understand, she said, "Mrs. Zohir, I regret that my Arabic is limited to a very few words."

"Rested, you?" Mrs. Zohir asked in accented English.

"I am, thank you."

Mrs. Zohir inclined her head. "Please, sit, you."

Linnea eased into a chair facing her. From the research she'd done after she'd married Malik, she knew that Arabic custom was to preface conversations with more than one polite inquiry into each other's state of health, but, wanting no misunderstanding about why she was here, she plunged directly into an explanation. "You are, I imagine, aware I'm in your country to find my lost daughter. I'm the only one who can identify her so I persuaded your grandson to bring me here with him. I'm grateful for your hospitality."

Mrs. Zohir waved a hand. "Welcome, you." She frowned. "Confused, me. Child, Talal already bring America."

Linnea explained as best she could about Talal delivering a little girl who was not her birth daughter. "I came to Kholi because I must find my lost child," she finished.

The older woman steepled her hands, murmuring in Arabic. After a moment her hands dropped back into her lap and she said, "Angry, the king." She tilted her head and examined Linnea all over again.

"Ailia!" she called. When her companion appeared, Mrs. Zohir spoke in rapid Arabic, evidently sending Ailia off on some errand. "Power, the Kholi king," Mrs. Zohir told Linnea. "Power, the *ulema*."

No argument there, even if she didn't quite grasp what Mrs. Zohir was getting at. When Ailia reappeared, she began to understand. Talal's grandmother was concerned about Linnea meeting the king while he was out of temper. That must be why Ailia was offering a long-sleeved white silk jacket and a white silk scarf.

Linnea shrugged. She had no objection to covering her arms and her head if Mrs. Zohir thought doing so would be more acceptable to the king. She allowed Ailia to help her into the jacket and to place the scarf over her head and drape it around her neck.

"Waiting, the car," Mrs. Zohir announced, surprising

Linnea. The car from the palace? Had it been here all along?

Mrs. Zohir rose from her chair and walked slowly toward the entry. She was as tall as Linnea, and though not actually stout, she had a matronly figure. Before reaching the door, she pulled her black scarf up over her head and held an end of it across her face.

A dark-skinned servant girl opened the door, then Mrs. Zohir exited and climbed deliberately down the two steps to the drive where a uniformed guard stood beside the car. He smiled at Mrs. Zohir and, to Linnea's surprise, gave her a quick hug.

"Ameen, boy of sister's son," the older woman said. "Miss Swanson, Ameen."

"I am pleased to meet," Ameen said to Linnea.

"How do you do?" Linnea said formally.

"I am well," he answered, opening the rear door of the limo and helping his great-aunt inside. Linnea slid in next to her. Ameen closed the door and got into the front seat with the driver. Remembering Talal's warning about being escorted, Linnea realized Ameen must be doing double duty—a palace guard but also the requisite male relative of Mrs. Zohir.

The limo passed between the gates in the walls surrounding the Zohir house, and as they drove along, through the darkened limo windows she caught glimpses of other houses behind walls. Barren hills, small mountains, really, rose in the distance. Near their summits she saw square white buildings and round towers. There was very little greenery of any kind evident; apparently those who owned the houses hid their flowers and bushes in their courtyards like Mrs. Zohir.

"I've never met a king before," Linnea confessed.

Once seated in the limo, Mrs. Zohir had dropped the

end of the scarf. Linnea watched a mischievous smile turn up the corners of her mouth. "Never meet you before, King Hakeem," she said, and chuckled.

Linnea smiled, warming to Talal's grandmother, who was turning out to be far from the crabbed old crone she'd expected. But she was still nervous about meeting King Hakeem. What did one say to a king other than calling him Your Majesty?

Uncertain what to expect, she obediently removed her shoes like Mrs. Zohir, before being ushered into a large room with seat-cushioned niches along the walls, some larger than others, all with small-paned windows. Though elegant in its simplicity, Linnea was relieved this wasn't the king's throne room—if he had one. A strong-featured older man, somewhat corpulent, rose from a seat in an oversized bay-windowed niche when Linnea and Mrs. Zohir were announced. From pictures she'd seen, Linnea recognized King Hakeem.

"*Ya*, Noorah," he said, holding out his hands to the older woman and continuing to speak in Arabic. He gave her a hug before turning to Linnea. "Ms. Swanson, I regret any grief you have suffered," he told her in a cultured British accent. "You have my word this tragic error will be corrected."

Motioning to the seats in the niche, he added, "Please join me for coffee."

As Linnea seated herself, a servant came through the door pushing a cart. Behind him, Talal strode into the room and Linnea's heart lifted. He crossed to the niche, bowed to the king, kissed his grandmother on the cheek and sat down beside Linnea.

The servant arranged the cart in front of the niche, poured coffee into the small cups the Kholis seemed to favor and handed one to the king before serving the rest of them. King Hakeem waved him away and he exited, leaving the fruit-and-pastry-laden cart behind.

Linnea sipped the sweet, strong coffee cautiously, aware she dare not refuse the king's hospitality. This brew, like Mrs. Zohir's, was decidedly not decaf, and too much caffeine would have her walking on the ceiling.

"You are rested from your journey?" King Hakeem asked Linnea.

"I am, Your Majesty," she said.

"Very good." He turned to Mrs. Zohir and said, "You do not mind if we speak in English, my dear sister-in-law?"

Talal answered for her. "My grandmother has an adequate command of that language. She will not be upset."

"It is to be hoped, despite the unhappy circumstances bringing you here, that you will enjoy your stay in our beautiful country," the king said to Linnea.

"Mrs. Zohir's courtyard is most inviting," she said tactfully. "I expect to pass many pleasant hours there."

She was aware of Talal's swift sidelong look but ignored him. Did he think she meant to flout his warnings and go traipsing about Akrim on her own? She might be independent but she wasn't an idiot.

"Talal will soon bring before me those who violated my trust and they will be appropriately punished," the king said. "At the same time, he will present your daughter to you, the child you bore to Malik Khaldun." He spoke Malik's name as though he found it distasteful.

"Thank you, Your Majesty," Linnea said. "*Shukran.*"

He smiled at her use of the Arabic word, apparently

pleased she'd made the effort to learn a smattering of
the language.

"While Talal's search will prevent him from being
at your disposal," King Hakeem said, "my sister-in-
law will provide for your every need. I trust your stay
will prove satisfactory in every way."

Linnea had no doubt Mrs. Zohir would be a good
hostess, but one thing, one person would be missing
from what she could provide. Talal. Did the king suspect there was something between them? Had he hidden
a warning in his words?

He had no reason to be apprehensive about Talal being interested in her to the point of marriage. He must
not realize Talal didn't want any wife—foreign or
Kholi. Ever.

The king certainly didn't know that even if Talal felt
differently, she would never consider marrying another
Kholi.

One mistake was enough.

Chapter Ten

In the Zohir courtyard, Linnea reclined on a padded lounge in the shade of two date palms. In this secluded place, she wore the one pair of shorts she'd slipped into her luggage at the last minute and a T-shirt Karen had given her that read Lucky Joe's Casino in brilliant red across the front. Lucky Joe's and Nevada seemed a million miles away, even though she'd received a call from Zed letting her know Yasmin was well and happy.

Talal didn't seem any closer. He might be in the same country that she was, but she hadn't seen him in almost two weeks. Why didn't he let her know what was going on?

Was he following a promising lead? She missed him more than she'd thought possible, especially at night when she relived their evening under the Nevada stars. Right now, if she closed her eyes and conjured up an image of him, she could almost imagine they were na-

ked together on the blanket, his lips on hers, his hands
caressing her intimately....

The faint snick of someone cutting shrubbery in-
truded, ending her erotic reverie. She opened her eyes,
noticing an inner gate was ajar, a gate that was always
kept closed and locked if any of the household women
were in this larger section of the courtyard. She wasn't
alarmed, aware the smaller yard was also within the
walled enclosure around the house. A servant must have
forgotten to lock it.

But her daydream of Talal had fled. Sighing, she
picked up the book Mrs. Zohir had found for her, an
English translation of Arabic poetry and proverbs.

"Take advantage of your youth," she read, "life lasts
only an instant." She shut the book with a snap, feeling
she was lounging around growing older every second
while the only one she wanted to take advantage of her
youth with was nowhere near.

Why didn't Talal call?

Resolutely she thrust him from her thoughts, deliberately focusing on her surroundings. Unseen birds
chirped to one another from the palm fronds over her
head. The courtyard was peaceful, beautiful and fra-
grant. Aadel, Ailia's son, was tending the plants with
loving care. He also doubled as the chauffeur when necessary, his presence in the car enabling Ailia to run
errands for Mrs. Zohir.

He was reaching for the pruning shears when he apparently noticed for the first time that the inner gate was
open. As she watched him hurry to close it, something
whizzed though the air near the lounge and thudded into
the shrubbery under the palms. Wings whirred as several birds flew to a safer location.

Alarmed, Linnea sat up and looked around. There

was no one in the courtyard except her. She heard the crunch of the inner gate being pulled closed and the click of the lock, leaving Aadel on the other side. Whatever had been tossed into the shrubbery couldn't have been thrown by him—he'd been in her view at the time. Whatever it was had to have come over the wall from the outside.

Uneasiness crept over her—had she been the object of an attack? Rising, she probed gingerly into the bushes and almost immediately spotted the missile—a large grayish stone with a sheet of paper tied to it with twine.

Again she looked around. Yes, she was obviously alone. Apparently nobody from inside the house had seen what happened because no alarm was being raised. Aadel, intent on locking the gate before he got into trouble, evidently hadn't noticed anything, either.

Curious, Linnea retrieved the rock. Slipping the paper free from the twine, she dropped the stone and smoothed the paper to better read what was written on it. In English. Her heart began to thud. She had to be the intended recipient.

   Mrs. Khaldun,
I know where your daughter is. I will tell only you. Meet me at the Blue Café tomorrow at eleven in the morning. Alone.

There was no signature.

A shiver ran along her spine as she stared at the words written on the paper. Who had written this? Had he also thrown the stone? He? She nodded. In Kholi, the person who initiated this would certainly be male. It didn't surprise her that he knew who she was and why she was in Kholi. News traveled fast in any country. Mrs. Khaldun, he'd called her. Perhaps he didn't know her by any other name.

Mrs. Zohir, commanding one or another male relative as escort, had taken Linnea for several drives around the area. From a closer view, the white buildings on the mountain had proved to be the ruins—Turkish, Mrs. Zohir said. They'd also gone shopping in Akrim, and Linnea remembered seeing the Blue Café, the name spelled out in both Arabic and English. As she recalled, the place was just off one of the main streets and had looked respectable enough.

But, of course, she couldn't go there alone. She read the note again, telling herself she ought to show it to Mrs. Zohir. She knew, though, that Talal's grandmother would advise her to ignore the letter and allow Talal to find her daughter. No doubt she'd also repeat the Arab proverb that Talal had mentioned in New York: Patience is the key to solutions.

Linnea was fast running out of patience. For all she knew, Talal might still have no clue leading to her daughter. If he were hot on the trail, wouldn't he have called to tell her so? She decided not to mention the note to anyone. At least not right away. Not until she decided what to do.

Would this unknown man risk tossing the rock over the wall to her if he'd been lying about knowing the whereabouts of her daughter? It seemed unlikely to Linnea. She wasn't so foolish as to believe he wanted to help her out of the goodness of his heart—he'd expect some reward, probably money. She still had quite a bit in that account in New York that she never touched except in search of her daughter. Once he produced Yasmin, he could have it all.

But how could she get from the Zohir house to the café alone without running the risk of encountering a *muttawa*? The religious police were active in the city; she and Mrs. Zohir had met one face-to-face on their last shopping expedition and he'd given them a lengthy scrutiny.

Linnea had worn the white silk jacket, the white scarf over her head and her longest dress, an ankle-length denim, so not much of her had been exposed to tempt a male. In addition, she and the veiled Mrs. Zohir had been escorted by a uniformed male—many of the Zohir relatives seemed to be members of one branch or another of the Kholi armed forces. The *muttawa* had watched them but hadn't approached.

No, she didn't dare be seen on the street alone, even if she muffled herself in the Kholi black gown and veil. True, if she dressed like one of the black-clad anonymous women, no one would have a clue she wasn't Kholi. Unfortunately, a lone woman would still stand out.

She couldn't just "borrow" one of the Zohir cars— there were three in the garages—because women didn't drive in this country. Once she arrived at the café, she'd be safe enough with the writer of the note as her male escort. They wouldn't be related, but surely the *muttawa* wouldn't be suspicious enough to check identification.

The main problem was how to get to the café. Aadel popped into her mind. If he drove her, she wasn't likely to attract attention. She had some money with her— would he be susceptible to a bribe?

Linnea glanced about, crumpled the note in her fist and jammed it into the pocket of her shorts. She wasn't afraid of meeting a strange man—after all, they'd be among others in a café and he wouldn't be likely to want to call attention to himself. Naturally she wouldn't take any chances. If he proposed that she go anywhere with him, she'd refuse and suggest some alternative. As she perceived it, any danger would come from the religious police, not from the man she meant to meet.

The key to this clandestine meeting lay with Aadel. Was he unhappy enough working as a servant to take the risk of helping her for money? Linnea shrugged. The only way to find out was to ask him.

Her mind made up, she walked briskly toward the house, hardly noticing the heat of midday. Inside, the breeze from the rotating fans cooled the air to tolerable. For some reason Mrs. Zohir didn't care for air-conditioning.

Later in the day, seated in the main room sipping tea, she noticed Talal's grandmother eyeing her with a question in her gaze. She expected the older woman to bring up what was bothering her, but when Mrs. Zohir said nothing she grew fidgety.

Unless she's psychic, Mrs. Zohir can't possibly suspect anything, Linnea told herself. It's your imagination. Guilt can play havoc with your nerves.

She shouldn't feel guilty, because finding her daughter was the single most important thing in her life—but she did. She hated to be a sneak, to betray anyone's trust. What else could she do, though, given the circumstances? If Mrs. Zohir saw the note, it would be goodbye to any chance to meet the man who knew where Yasmin was.

"Come he should, Talal," Mrs. Zohir said at last in her odd English construction.

Linnea nodded, feeling exactly the same. Why hadn't he shown up before now? Or at least called? Still, maybe it was lucky he hadn't. He'd never allow her to go alone to the Blue Café.

Since she needed to study her phrase book to be able to talk to Aadel in Arabic, Linnea told Mrs. Zohir she was going to her room to rest. Actually, it was a relief to get away from the older woman, who seemed to sense something was amiss in Linnea's behavior. Fortunately, she had no way of discovering what it was.

Kholi custom made it very difficult for Linnea to approach Aadel. Women were not allowed to be alone with men unless they were related by blood or by marriage, which meant the servants were off limits, as well. Shortly before the evening meal, she finally caught a glimpse of Aadel in the main courtyard, tending to the flowers, and managed to slip out through one of the glass doors without being seen.

He started when he saw her, apprehension clouding his expression, and seemed about to flee.

"Wait," she ordered in Arabic. Having carefully memorized the words she'd need, she hurriedly went on. "Eleven tomorrow. Cafe Blué. You drive me. No one else. Your pay, fifty *riyals.*"

He gaped at her, but she saw a flicker of cupidity cross his face at her mention of money. He finally agreed.

"Good. I meet you garage tomorrow morning." Linnea turned and hurried back into the house.

She spent a restless night and overslept, waking from a distressing dream of being chased across an endless desert by faceless men. Shaking herself free of lingering traces of the dream, refusing to regard it as any kind of omen, she rose and faced the challenge of the day.

Mrs. Zohir had included a long-sleeved, black gown, complete with veil, in the clothes Maha had placed in Linnea's wardrobe, so she did have one. But she'd have to dress in western clothes first and cover herself with the voluminous garment after she got into the car. The problem would be to sneak the black outfit out to the garage. Even getting to the garage would have to be surreptitious because it wasn't a usual place for a woman to go.

By the time she was dressed, Linnea had worked herself into the spirit of what she told herself was a game where success meant she might recover her daughter. She meant to win this high-stakes game.

The hour between ten and eleven moved on turtle feet. She tried to avoid Mrs. Zohir, unsure she could conceal her eagerness to be on her way. That proved to be no problem since the older woman did not appear. When Linnea finally made it to the garage unseen, climbed into the limo and saw Aadel already in the driver's seat, she sank limply against the back seat cushions in relief.

She didn't know or care what story Aadel might have made up for his reason to take the car out. Despite the dark-tinted windows, she crouched low to avoid being seen until the gates closed behind them. Then she sat up quickly and pulled the voluminous black gown over her head, arranging the shawl part to cover her hair. Last of all she pulled down the veil.

Aadel didn't look or speak to her as he drove toward the café. Which was just as well since she probably couldn't have understood him. She cringed when she saw a *muttawa* along the route, then chided herself. He had no way of knowing who was in the limo. Nothing would go wrong.

After pulling up to the Blue Café, Aadel stayed where he was, reaching his hand back through the open window separating them. She placed the money in his hand and let herself out of the car. As she hurried toward the door, a white-robed Kholi male, a stranger, stepped forward.

"Mrs. Khaldun?" he said in a low tone.

She nodded, glad she didn't have to face walking into the café by herself. Every eye would have been on her, a lone woman in public.

A hand on her elbow, he led her inside, maneuvering around other people and tables until he reached a door. In passing she noted some Western men and women among the customers. Opening the inner door, he motioned for her to enter. She paused to glance inside. Seeing it appeared to be merely a small, private dining area—they did need privacy—she went in. He followed her into the curtain-draped room, closing the door behind them.

Talal stormed into his grandmother's house. "Where is she?" he barked at Ailia. "Where is Ms. Swanson?"

"In her room, if anywhere," Ailia said.

Not pausing to decipher her meaning, Talal marched through the house, throwing custom to the winds as he headed for Linnea's room. Her door was closed. He banged on it. Receiving no response, he flung it open. The room was empty.

"If she's not here, she is nowhere," Ailia said from behind him.

"She can't have disappeared," Talal said. "Where's my grandmother?"

"I'm here," Grandmother Noorah said in Arabic, coming up to where Ailia waited in the hall. She nodded to her companion. "Go along, please." When Ailia was out of hearing, she said, "I suspect Miss Swanson has bribed Aadel to drive her somewhere. Ailia fears for him. With reason."

"Where is Aadel?"

"Driving the limo, of course. I was too dense to suspect at first when he claimed the car needed servicing." She sighed. "As I told you when I called you last night, I knew in my bones the girl was up to something devious. She's incapable of hiding her emotions. That may be a characteristic of American women, because your mother was like that, too. Alas, I didn't associate until too late what Miss Swanson might be up to with Aadel's explanation about the limo needing servicing."

"Where would he take her?" Talal demanded.

His grandmother shrugged. "Only Allah knows."

"Is the phone still in the car?"

"I have never had it removed."

Talal strode to the nearest house phone and punched in the numbers, drumming his fingers against the table while he waited for a response. He might have known Linnea would break her word, would betray him. All women were betrayers, sooner or later.

When Aadel's voice came on the line, Talal shouted at him, "Get home fast. Now. The longer it takes, the angrier I'll be."

Talal was at the gates waiting when the limo came in sight. He strode toward the car. Aadel stopped when he saw him and Talal flung open the driver's door, resisting an impulse to choke the life out of the miserable dog.

"Where did you take her?" he demanded.

"The—the Blue Café," Aadel stammered, his face pinched with fear.

"Get out!"

Aadel stumbled from the car, Talal slid behind the wheel, turned the limo around and roared off. Luckily, it wasn't far. If only he could get there before she caused an incident.

"Who are you?" Linnea asked the stranger as she faced him across the small table. Tea glasses sat in front of them.

"A man who knew Malik," he said. "My name is not necessary." He leaned back and took a sip of his tea.

"Where is my daughter?" she demanded, flipping back the annoying veil. Almost immediately she regretted the move because his eyes gleamed lasciviously as he stared at her unveiled face. She frowned.

He smiled. "We must first discuss terms."

"You want money, I suppose." Despite her growing distaste for him, she tried to keep her tone neutral, to show no emotion. "How much?"

"Do have some tea." He took another swallow. "It's such a pleasure to be sharing a table with an attractive woman."

She bit back a pithy rejoinder. "I'm not here to drink tea," she said as calmly as she could. "I asked you what your terms were. I'd appreciate an answer."

"Perhaps a part of those terms are to enjoy a glass of tea with a charming woman."

What an obnoxious man! He reminded her of Malik, who'd always assumed he was irresistible to women. Though tempted to fling her glass of tea in his smirking face, she hung on to the skirts of her growing anger with determination. Losing her temper would accomplish nothing.

"I'm not here to be charming, I'm here to recover my daughter," she said firmly.

She might have been talking to a post. "I had no idea Malik Khaldun's wife was so beautiful," he murmured.

"I am not Malik's wife." Anger laced her words. "Nor his widow. We were divorced long before he died. I rejected his name at that time and resumed my own. I am not Mrs. Khaldun, I'm Ms. Swanson. Where is my daughter?"

Without warning, he rose and edged around the table. She sprang to her feet, knocking over her untouched glass of tea. "Keep your distance!" she cried, backing away as he reached for her.

The door slammed open. At the sound she noted a look of satisfaction cross the man's face before they both turned their heads to look at the intruder. Scowling, Talal kicked the door shut. "You flea-bitten son of a licentious she-camel," he snarled in Arabic, "take your filthy hands off the woman."

The man backed away from Linnea, shock written all over him. Talal put himself between her and the dog of a Kholi she was with. He'd deal with her later. Before he could make any other move, the door opened and a skinny, wizened *muttawa* sidled into the room, his suspicious gaze flicking over the three of them.

"Cover your face, woman!" he snapped in Arabic. "Have you no shame, cohabiting with two men?"

"Stop!" Talal ordered, holding up a hand as the *muttawa* advanced toward Linnea. "I am Prince Talal."

"I know you, Prince," the man said. "My business is not with you but with this slut of a foreign woman."

The truth struck Talal. A setup. The man knew he'd find a foreign woman in this room with a Kholi male she wasn't married to, knew because someone had notified him ahead of time. He shot a venomous glance at the man, promising death at the very least, then confronted the *muttawa,* desperately trying to think of a way to extricate Linnea from this mess.

"The woman is with me," he said.

"What difference does that make?" the man demanded. "She is still a whore and it is my duty to arrest her."

It dawned on Talal there was only one way to save her. Thanking Allah that he'd arrived before the religious police came on the scene, he drew himself up and glared at the *muttawa.* "How dare you insult my wife?" he snapped. "And me, as well." He drew Linnea to him, pulled down her veil and put an arm around her shoulders. "Can my wife and I go nowhere in my own country without being harassed?"

The *muttawa's* mouth dropped open. When he recovered enough to speak, he bowed his head briefly and muttered, "You should have told me sooner, Prince. I apologize." He scuttled through the door and vanished from sight.

"Talal!" Linnea cried. "He's getting away."

For a confused moment he thought she meant the *muttawa,* then realized the dirty dog who'd contrived this imbroglio was disappearing behind a curtain, evidently through a hidden door. Not daring to leave Linnea alone, he grasped her hand and thrust the curtain aside, revealing a door into a short hall which proved to lead into the street.

By the time Talal threw open the street door, there was no sign of the man. Burdened as he was by Linnea's presence, he realized pursuit would be futile.

He'd left the limo, motor running, in the street in front of the café. As he expected, the car was still there,

unmolested, the Zohir crest on the license plate deter-
ring authorities as well as the criminal-minded.

He handed Linnea into the front seat, skirted the limo
and slid behind the wheel. He pulled away, made a turn
and headed back toward his grandmother's in silence.
Before reaching her house, he pulled off the road into
a street with few houses that ended against a rocky hill-
side, stopping there.

"What in the name of a thousand ghouls were you
doing in that miserable café?" he growled. "Take off
that veil so I can see your face when you tell me."

Linnea, her hands shaking from the frightening en-
counter with the *muttawa,* shoved the veil aside and
reluctantly met Talal's gaze. "He told me he knew
where my daughter was," she said in a small voice.

"How?" Talal's voice snapped like a whip.

She explained about the stone thrown over the wall
with a message attached. "He addressed the note to
'Mrs. Khaldun,'" she added.

"So you decided to break your promise to me instead
of telling my grandmother about the message."

The controlled anger in his voice put her back up.
"Was I supposed to continue lounging around waiting
for a call from you?" she cried. "A call you never
bothered to make? She's my daughter—I had to meet
the person who wrote the note and find out—"

He cut her off. "Do you realize how close you came
to being detained by the religious police? Which is exactly what this Kholi dog intended to happen."

Linnea blinked. In her shock and fear, she hadn't put
it all together. Recalling the momentary smug look on
the man's face when the door opened the first time, she
realized he must have been expecting the *muttawa.*
What a surprise he must have gotten when Talal stood

there instead. Thank heaven Talal had arrived first—she shuddered to imagine the consequences if he hadn't.

"He led me on," she muttered, biting her lip. "But why would he want to sic the *muttawa* on me? Why harm me?"

Talal slammed his fist on steering wheel. "Don't you understand? In Nevada they'd offer one hundred to one odds that he's the man I'm looking for. Placing you in jeopardy would have deflected me, giving him time to make plans to flee Kholi. He knows he's doomed if he remains in the country."

"I never saw him before. Who is he? Do you have any idea?"

Talal nodded. "The last surviving cousin of Malik's. Though he wasn't the man who delivered Yasmin to the king, we've located that man, and with some persuasion, he told us Basheem Khaldun paid him for the errand. Apparently you didn't meet Basheem during your marriage."

"I met very few of Malik's relatives. His parents were dead and he didn't seem to have anyone close. There was a cousin I knew and disliked very much, but this man wasn't him."

"Possibly that was the cousin who was killed with Malik in the accident."

Which hadn't exactly been an accident, she assumed. "If that man in the café was related to Malik he must know where Yasmin is," she said. "Why wouldn't he tell me? I was willing to pay him, but he refused to discuss terms. Instead he—" She broke off, not wanting to reveal how he'd started coming on to her. It was clear now that he'd wanted the *muttawa* to find them in a really compromising situation. What an idiot she'd been!

"Once I get my hands on him I'll choke out all the filthy dung-eater knows," Talal growled. He started the motor and maneuvered the limo around on the narrow road. "I'm taking you back to my grandmother's," he said, scowling. "You are not to leave her house under any circumstances, do you understand?"

She bristled at his commanding tone but merely nodded. He had a right to be angry: she hadn't exactly distinguished herself today and he must resent being forced to rescue her. What, she wondered, had he said to make the *muttawa* back off?

"If you betray my trust one more time," he went on, "I'll have your visa revoked and ship you back to America so fast you won't have time to draw breath."

"I promise I won't venture outside the Zohir walls," she said more meekly than she felt. True, she owed him, but she didn't appreciate being treated as though she were a child.

"Your promises have proved worthless," he said curtly. "Like all women, you've proven to be an expert at betrayal."

Offended, she stared at him. His face set and cold, he didn't so much as glance her way.

Hurt and angry, she retreated into herself, huddling into the ugly black dress covering her from head to toe. Why had she let herself believe Talal wasn't a typical Kholi male? Couldn't he understand what she'd done was because of her urgent need to find her daughter? Once Yasmin was safe in her arms she'd thank him, of course, but she'd make it clear she never wanted to see or hear from him again.

Kholi women, having little choice, had to put up with their overbearing, arrogant men, but she certainly didn't intend to put up with this one.

Chapter Eleven

Talal pulled up in front of King Hakeem's summer palace, slid out and allowed the waiting servant to park his car. He'd called from his grandmother's requesting an audience with the king so he knew he was expected.

The guards waved him through the inner doors, directing him to the sitting place, the king's favorite room. Once he reached the room, he kicked off his sandals outside the arched entrance and padded across the carpeting toward the bay-windowed seating niche the king preferred.

"*Ya*, Talal," his great-uncle said as he approached, "sit here by me." The king motioned to a servant standing by and the man glided from the room, going, Talal knew, to fetch tea.

"You are well?" the king asked. "You seemed disturbed on the phone."

"I am physically well," Talal responded. He was not

looking forward to explaining his run-in with the *muttawa* but he knew it was better King Hakeem hear the news from him.

His great-uncle eyed him consideringly. "The woman?"

"She's created a problem," Talal admitted, and began to relate what Linnea had done, including the confrontation in the Blue Café and his identification of the man Linnea had gone there to meet, the Khaldun cousin who'd unfortunately escaped. He paused when the servant brought the tea and resumed once again when he left.

"I saw no way out of the dilemma but to tell the *muttawa* she was my wife," he explained.

He sipped the sweet, hot tea as he waited for King Hakeem's comments, draining the cup before the king spoke.

"I assume you alerted the national guard," he said. "With luck they'll prevent this dog of a Khaldun from leaving the area and we'll have him trapped. I look forward to his beheading."

Talal waited again, aware the king hadn't finished. He'd placed himself in an awkward position by lying, and he half expected to hear the king demand he put Linnea on the next plane to America.

"As for the woman," King Hakeem said at last, "the problem resolves itself once you marry her. The lie becomes the truth, and as her husband, you can directly control her waywardness."

Talal stared in consternation at his great-uncle, unsure he'd heard him correctly.

The king smiled. "Marriage is, you must admit, the perfect solution. It's past time you took another wife, and while I'd prefer she be a Kholi, necessity makes her this American woman we have wronged. So justice is served.''

Talal swallowed. Suppressing his own objections to the king's solution, he said, ''She won't be happy with your decree.''

The king waved his hand. ''Nonsense. Any woman would be pleased to be your wife. You will easily persuade her, I am sure. If she does prove to be recalcitrant, I have a stick to use. As I recall, you said she wants to keep the little girl we were led to believe was hers. If she gives you any trouble, tell her that unless she's married to a Kholi so the girl may be raised properly, I intend to reclaim the child you delivered to her by mistake.''

He leaned back in his chair and sipped his second cup of tea. ''The wedding will be private, family only, here in the palace. To avoid conflict, I'll inform everyone that you married her in America and we're repeating the ceremony in Kholi to make it official.''

Talal knew enough not to argue. What King Hakeem referred to as a solution was really a royal command and not to be defied. If he weren't the intended groom, he could even admire the appropriateness of the proposal. With one stroke the king obliterated a lie and, at the same time, put Linnea under Kholi control.

Whether Talal wished to marry her—or to marry at all—was of no concern to his great-uncle. He cared even less about Linnea's wishes. A king's decision about what's best for everyone isn't necessarily acceptable to those concerned, and in this case, Talal could see no way out.

''Now that the immediate problem is solved,'' the king said, ''you can devote yourself to running down that camel dung of a Khaldun. After a brief honeymoon, of course. No man should be denied that reward.''

Gritting his teeth, feeling like a sacrificial lamb being led to the slaughter, Talal asked, ''When is the marriage ceremony to take place?''

''Tomorrow. The sooner the better. You and your new wife will move into the palace where she can be well guarded. To avoid any last-minute crises, bring her here today with your grandmother as her chaperone. I look forward to many discussions with Noorah—she's long been my favorite of all my brothers' wives. As you age, you begin to respect intelligence in a woman, and truly intelligent women are rare, you know.''

Numbly, Talal agreed.

When he left the palace he drove directly to his grandmother's. On his arrival he sought her out at once, finding her in the main room. ''Where's Linnea?'' he asked.

She raised her eyebrows. ''No longer Miss Swanson?''

''Hardly. I'm marrying her tomorrow at the king's command. You're to accompany her to the palace immediately, where we'll all be staying for the time being.''

He wasn't sure how she'd react to his abrupt announcement, but at the very least he expected exclamations of surprise and concern.

Instead, his grandmother rose from her chair, saying, ''Then I'd best alert the household to begin packing.'' She laid a hand on Talal's arm. ''Your bride-to-be is in her room. I'll have her fetched here so you can explain the circumstances to her.''

Talal took a deep breath. ''You're taking this calmly.''

"What else do you expect? I'd begun to despair of you ever marrying again. Allah did not design men to live alone. As I've told you, in some ways Linnea reminds me of your mother. I regret I wasn't able, at that time in my life, to accept her, a foreign woman, as my son's wife. Had I done so, the entire course of our lives might have been different. I intend to take this second chance, to accept Linnea as my beloved granddaughter, and so make up for my long ago failing with your mother. At your leisure you might let me know why King Hakeem issued this interesting decree." She patted his arm before leaving the room.

Aware he'd been warned against heading for Linnea's bedroom, he paced up and down where he was. Seeing Aadel in the courtyard watering flowers, he controlled his impulse to rush out and throttle the man. If Aadel had refused to drive Linnea, this entire miserable affair might well have been avoided.

How would she react to the king's order? Her experience with Malik had obviously made her wary of marriage—especially to a Kholi. On the other hand, she'd certainly been willing to make love with him on that night in Nevada. For the first time in this tension-filled day, he smiled. All was not negative; after tonight he'd be sharing Linnea's bed....

Linnea found Talal staring out the window when she walked into the room. "You wanted to see me?" she said defensively.

He whirled around. "You failed to ask what I said to the *muttawa* to convince him not to haul you off. Aren't you curious?"

"I did wonder," she admitted.

"I told him you were my wife."

She blinked, taken aback for a moment before com-

mon sense came to her rescue. Obviously Talal was
Kholi and she foreign—no blood relation there. Marriage would have been their only possible relationship.

"Quick thinking," she said.

"Unfortunately my brilliant lie has backfired. The
king was not at all pleased. As you know, the *ulema*
has embarked on another of their attempts to gain control of the country. At this time, King Hakeem must
tread carefully to avoid giving them any ammunition to
use against him. My lie would be just that."

"Would be?" she echoed, tensing. What was he
leading up to?

"The king has ordered us to make that lie the truth."

She heard his words but they refused to make sense.
Make a lie the truth? "You can't possibly mean the
king has ordered us to marry!"

He shrugged.

"But he can't do that. I'm an American citizen, not
a Kholi."

"He can and he has."

She drew herself up. "I refuse to obey such a ridic-
ulous command and I'll tell him so to his face."

He smiled wryly. "You mean you don't find me irresistible?"

"That's neither here nor there. How I feel about you,
I mean. I have no intention of marrying a Kholi and
you are one. I simply will not do it."

"You will. We'll be married tomorrow at the king's
palace."

Anger steamed through her as she searched for words
scathing enough to sear his arrogant hide.

"Don't bother to raise your voice at me," he said
before she could speak. "Marrying you—or anyone—
is not my idea. But I have no choice except to obey my

king. As for you, he threatens to bring our little changeling Yasmin back to Kholi and keep her here, away
from you, unless you're married to a Kholi.''

"He can't do that!" she cried.

"You know he can. And will. King Hakeem doesn't
make idle threats. Make no mistake, he has the law on
his side, because Yasmin is Kholi.''

Balling her fists, Linnea fumed wordlessly, unwilling
to accept his ominous words as they penetrated deep
into her heart. Yasmin was hers!

But not by law. Admitting the truth, she collapsed
onto the couch, all the fight leaving her. "I don't want
to get married," she whispered.

Talal eased down beside her. "Neither do I.''

She looked at him and saw her own confusion and
unhappiness reflected in his eyes. "I guess we really
don't have any choice, do we?" she said, and burst into
tears.

His arms went around her and she wept on his shoulder in long shuddering sobs as he gently stroked her
back, murmuring in Arabic, the soft, melodious words
easing her distress.

"From joy, the tears?" Talal's grandmother's voice
jolted through Linnea. She pulled away from Talal and
searched her pockets for a tissue.

His grandmother handed her a lace-edged handker-
chief.

"Thank you, Mrs. Zohir." Linnea managed to choke
the words out as she mopped her wet face.

"Grandmother Noorah," the older woman corrected
her, holding a hand toward Linnea. "Come, we pack.''

Linnea glanced at Talal. "Pack?''

He nodded. "We're moving to the palace. Now.''

Everything happened far too fast for Linnea. She felt

she'd scarcely had time to draw breath before she found herself riding in the back of the limo with Talal's grandmother, whom she'd now be expected to address as grandmother, too. In the front, she noticed Aadel drove, as usual.

Apparently seeing her glance at him, Grandmother Noorah said, "Punish Aadel, unhappy, Ailia. Not hurt Ailia, me."

Evidently Aadel was getting off scot free. Since it was really her fault, too, Linnea was relieved for him. She, though, was being punished in a way she never dreamed could happen.

Deciding she had to get what kept bothering her off her chest before they reached the palace, she turned to the older woman and said, "I hope you don't mind about Talal being forced to marry me. You must have hoped he'd take another Kholi wife."

Grandmother Noorah smiled at her. "Make good wife, you. Welcome, Linnea."

Linnea's heavy heart lightened a little at this unexpected welcome into the Zohir family.

"Many sons, Talal," the older woman added. "With Linnea."

Sons? Children? She and Talal? Sudden warmth seethed through her and settled deep inside as she realized she and Talal would be sharing a bed. Isn't that what she'd wanted?

Not exactly. Lovemaking wasn't marriage. And the idea of them having children shook her. Actually they already *had* children. Danny was Talal's son and Yasmin her daughter. They'd share their little changeling, too. Three children and they weren't yet married.

Children should have a father as well as a mother, but she would have preferred to choose for herself. Not that she found Talal physically undesirable. Imagining him lying beside her at night sent tingling waves along her spine.

Even though he didn't want to marry her—or anyone—as he'd said, surely they'd be sharing a bed. Or would they? Recalling that in Kholi a man could divorce his wife by merely saying so gave her pause. Maybe Talal intended this to be an on-the-surface-only marriage, the ceremony meant merely to pacify the *ulema.*

"Bring trunk, me," Grandmother Noorah said, obviously referring to the mound of baggage in the truck following them. "Worry not, Linnea. Come they will, the dressmakers."

Trunk? Dressmakers? As she pieced the older woman's meaning together, it dawned on Linnea that a bride needs a gown. What she'd wear had been the least of her worries until this moment. If she was being forced into this marriage, she damn well wanted to look her absolute best.

"Wedding gown?" she asked.

Grandmother Noorah smiled. "Shape much same, Linnea and Talal's mother. Gown in trunk. Make fit, the dressmakers."

She was to wear the gown Talal's mother had been married in? Linnea drew in her breath, more disquieted than ever. No doubt the dress was beautiful, but to wear it meant linking herself to Talal in a way she hadn't expected. And didn't want?

What *did* she want? Linnea hugged herself, feeling she was being rushed down a steep slope to an unknown and frightening destination at the bottom. More than once she'd insisted she'd do anything to keep her changeling daughter, and now her bluff had been called by King Hakeem himself.

When they arrived at the palace, the limo stopped at a different entrance than the one Linnea had seen before. When they reached the door, it opened and they were greeted by a veiled woman in a Western-style dress who led them down a short corridor and through another door into a small room. Once inside, she threw off her veil, revealing a young face, and hugged Grandmother Noorah. Then she stepped back and examined Linnea with open curiosity.

From the introduction, Linnea learned she was Sahar, a grand-niece of the older woman.

"Come," Sahar urged in English, taking Linnea's hand. "Everyone is eager to meet the girl who finally captured Talal." She smiled. "Many have tried!"

When they arrived in a large room furnished with many couches and chairs, Linnea's first impression was that she'd entered a woman's convention. As she was introduced to one after another, she realized they were all somehow connected to the Zohirs and that this was the palace's women's quarters, the *hareem*.

To Linnea's relief, all of the younger women and a few of the older ones spoke English. Except for Sahar and the king's wife, Wajeeh, she made no attempt to try to connect names with faces; that would have to wait until she wasn't so overwhelmed.

Wajeeh's gracious welcome made Linnea feel these relatives of Talal's didn't resent her presence, but their avid interest in the details of how she'd met Talal made her uneasy. There were just too many questions from too many people, all coming at once.

Grandmother Noorah evidently noticed because she announced, "Rest, Linnea must."

"Yes, the bride must be well rested for her wedding night," one of the younger women said, giggling.

"Especially if the groom is Talal," another added.

To the sound of teasing but good-natured laughter, Linnea left what she couldn't help thinking of as the women's assembly hall, led by Sahar to a suite of rooms she apparently was to share with Grandmother Noorah. She sat on the bed, her head roiling with confusion. What was she doing here? What was she letting herself in for? Finally she kicked off her shoes and stretched out.

She woke to find a light cover over her—unlike Grandmother Noorah's, the palace was air-conditioned. The older woman stood beside the bed. "Awake. Good," she said, and walked briskly to the door, letting in two diminutive women in black, announcing, "Dressmakers."

The fitting was not limited to the wedding gown, a surprisingly well-preserved and gorgeous pearl-studded cream silk dress, long, with a high waistline, but also to other clothes, apparently from Talal's mother's trousseau. His grandmother's memory was accurate, Linnea decided. She must be shaped much like his mother because very few alterations were necessary. Linnea had never donned designer clothes before and she was amazed at the timelessness of the outfits.

While the dressmakers fitted and pinned, a servant entered with a cart containing many boxes of new shoes for Linnea to try on. She'd already decided it was useless to question any of the preparations, so she obediently chose the shoes that fit comfortably. The rest were carted away.

"This all seems like a dream," Linnea said after the dressmakers left with the clothes and she was sitting in a chair sipping the inevitable tea from a tiny cup. "Talal—I mean, I never expected—" she broke off, unable to put her confusion into words. Grandmother Noorah, seated across from her, smiled. "Love like sandstorm," she said. "Take by surprise."

"But he—but I—" Linnea began, and again stopped. Talal's grandmother knew the king had ordered the marriage—why did she speak of love?

Someone tapped at the door, and a woman carrying what appeared to be a large attaché case entered on Grandmother Noorah's invitation. She didn't look or act quite like the other female servants.

"Boshra Guttrah, at your service," she said, nodding to the older woman, then to Linnea. Placing the attaché case on the table, she unlocked and opened it, removing velvet-covered cases and setting them onto the table.

"From jewelers, you?" Grandmother Noorah asked.

Boshra nodded. She opened the lid of one of the cases and walked over to Linnea, who blinked in disbelief at the soft shimmer of gold and the glint of light off what had to be diamonds. She'd never seen such large diamonds or so many clustered together as in the necklace and earrings in the case. Grandmother Noorah glanced at the jewels and waved the case away, saying, "Not right, no."

When Linnea realized she'd have to choose and to wear jewels from one or another of these cases, her mind went blank for a time. Numbly she allowed Grandmother Noorah to pick the necklace and earrings she felt were appropriate—diamonds and emeralds set in gold, elegant rather than ostentatious.

The last case, though, contained smoky gems that

gleamed golden when held to the light. Involuntarily, Linnea reached for the necklace, awed by its beauty.

"Topaz," Grandmother Noorah said. "Yes."

"Thank you," Boshra said, setting the two cases aside and replacing the others in the attaché case, which she locked. "May you wear the jewels in good health," she added before exiting.

"All this is too much," Linnea said, gesturing at the jewelry cases. "Too much."

"Not for wife of Talal."

Maybe not, but she felt like an imposter who was only going to pretend to be his wife for the benefit of the king.

Their evening meal was served in private, to Linnea's relief. She couldn't face any more questions, not today. In the back of her mind she'd been expecting to see Talal, but as the evening drew on, she realized she wasn't going to. With the exception of the king, no man could enter the women's quarters, and she suspected that, by custom, the bride was meant to stay secluded until the ceremony.

She'd counted on talking to Talal because he was the only one who truly understood, who could reassure her, reminding her that there was no choice for either of them. He was the only person she could share her doubts with because she knew he had them, too.

Though she could question his grandmother about the actual ceremony, Linnea decided not to. Knowing more would merely give her something additional to unnerve her.

"What was Talal's mother like?" she asked finally, seeking to distract herself from her worrisome thoughts.

"Some like Linnea. Try be good wife, her. Die, my son, too soon. Mourn, she. Wish go home." The older woman shook her head. "Wrong, my husband. Wrong, me. Make stay. Run away, she. Take Zeid. Lose him, we. Jaida, never see. Wrong, us."

Unexpected tears filled Linnea's eyes as she listened to this sparse account of the tragedy that had separated Talal and Zed for so many years. She could feel his grandmother's grief at what had happened and she felt for the fear and heartbreak Talal's mother must have suffered.

She tried to stem her tears, but what the Zohirs had suffered reminded her of her own agony when Malik abducted their baby. Would she ever hold baby Yasmin in her arms again? In Kholi, she was closer to her but they were still apart. "My baby," she said brokenly.

"Truth find, Talal will," his grandmother said, rising from her chair and crossing to pat Linnea's shoulder. "Strong, he. Loyal. Keeps word."

Her praise of Talal dried Linnea's tears as she mentally added up her own description of him. Arrogant. Intolerant—hadn't he called her a betrayer? Why? What had she done that was so terrible? Tried to find a lost daughter, that's all.

Wiping her eyes, she looked up at Grandmother Noorah and asked impulsively, "Why does Talal believe all women betray men sooner or later?"

His grandmother walked to the curtained windows that faced the women's courtyard and stood there, her back to Linnea, who bit her lip, afraid she'd upset her.

"Desert," the older woman said finally, without turning. "Desert *is* Kholi. Bedouins, we all once. Desert dwellers. Bedouin blood, his wife. Jealous, she. Died in desert, she. Not forgive her, Talal."

Linnea rose and crossed to her, putting an arm around

her shoulders. "I'm sorry I asked, sorry I upset you. I didn't mean to."

Grandmother Noorah turned to her. "Forgive he must, Talal. Someday. Help him, you."

Those words returned to haunt Linnea after she went to bed. Help Talal? How? Even if she knew how, he wasn't likely to let her. She still was in the dark as to the sequence of events that caused his Kholi wife to die in the desert, and she doubted if he ever meant to enlighten her.

Tomorrow he'd be her husband. She wanted, she needed him right now, needed to be held close, to feel his desire match hers, to share with him the only thing she feared they could ever share.

In the men's quarters, Talal paced his room. The evening had been pleasantly enough spent with relatives. He'd survived the usual prewedding chaffing and jokes by shutting his mind down so the words passed by without meaning. Alone, though, he couldn't avoid thinking about tomorrow.

He wouldn't even consider having an alcoholic drink in Kholi but, at the moment, he wished he were in Nevada with Zeid, the two of them sitting in Lucky Joe's with J.J., having a couple of beers. Later, when they were alone, he and Zeid would talk. Only to his twin brother could he speak the truth, reveal his inner self. What he wanted to say couldn't be shared over the phone, he'd have to be face-to-face with Zeid.

Even to Zeid, though, could he admit how urgently he wanted Linnea? The thought of her in bed in the women's quarters, so near but so inaccessible, tortured him. Would making her his wife cure his obsession with her? Once he had the right to make love with her any time he wished, perhaps his intense desire for her would diminish. Intimacy might lead to a cure.

He hoped so. Never had he been so plagued by his need for any woman. No one would ever know how difficult it had been to stay away from her for these past several weeks. But marriage when he'd vowed not to get into that decidedly unblissful state again? Too drastic a solution!

What had his grandmother been referring to when she said Linnea reminded her of his mother? When he was very young, because she wasn't real to him, he'd endowed his mother with such virtues as loyalty and sacrifice. As he grew older, though, his buried resentment—why had she taken Zeid instead of him?—made him feel betrayed.

He still hadn't completely overcome his sense of her betrayal. As he saw it, betrayal was a woman's flaw. Any Kholi male who committed that crime had lost his Bedouin roots, had lost his true identity, was no longer a man.

Grandmother Noorah, whom he loved with all his heart, had also betrayed him by keeping her secret, by shutting him off from his twin for so many years.

His wife had betrayed him.

Talal blinked, suddenly realizing that, after tomorrow, he'd have to think of her as his first wife. He wouldn't have to wait for betrayal by his new bride-to-be, she'd already damned herself.

Chapter Twelve

The sun was up when Linnea woke dazed and groggy from an almost sleepless night. Sahar stood beside her bed.

"The servant brought your tray some time ago," Sahar said. "You must rise and break your fast because there's much to be done and little time for you to get ready."

Sahar left her, and Linnea, though she had no appetite at all, nibbled on the grapes and poured a cup of Kholi coffee, wondering if ever again she'd taste good old American decaf. As she sipped the strong brew, to keep her mind from what was yet to come, she took a deliberate inventory of the bedroom suite. *Lavish* and *lush* were the words that occurred to her. The polished furniture was beautiful, but there were too many pieces crowded in for her taste.

She preferred Grandmother Noorah's spare style. Reminded she was sharing this suite with her, she wondered where the older woman was. Finishing the coffee, she set her cup down, contemplated pouring another and shook her head. Her stomach felt unsettled enough.

Someone tapped on the door, and a moment later it eased open and Sahar peeped in. "Time for the bath," she said, beckoning to Linnea.

Confused—the suite had a fully equipped bathroom—Linnea rose. Sahar took her by the hand and led her down a hall into a large tiled room where she saw what she at first took to be a small swimming pool. As Sahar coaxed her closer, she saw that it was the largest bath she'd ever seen. The scented water steamed, bringing her the fragrance of roses.

Sahar motioned and three young servant girls appeared. "They'll bathe you," she told Linnea. "It's our custom, a purification of the bride."

Linnea eyed the three girls uneasily, aware she couldn't refuse what was custom even though she'd much rather bathe herself. One of the girls slipped the nightgown off over Linnea's head, another urged her into the bath. To her surprise, Sahar lingered, watching as she descended the several steps into the bath. Was this also custom?

As if reading her mind, Sahar said, "A female relative of the groom must see the ritual is carried out properly." Her gaze assessed Linnea. "I was told you bore a child to your first husband," she said. "It's remarkable how you've kept your figure. One would never know."

Unused to such frankness from a stranger, Linnea found herself blushing, which amused the servant girls, who giggled.

At first she submitted resignedly to the soaping and

rinsing, but, as the rose-scented water frothed around her, their gentle ministrations began to relax her, even making her drowsy. The girl washing her hair massaged her scalp with such skill she sighed with pleasure, closing her eyes. She was almost sorry when Sahar clapped her hands, indicating custom had been satisfied.

As Linnea emerged from the bath, one girl wrapped a soft towel around her while another began to pat her dry and the third rubbed her hair with a smaller towel. By now she was almost accustomed to their attentions. When they were satisfied she was sufficiently dry, the towels were whipped away, leaving her naked.

Sahar stepped forward, a small open jar in her hand. She reached into the jar and, with delicate fingers, dabbed a creamy pomade onto Linnea's temples, behind her ears, to her wrists, under her arms and lastly to her ankles. The smell, strong at first, gradually faded to a faint, pleasantly spicy odor.

"A Zohir family secret recipe," Sahar said, smiling. "You are now irresistible to men."

Linnea slipped on a white silk robe held by one of the girls, who gestured toward a dressing table with hinged mirrors. She walked over and seated herself on the padded stool and a servant she hadn't seen before appeared and began to dry her hair. Afterward she brushed and arranged Linnea's curls into an upsweep. Sahar handed the woman a glittering golden chain which she proceeded to thread into the upsweep. Belatedly Linnea realized the glitter came from diamonds set into the gold. Another servant came in with a tray of cosmetics, which she skillfully applied to Linnea's face.

Before she could leave the room, Sahar covered Linnea's head and face with a gossamer white veil. "To conceal the beauty of the bride," she murmured.

Bemused by the exotic pampering, Linnea returned to her room to find Grandmother Noorah waiting with a servant and one of the dressmakers in attendance. Off came the robe, on with new, lace-trimmed wisps of silk lingerie, everything white, including a garter belt and hose. Last of all the gown, now a perfect fit, the luster of the pearls glowing softly against the creamy white satin.

Grandmother Noorah herself placed the diamond-and-emerald necklace around Linnea's throat and inserted the matching earrings into her lobes. Linnea had feared the necklace would diminish the effect of the pearls; instead it enhanced them.

She'd deliberately looked at the gown, the necklace, at those helping her, anywhere but at her image in the cheval mirror. But, finally, she was made to face herself as Grandmother Noorah affixed to her head the gold tiara that held up the bridal veil.

Almost fearfully Linnea stared at her image and sighed in relief. The stunning woman staring back at her bore little relationship to Linnea's own view of herself. It would be all right—the woman in the mirror was to be Talal's bride, this woman could and would get through the ceremony unfazed.

Down came the veil, giving her the temporary anonymity of a bride. She was as shrouded in white as any Kholi woman in the ritual black gown and veil.

At the door, Sahar handed her a bouquet of white rosebuds and Linnea clutched the bridal bouquet with her white-gloved hands like a protective talisman, telling herself what was happening was not real. The other woman, the one who'd been bathed and scented and gowned and jeweled, would deal with it; she wouldn't have to.

With Grandmother Noorah on one side and Sahar on the other, she glided down the hall in a trance. Before they reached what she called the assembly hall, she was startled into awareness by a wild shrieking, accompanied by the rat-a-tat of drums. From one side of a connecting hall crossing just ahead, three lavishly costumed women beating handheld drums danced into sight; from the other side, three women in flowing draperies that left their abdomens bare wriggled into place next to the drummers.

Belly dancers, Linnea realized in amazement.

The assembly room doors were thrown open, and with another series of wild shrieks, the drummers and dancers preceded the bridal party into the room. By the time Linnea entered, numerous guests lined up on both sides of the hall were making strange clicking noises with their tongues.

"Bedouin wedding ritual," Sahar whispered.

Allowing the woman in the mirror to take charge, Linnea followed the chanting drummers and the belly dancers the length of the hall and then halfway back to a dais set several feet above the floor. Sahar escorted her to one of the two elaborately decorated chairs on the dais, leaving her sitting alone there while the drummers and dancers marched and wriggled back to the entrance and exited.

Once they'd disappeared, three white-clad men entered the hall in their robes and headdresses. Talal, in the middle, stood half a head taller than either of the others. She watched as he and his escorts made the same promenade down the hall and back to the dais. One of the men escorted him to the chair next to her and left them.

A man emerged from the line of guests, climbed onto the dais and began speaking in Arabic. Talal repeated some words after him. Looking at Linnea he murmured more Arabic. Realizing she'd be expected to echo his words, she listened carefully and did the best she could. After many invocations to Allah, the man stepped down from the dais.

Immediately the guests approached, filing one by one past the dais, all speaking to the bride and groom in Arabic. Linnea, still wearing the veil, murmured *"Shukran"* until her lips felt numb. No one seemed startled so she assumed it was correct to thank them.

Eons passed before the last guest had his or her say. Linnea started to breathe a sigh of relief, cut short when Talal leaned close and whispered, "Now the wedding feast."

By the time they reached the food table, laden with every possible delicacy, she'd gone beyond rational thought. Turning to Talal, at her elbow, she whispered, "Please can't we leave?"

"They don't expect us to stay," he murmured as, arm about her waist, he escorted her through the crowd toward the door. She didn't have a clue where he was taking her, but she soon realized it wasn't going to be to her room. After being led by him through a maze of corridors, she found herself in a large, overly decorated room with a vast round bed draped in white velvet in dead center. Another, smaller room led off it.

"The bridal suite, for lack of a better name," Talal told her with a crooked smile. He took hold of the edges of her veil and slowly lifted it from her face, then removed the tiara and veil altogether.

Gazing into his smoldering eyes, her numbness vanished like ice in the heat of the sun.

"You're very beautiful," he said, "but I hardly recognize you."

"That's because I'm the woman in the mirror," she told him.

"She's not the woman I want." The huskiness in his voice thrilled through her. "But I'll find the other, she's here somewhere." Talal's fingers pulled out the pins holding her upsweep in place, the diamond-studded chain slithering to the floor. He ran his fingers through her hair so that her curls fell into their customary place.

"You smell good," he murmured.

His touch made her feel as if she couldn't draw enough air into her lungs to keep breathing, but she forced a light tone. "That's because I'm wearing a secret, irresistible scent."

"I have my own secret," he whispered against her lips. "You'd be equally irresistible without it."

She opened her lips to his, tasting him, familiar yet strange and exciting. His arms went around her, holding her close, and she melted against him.

"The gown," she managed to gasp after a long moment. "It was your mother's."

He let her go, turned her around and began to undo the buttons that held the gown together, his lips touching the exposed flesh of her upper back as he continued unbuttoning until the gown fell into a heap around her feet. He drew the long satin slip over her head and off, tossing it aside, then turning her to face him, held her away and stared at her with such evident desire that her insides turned molten.

Reaching behind her, he unhooked her bra, cast it aside and cupped his hands over her breasts, whispering to her in Arabic. "English doesn't have the words I need for your beauty," he said as he bent to taste each breast.

He lifted her, tipped her backward onto the bed and removed her shoes, then unhooked the garters on the belt, sliding her stockings down her legs. Off came the belt, then he knelt and ran his tongue over her inner thighs, sliding his fingers inside the wisp of a pair of panties she wore, finding her warmth and caressing her until she moaned in agonized pleasure.

Hooking his fingers in the elastic rim of the panties, he pulled them off, eased her legs apart and teased her almost beyond bearing with his mouth. She was gasping for breath by the time he stood, tore off his shoes and socks and flung his robe aside. She caught a glimpse of the white shorts he wore underneath and then they, too, were gone. Quivering with need, through half-closed eyes she stared at his revealed maleness.

He dropped onto the bed and pulled her around so she lay on her back next to him. "My princess," he murmured, before rising over her.

Opening to him, she cried his name as he plunged into her, waves of fulfillment already beginning to dance through her. His deep thrusts took her higher and higher as she moved with him in perfect harmony.

Afterward, as she nestled drowsily against him, she remembered what he'd called her. *Princess.* Good heavens, she actually was one now that she'd married a prince of the royal family. A memory from the Nevada night they'd shared slid into place. "When we saw that shooting star," she said, "you warned me to be careful what I wished for."

"So I did." He nuzzled her ear. "And you've been properly punished, Princess Linnea."

"Have I?" she inquired archly, sliding her leg over his, reveling in the delicious sensation of skin against skin. She touched her tongue to his chest, finding he tasted faintly of salt and musk. He slid his hand over her hip, tracing its curve, making her discard every thought except one—Talal lying next to her. His nearness, his scent, his taste, his touch filled her senses, shutting away all else.

Aching need beginning inside her once more, she ran a hand along his lower abdomen, down and down until she felt his nest of hair, then the hard evidence of his desire.

Talal groaned when her hand closed around him. "My little falcon," he said huskily. "Still wild as the wind. I will tame you yet."

His need for her was as powerful as if they hadn't made love for a millennium. He pulled her to him, kissing her with unsated passion that filled him with fire. Her heated response pushed him past reason, past anything but his driving urgency to be sheathed within her pulsating warmth.

He took her with no preliminaries and found, to his delight, that she needed none. Wrapping her legs around him, she matched his eagerness, climbing to the peak along with him, her cries mingling with his groan of release.

This time he sank into total oblivion afterward.

In the morning they bathed together, making slow, sweet love in and out of the tub, feasted on dates and apricots and drank the Kholi coffee he loved. The day was theirs as his great-uncle had promised and they didn't leave the suite or dress. Servants knocked at discreet intervals to bring more food and collect the residue of previous meals.

Surely, after this passion-filled interlude, his obsession with Linnea would lessen and gradually vanish, allowing him to view her objectively. But, for now, he was completely immersed in her, wanting her within arm's reach so he could touch her and caress her between the highs of lovemaking.

Linnea refused to think beyond the moment, each one filled with a new delight of discovery. Her world, for now, consisted of Talal—no one, nothing else was necessary. He inspired heights of passion she'd never believed herself capable of. He was the most sexy, most desirable male in existence and the only one she'd ever want.

Whether this exquisite delirium would last or not, she didn't care. This day was a gift shared by the two of them, a day she'd remember until she died. He was her prince in more ways than one.

They made love, slept, woke, ate, made love again, bathed, napped entwined, their only speech words of endearment, in Arabic and English, as he translated his murmured phrases for her. When night cloaked the world, she fell asleep knowing she'd lived the happiest day of her life, a day to cherish forever.

When Linnea woke in the morning, sunlight crept into the room around the blinds, reaching its rays toward the vast round bed where she lay alone. She tried not to feel deserted. Talal had told her he'd resume his hunt for Malik's cousin Basheem at daylight. Though she realized the sooner the man was found, the sooner she'd be reunited with her daughter, she missed Talal's presence.

A tray of fruit and coffee sat on the table near the bed. Sighing, she rose to break her fast and begin the second day of being a princess. She grimaced at her mirror image.

"Where's the golden hair and blue eyes that were supposed to go with the deal?" she muttered. "For that matter, where's the prince who left you without so much as a note?"

The knock on the door ended her solitude. A servant girl entered, saying her name was Lawand. She opened an ornate wardrobe filled with clothes, none of which Linnea recognized as hers. Some were the altered designer clothes that had been Talal's mother's, but others were new, ones she'd never seen before. The girl extracted a gold sleeveless dress and held it up for Linnea's approval.

Though the dress was more elaborate than Linnea would have preferred, she agreed to the choice rather than interrogate the girl about where her own clothes might be. She'd tackle Grandmother Noorah about them later. She didn't allow the girl to help her bathe or dress, though. That had been a one-time affair as far as she was concerned.

The lack of sleeves and the shortness of the skirt convinced Linnea she'd be restricted to the women's quarters once she left this room. Was the honeymoon suite in no-man's or no-woman's land? she wondered.

When she was dressed, the girl opened a door Linnea hadn't yet used and she saw her guess had been more or less accurate, because the door, which the girl carefully locked behind them, handing Linnea the key, led the way into the women's quarters.

Linnea pushed away her sensation of entering a cage, telling herself she was overreacting, and in any case,

she wouldn't be here forever. But the feeling muted the
glow left over from her day with Talal. By the time she
reached the suite where Grandmother Noorah was staying, sober reality had taken hold. There was more to
her relationship with Talal than lovemaking. They were
married. And he was Kholi.

Grandmother Noorah was not in the room. Sahar,
coming by, told her the older woman was with the king.
"They're old friends," Sahar added. "Do come into the
courtyard with me, many of those our age are eager to
get to know Talal's wife and to ask questions about
America. Do you really live the way the movies and
TV would have us believe?"

"Not exactly," Linnea told her as she permitted herself to be led through an outer door into the courtyard.

A riot of flowers bloomed against a background of
greenery. Palms and evergreens provided welcome
shade while a fountain splashed soothingly in the background.

Seated in a lounge chair amid a bevy of young Zohir
women, she spent the next hour fielding questions and
trying to be tactful in her answers while still telling the
truth about her country. When the questions turned
more personal, she excused herself. What was between
her and Talal she intended to share with no one, not
even the tiniest detail.

Inside the *hareem,* she found Grandmother Zohir had
returned to the suite. "*Ya,* Linnea," the older woman
said. "Happy, you, *Inshallah.*"

Linnea smiled. Nothing, she was learning, was taken
for granted by the Kholis, everything was subject to
God willing. Perhaps they were wiser than she knew.

"I'm happy," she said, the truth as far as it went.

"I'm curious about my clothes, though. Everything in my wardrobe seems to be new."

"Trunk, old clothes, you," Grandmother Noorah said. "Gone, truck."

Assuming she meant the trunk with her clothes in it had gone back to her house, Linnea bit back a protest. She could hardly complain about receiving a closet full of new clothes in exchange for what she'd brought to Kholi. But those clothes were hers and familiar. She didn't feel the same in the dress she was wearing; she half expected to look in the mirror and see the woman who'd taken her place for a while yesterday, the woman who'd survived the wedding ceremony.

"Hunting, Talal," Grandmother Noorah said. "Soon catch Khaldun dog. Soon hold daughter, you."

Linnea sighed, praying her words would come true. Soon.

As the days passed with, again, no word from Talal, Linnea grew restless. Though she'd begun to feel at ease with Sahar, she couldn't feel comfortable in the *hareem* as even a temporary home. Many of the other women, including Sahar, went off on escorted shopping excursions and other jaunts that she wasn't invited to join, which made her suspect the king had issued an edict restricting her to the palace.

"King Hakeem believes I can't be trusted," she fumed to Grandmother Noorah. "Does he think I'll run off?"

"Ruthless, Khalduns," the older women reminded her. "Not safe, you."

"I'd stay with the others if I were allowed to go," Linnea protested. "And I certainly wouldn't dream of leaving the palace grounds by myself. Not after what happened at the Blue Café.'' She shook her head. ''Here I am, married because of that little misstep.''

''Careful, king.''

''But I'm beginning to feel like I'm in a cage,'' Linnea cried. ''And please don't tell me patience is the key to solutions, even if it is true.''

Grandmother Noorah spread her hands. ''No patience, youth. Wait, Linnea. Return victorious, Talal.''

''Yes, I know, but why can't he call?''

''Hunter, Talal. Warrior. Battle first, wife later, warrior.''

In other words, first things first and wives came second. Still, did that mean he couldn't pick up a phone? Where *was* he? Why couldn't he come back to the palace at night? She might not be entirely happy about the marriage, but she missed him acutely at night. She could only assume he didn't feel the same about her.

Time inched along, one day after another. By now Linnea understood why lions and tigers in zoos, deprived of their freedom, paced back and forth endlessly. If she were the falcon Talal had called her, she'd fly over the walls and search for him.

And then King Hakeem sent for her. Wearing a long, exquisitely fashioned white dress she found in her wardrobe and swathed in a white veil, she entered the main corridor of the palace, accompanied by Talal's black-clad grandmother. While appreciating the variation in her restricted life, she fretted over the reason she was being summoned. Was the news good or bad?

Neither, as it turned out. The king greeted her graciously, announcing he was taking her to the far end of the palace compound. ''No doubt you, an American woman accustomed to being active, grow bored with this sedentary life," he said, "but you must be guarded until Talal is successful."

Without giving her a chance to ask how close Talal might be to success, the king continued. "I'm taking you on an excursion to visit my birds. Are you familiar with falconry?"

"I know what it means," she said. "I've never seen falconry practiced."

"I regret I can't take you on a hunt," he told her. "Perhaps, later, Talal will. For now, you'll meet my brave Sakar birds, keen hunters all."

They rode through the grounds to the falconry on an electric cart driven by King Hakeem himself, four of the palace guard jogging alongside. Once there, the king strapped a thick leather band about his wrist and unleashed and unhooded a bird from its roost pedestal. He offered his wrist, and after moving back and forth on the perch, the bird half raised its wings, subsided, then hopped onto the leather wristlet.

Though smaller than the hawks Linnea had seen spiraling high along the Hudson River in New York, the Sakar falcon seen face-to-face impressed her. The fierce eyes glaring at her, the sharp talons and the cruel, hooked beak marked the falcon as a hunter of prey.

"How is it possible to train such a ferocious bird?" she asked the king.

"The falcon must first learn who is master, then be trained to respond to rewards. But the bird is never completely tamed. You see I hold the leash lest the falcon decide to fly without my order." King Hakeem smiled. "The joy of owning a Sakar is to possess a wild falcon that responds to your command but is never meek or cowed. As did our Bedouin ancestors, we respect such a nature."

Though Linnea enjoyed the outing, the king's words haunted her after she'd returned to the *hareem*. To possess, to command, always holding the leash.

When Talal had called her his little wild falcon she'd taken it as an expression of affection, and she still hoped that was what he'd intended. She tried to thrust away the unpleasant possibility that she was responding to him much as the Sakars responded to their masters. His lovemaking rewarded her in ways she hadn't dreamed of, but whether he intended it or not, was she being trained to accept him as her master?

She didn't want to ever be possessed, to be commanded, to be leashed. But isn't that exactly what Kholi husbands did to their wives?

To rid herself of her disturbing thoughts, she thrust open the outside door to the women's courtyard and stepped into the gathering dusk. A few stars glittered in the evening blue of the sky, reminding her of Talal. She sighed and wandered along the meandering paths that all led, sooner or later, to the fountain. No other women were in the courtyard; this was the time they gathered in the main room to share their day and to tease one another about husbands. Tonight she didn't feel like joining them.

Hearing the door open, she looked to see who was coming out. A slight figure stepped into the courtyard, closing the door behind her. In the dusk it was impossible for Linnea to tell which of the women it was. Not wanting company, she left the fountain area, where the splashing water was lit by colored lights, and walked deeper into the shadows.

Apparently the woman had seen her because, looking back, Linnea saw she was following her. Resigned, she stopped and waited, soon realizing it was a servant, not one of the Zohirs.

The girl thrust a sealed envelope at her and hurried away before Linnea could say a word. Back in the dim glow of the fountain lights, she read her name, *Linnea,* on the front of the envelope. Her heart leaped. Talal! He'd finally remembered she existed.

Chapter Thirteen

Standing beside the fountain in the women's courtyard, clutching the envelope to her heart, Linnea was torn between ripping it open immediately or waiting until she reached the privacy of the bridal suite to read the contents. Impatience almost won, but then she decided one of the women might look out a window, see her reading the message and ask what Talal had to say. She didn't want to share a single word of his with anyone.

Reentering the quarter, she hurried along the corridors until she reached the locked door of her suite, which was not a part of the *hareem*. She unlocked the door and, once inside, crossed to sit on the bridal bed, where she tore open the envelope.

She scanned the first few words and frowned. The message wasn't from Talal.

I will deliver your daughter to the palace tonight. Open the courtyard door to your quarters at midnight. Have money ready. Do not tell anyone or I will kill the child.

Though there was no signature, she knew who'd written it. Basheem Khaldun.

Linnea stared at the words, her heart hammering. Kill Yasmin? She shuddered. Did he mean it? She dare not take a chance. On the other hand, could she believe he actually would deliver Yasmin to her? Could she believe anything a Khaldun might promise?

She bit her lip in indecision. If only Talal were here. He must know Talal was not at the palace or he wouldn't take such a risk. What should she do? Show the letter to the king so he could have the guards set a trap? She shook her head. Yasmin might be killed before they captured this dangerous cousin of Malik's.

He must know I wouldn't leave the grounds after what happened before, she reasoned, so he'd found a way to get inside. She couldn't imagine how he could possibly manage to elude the guards to get in without being challenged, but he obviously believed he could. He must have bribed the servant who'd brought her the message. How? Linnea wished she'd paid more attention to the woman. As it was, she couldn't possibly identify her.

What should she do? She ought to be safe enough within the palace grounds to risk doing what he asked. Except she hadn't enough money with her to pay him what he must want. Her gaze fell on the velvet jewel cases atop one of the mahogany chests. Her bridal gifts. Gifts she hadn't really wanted, at least in the case of the diamond-and-emerald necklace and earrings.

She shouldn't even consider giving him the jewels.

Yet Yasmin was worth the world to her. And the jewels *were* hers. How much of a risk would she be taking in the exchange? She'd have to be sure Yasmin was in her possession before handing him the jewels. Then he'd leave in a great hurry, anxious to escape before she could sound an alarm. Wouldn't he? She drew in a shaky breath, twisting her hands together. How could she possibly decipher what might be going on in his mind?

If he had Yasmin, and she had no reason to believe he did not, she must keep that most important fact in focus. She didn't see where she had any choice but to take a chance on doing as he asked.

In her anxiety for Yasmin's safety, she couldn't swallow a bite of the evening meal. Pacing back and forth in her room, she wondered how Basheem had been able to elude the national guard and all the others searching for him. She then began to worry how close Talal was. If Talal was hot on the trail, he might arrive at the palace before Yasmin had been safely delivered to her. What then?

A tapping at the door startled her. When she unlocked and opened it, Sahar stood there.

"We're having a party," she said. "In your honor. I've come to fetch you."

The last thing Linnea wanted to do was attend a party, but a glance at her watch told her it was only eight. With four hours to get through, perhaps being with others might offer some distractions. Besides, she'd been avoiding Talal's relatives lately due to her own restlessness. They'd done their best to make her feel welcome and the least she could do was attend a party held in her honor.

Indicating her casual cotton dress, she said, "Will this do?"

Sahar smiled. "What you're wearing isn't important—you'll see."

When they reached the assembly hall, Linnea found all the furniture had been shoved down to one end of the room, leaving almost half of the room bare except for the carpets and a multitude of fat, colorful pillows lining the walls. The lights had been turned off in favor of candles burning in sconces on the walls.

Two women strummed the strings of exotic instruments resembling zithers. The scent of sandlewood incense swirled around her. Not seeing Grandmother Noorah nor Sahar, she sat down next to Huda.

A tattoo of drumbeats began, and Sahar slithered around the edge of a three-paneled screen near the door. Gone was her bright pink Western-style dress, her high heels. Barefoot, with bells chiming on ankle chains, she wriggled slowly, sensuously, toward the center of the part of the room that was in use. Her costume was similar to those worn by the belly dancers at the wedding, leaving her bare from just under her breasts to her lower abdomen.

Sahar's transformation involved more than the change of clothes. She'd become some exotic creature from Kholi's past. Or maybe not so very much past, Linnea amended, as two more costumed women slipped around the screen and wriggled their way toward Sahar. One was older, plumply attractive, the other a girl barely into her teens. Both carried tambourines, shaking them above their heads.

After they reached Sahar, she advanced toward Linnea, still dancing, and reached down and offered her hand. Uncertain what to do, Linnea put her hand in Sahar's.

Sahar pulled Linnea to her feet, stopped dancing and urged her captive toward the screen. Once behind its concealment, Sahar lifted a gauzy garment from an open chest and handed it to Linnea, saying, "Please put this on."

"This is a costume like yours," Linnea protested. "I can't belly dance."

"That's because you've never tried. All women can learn the dance, though some perform better than others. We'll teach you."

"But I don't—"

"You must. How else can you keep your husband interested once the honeymoon ends?"

Taken aback, Linnea couldn't immediately find an answer.

"No one will mind you're a beginner," Sahar insisted. "We all were once."

Realizing she'd be labeled a poor sport if she didn't at least make an effort to participate, Linnea nodded reluctantly. "I'll try."

With no mirror available, she had no idea how she looked as a belly dancer, but the costume was comfortable and she rather enjoyed the bells on her wrists and ankles jingling with the slightest motion. With more confidence than she felt inside, she emerged from behind the screen with Sahar.

Immediately all the women began clicking their tongues, making the same sound as at the wedding. The drum beat slowed. Linnea padded to the middle of the room feeling the invisible support of the women watching her, realizing they'd accepted her as one of them.

She might make a fool of herself but suddenly that didn't matter.

Doing her best to match the rhythm of the drummers, she tried to copy the sinuous movements of Sahar and the others, finding the dance was not as easy as it looked. After a time the young girl reached up and grasped Linnea's hand, placing it across her abdomen as she gyrated. Startled for a moment, Linnea finally understood the girl was trying to show her what muscles to use. She smiled and nodded.

As she continued to try, to her surprise, she slipped into a more natural rhythm, one that seemed to well up from inside her. She began to imagine she was alone with Talal, dancing just for him, and her movements turned languorous. Applause from the watching women ended that fantasy and she paused.

"We can see you have the soul of a belly dancer," Sahar told her. "Practice and you will become more and more accomplished."

"Your reward will come from Talal," Huba called. Her giggle was echoed by general laughter.

"It's true," the plump dancer insisted. "Why do you think I have five sons?"

The women insisted on offering her tea and a variety of fruits and other delicacies. To refuse would insult them, she knew, so she ate what she could, then begged to be excused, thanking them for the lesson. On her way to the door, she retrieved her clothes, telling Sahar she'd return the costume later.

"No need, we had the dressmaker fashion it for you. The costume and the bangles are a gift from all of us, a gift from the heart. What is life if you can't please your husband?"

Linnea returned to her suite, marveling at how the

Kholi women's lives revolved entirely around their husbands. Not that marriage wasn't important, but spending a life confined to a *hareem* seemed impossibly constricting to her.

When she was back inside her suite, she locked the door, then glanced at the clock. Eleven. The belly dancing lesson had temporarily distracted her, but now tension tightened her muscles again. She plucked one of the jewel cases from the chest, opened it and lifted out the necklace and earrings, the diamonds and emeralds glimmering in the light. Wrong or right, she'd use them in place of money.

A servant had been in to draw the blinds and turn down her bed. Still holding the jewelry, she padded over to the door to the courtyard and peeked through the blinds, seeing only the few lights set here and there among the shrubbery. Turning off the lights, she waited until her eyes adjusted to the dark, then pulled open the blinds and stared through the glass of the sliding door again. Nothing moved in the darkness.

She had to change from the costume before midnight, but she lingered a moment to look at the stars in the night sky, sliding the bracelets from her wrists and tossing them on the table near the door. Was that constellation Orion? She unlocked the door and eased it open far enough to stick her head and shoulders out to see the sky more clearly, trying to remember what Talal had said about how to locate Orion. Warm air scented with gardenias washed over her, mingling with the artificially cooled air in the room.

Staring intently at the sky, she didn't at first notice when the lights amid the shrubbery went out. When she did, alarmed, she started to draw back into the room. A hand grasped her arm and yanked her into the night.

From behind, an arm hooked around her neck, choking her.

"Please," she gasped. "I can't breathe."

"Good." She recognized Basheem's voice. "Feel this." Something sharp pricked her bare torso and she flinched. "A knife," he said. "Fight or scream and you die."

"Yasmin..." She managed to choke the words out. "My daughter."

He chuckled. "Do I seem that much of a fool? You're the one I wanted. You're my ticket out of Kholi."

Not releasing his hold, he dragged her, choking and gasping, across the courtyard. Dizzy from lack of air, Linnea felt the necklace slip from her grasp. When they came against the outer wall, the earrings fell out of her hand.

With his knife pricking her between the shoulder blades, he forced her up a rope ladder ahead of him. At the top, he pushed her so she half fell, half jumped down the other side of the wall, stumbling and falling to her knees. As she struggled to her feet, she heard a shout from the courtyard side of the wall. "Linnea!" someone called.

Talal!

"One sound from you and you die," Malik's cousin snarled, yanking her to her feet and tying a thong around her wrists. Pulling her by a long end of the thong, he forced her toward a car parked across the road and then into it. He shoved her into the back seat, climbed into the front, revved the engine and roared off.

Linnea sat up, swaying back and forth as the car squealed around corners, and tried to figure a way to escape. There were no handles on either rear door and a heavy glass window separated the front from the back so she couldn't reach the driver. Even if she could open a rear door she'd be killed if she tried to jump from the car at this speed.

Something pricked her thigh, and, feeling awkwardly with her bound hands, she discovered the wire of one of the earrings she'd lost in the palace courtyard had snagged in the filmy material of the costume she still wore. She started to work it loose and then shook her head, leaving the earring where it was. Maybe she could find a way to use the earring later. A faint hope but better than none. The ankle bracelets she hadn't removed tinkled with each movement she made.

She twisted around to look through the back window, searching for any sign of pursuit. Headlights shone far back along the road, but she had no way of knowing who drove that car. She prayed it was Talal. She concentrated on trying to free her hands, but the thong was tied too tightly.

Her mind skittered away from any thought of Yasmin. At the moment her position was too precarious to be distracted by worry. She had to use all her wits to get away from her captor. But how?

Maybe if she knew where he was taking her she could form some kind of plan. Clearing her bruised throat, she said, "Can you hear me? Where are we going?"

Basheem didn't answer.

Either the intercom wasn't working or he didn't choose to answer. What now?

If he stopped, she should try to leave something to mark their trail. She reached for the earring again, then shook her head. The silver ankle bells would be better.

With much effort, she worked one of the ankle chains loose and held it in her left hand.

She tried to peer from the windows of the car but could see no lights, and the tinted glass made anything else difficult to make out in the darkness. From the more labored sound of the car's engine, she deduced they were climbing, and she tried to picture the mountains around Akrim as she'd seen them on the drives with Grandmother Noorah. Visions of white buildings and towers rose in her mind.

Were they heading for the Turkish ruins? On the other side of the hills where the ruins stood, as she recalled, the road led to the border of Yemen. But hadn't Grandmother Noorah mentioned that the border was many klicks, as she called kilometers, off and also unfriendly?

She twisted around again to look through the rear window. No headlights followed. Huddling on the seat, she tried not to give way to the panic she felt hovering over her.

Suddenly she was thrown onto her side as the car swerved into a right-angle turn. As she straightened, she began to jounce up and down as they negotiated what was apparently an extremely rough road. The ruins? She thought she could see white blurs through the tinted windows. They must be off the main road—why had he turned in here? No one lived in the ruins. She'd been told Bedouin nomads had formerly camped among the ruins but rarely did so these days—the city below had grown too large for them to be comfortable setting up a camp so close by.

The car stopped, he climbed from it and reached to open the back door from the outside. She tried to swallow her fear. He'd told her bluntly enough that she was his ticket out of Kholi, so she no longer believed he had any intention of leading her to Yasmin. The stop here was for some other reason. Dread tightened her muscles.

He grasped the dangling end of the thong binding her hands and yanked her from the back of the car. As she stumbled out, a flash of defiance sizzled through her growing terror. "Where is she?" Linnea demanded. "I'm beginning to think you don't even know where my daughter is."

"You're wrong." He tugged on the thong, forcing her to follow him up an overgrown path that hurt her bare feet.

Linnea fought down the flicker of hope in her heart. No, Yasmin wouldn't be hidden somewhere in the ruins. It made no sense for him to bring her daughter here if what he meant to do was flee the country with Linnea as hostage. She clutched the chain of bells tightly. Not yet.

She bit back a cry as she stepped on something sharp, refusing to give him the satisfaction of hearing her gasp in pain. The moon, past full and waning, shone down, adding an eerie dimension to the square white building looming up ahead of them. On her daylight tour she'd thought the Turkish ruins exotically lovely. By night they seemed ominous.

He forced her on until at last they reached the doorless building. Linnea dropped the belled chain at the threshold, the continual tinkling of the other chain still around her ankle covering the sound. She limped inside, following his pull on the thong, the floor, littered with debris, adding additional agony to her injured foot. She'd done all she could to mark her trail, but if no one pursued, she'd done so in vain.

Talal. She whispered his name under her breath, holding it in her mind like a talisman of hope.

Her captor paused after entering an inner room. He crouched, yanking her down onto her knees. Producing a tiny penlight from his pocket, he flashed it into her eyes, blinding her for a moment. Then his light roamed over her body, making her stiffen in renewed fear. She saw the glint of the light on the blade of his knife as he raised it and she shrank back.

He pulled her closer, the knife slashing at the thongs binding her hands together. She blinked in surprise at her unexpected freedom. He grabbed her wrist, stood and pulled her with him.

Releasing her, he said, "Undress. Now."

She stared at him in horror.

"Afterward you can put on the woman's gown," he told her, gesturing to a heap of blackness on the floor near where a rug was laid atop the rubble. "First we'll take our pleasure."

"No!" she cried, edging away from him.

The flashlight fell from his hand onto the rug as he grasped her wrist, shoved her into the corner where two walls met and traced the tip of his knife along her bare midriff. Beads of blood appeared. "You will undress for me," he growled.

Though the tiny beam of the fallen penlight now illuminated the opposite wall rather than being focused on them, there was enough light for Linnea to cringe at the avid anticipation in his eyes. Enough light for her to fear the knife that was forcing her to his will. Enough light for him to gape at her nudity once she'd removed her clothes. Enough light so she'd be forced to watch him rape her afterward. The thought made her gag.

Was there no escape? Stalling, she mumbled, "I'll

take off the ankle chain first.'' As she reached down, her fingers brushed against the earring caught in her costume. Hiding what she was doing with her hand, she unhooked the wire and carried the earring with her while she fumbled with the chain around her ankle. Bells tinkled when she finally released the catch and tossed the chain aside.

''Hurry up!'' he snapped.

He had her penned in this corner; she couldn't get away. Taking a deep breath, her gaze pinned to the knife he threatened her with, Linnea regretted she'd never taken any defense classes for women. Even if she had, though, she couldn't imagine how she'd be able to disarm him before he could use the knife on her.

Slowly, reluctantly, she raised her hand to the tiny buttons on the front of the costume's top.

A wild, ululating howl froze her in position. In a blur of motion, a figure—Talal!—leaped at her captor through the archway and Basheem swung around to face him.

''He's got a knife!'' she screamed.

As if by magic a knife appeared in Talal's hand, too. They circled each other, close to her. Too close. She sidled from the corner, backing up until several feet separated her from the two men. Breath hissed between her teeth as her captor lunged at Talal, slashing downward with his blade. Talal leaped aside, whirling to deliver his own blow. Blood stained the shoulder of Basheem's white robe.

She saw Talal through different eyes, a man fighting for his woman, fighting for her. Love she'd refused to admit to swept into her heart, making her lift a hand to her breast as though to try to contain the feeling. Why hadn't she realized her love for him was too great to be imprisoned behind the barriers she'd tried to erect?

When Basheem came even with the archway, he suddenly turned and fled. Talal raced after him. Left alone, Linnea grabbed up the penlight and searched the room for any possible weapon she might use, coming up blank. Finally she twisted the hook of the earring wire straight and gripped it in her hand so the wire was free to jab with. Not much, but the best she could do. Putting her back to a wall, she waited apprehensively, fearing that, if she moved, Talal wouldn't be able to find her once he disposed of the enemy and returned here.

Besides, if she left, she wouldn't dare use the light and, in the darkness, might blunder into Basheem again and wind up as his hostage. At the same time, she longed to get into the action, to do her part in capturing this evil Khaldun.

Running footsteps alerted her, she tensed, prepared for anything. Talal burst through the archway, his glance searching the room. When he located her, he paused momentarily, his attention distracted just long enough for him to step on her discarded chain of bells. His foot twisted under him and he lurched sideways, falling onto his back despite a desperate attempt to stay on his feet.

Shrieking in triumph, Basheem bounded into the room and, knife in hand, flung himself at the fallen Talal. Crying "No!" Linnea darted forward and thrust the stainless steel earring wire as hard as she could into the back of Basheem's neck.

He cried out and clapped a hand to his nape. Talal rolled free and leaped to his feet in time to avoid a thrust of his opponent's knife. He thrust at the Khaldun dog, aiming for his knife arm. His blood beat with the need to kill the dung-eater but, controlling his battle rage was the knowledge the king would resent being deprived of a beheading.

At that moment the man twisted and Talal's knife slid in between the ribs instead. With a sickening gurgle, Basheem collapsed onto the floor, frothy blood oozing from his mouth. Talal grimaced as he stared down at him. Got him in the lungs. He wasn't likely to survive long.

"Talal!" The alarm in Linnea's voice made him whirl.

Three Bedouins in desert dress, the ends of their checkered red-and-white headdresses folded back, stood in the archway, knives in hand.

"Prince Talal," the oldest one said. "We heard your call. We came."

Talal hadn't realized he'd uttered the primitive howl that was the fighting call of his ancestors' Bedouin clan. The sight of Linnea at the mercy of a Khaldun had short-circuited his brain.

He strode to the men, embracing them one at a time. "Thanks to Allah, you were within earshot. I won't forget."

The eldest smiled. "We were camped for the night at the far edge of the ruins and arrived late, Prince. You needed no help."

"I ask your help now," Talal said. "My enemy must be taken to a hospital."

The old Bedouin shrugged. "Why bother?"

"We need information from him before he dies," Talal said. "So we save him. His car is down the track. Can you drive him to the city and remain with him until I arrive at the hospital?"

"You ask, Prince, we oblige," the Bedouin said.

"As I will do in return one day." He bent, extracted car keys from a pocket of Basheem's robe and tossed them to the old man. Without further talk, the three men lifted the unconscious man and bore him from the room. Talal strode to Linnea and wrapped his arms around her.

She hugged him close. "Thank heaven those men were friendly," she murmured. "They frightened me."

"Some of my Bedouin relatives," he said, breathing in the fragrance of her hair in bemused relief.

"Who in Kholi aren't you related to?"

Detecting the quiver in her voice, he eased her away. "Time to get you back to the palace." Seeing her wince as, an arm around her waist, he urged her through the archway, he noticed her bare feet and the bloodstained footprints she'd left on the filthy floor.

Muttering in Arabic, he swept her into his arms and strode from the ruins, heading for his car.

Against the odds, he'd found Linnea in time to save her from defilement by that miserable Khaldun. In all his life, he'd never been given a more precious gift.

What he felt for Linnea was far more than the normal lust of a man for a pretty woman. He knew he'd protect her with his life if necessary, but *love* was a word he'd never offered any woman because he shied away from lying. Even now, carrying the woman who meant more to him than anything else, the word caught in his throat, refusing to pass onto his tongue.

Chapter Fourteen

Talal drove back to the palace with one arm around Linnea. She huddled against him as though he was her only anchor in a sea of chaos. Before they reached the palace, though, she'd recovered enough to begin asking questions.

"I heard you call my name," she said, "but he—Basheem Khaldun—had that knife and I couldn't answer. I tried to leave a trail for you to follow. Did you find the necklace and the earring?"

His arm tightened around her. "That's one of the reasons I was able to locate you in time. We'd traced Basheem to the ruins earlier, but he was gone by the time we reached them. Once I found he'd abducted you, I was sure he'd head back to his lair. When I discovered the ankle chain outside the ruined building, I knew where he'd taken you."

He wasn't yet able to share with her how he'd felt

when he arrived at the palace and found her gone. He'd been close on Basheem's trail when he'd realized with a sickening certainty that trail was leading him toward the palace. Toward Linnea. Knowing Basheem meant to harm her, he'd finally understood just how much she meant to him and he was terrified he'd be too late—as he almost had been.

"I tried not to lose my head," she said.

"You're as brave as any man I know," he told her.

By the time they reached the palace Talal's fury at the ruthless dog who'd abducted her had reached explosive proportions. He carried Linnea into their suite at the palace, damping down his rage with difficulty. Her injuries needed tending and he meant to take care of her himself.

After easing her onto the bed, he directed the servants he'd summoned to run bath water and fetch first aid supplies. As they hurried away, Linnea beckoned him close. He bent down and she whispered, "Don't leave me alone with any of them. One of the women servants is connected to him." She shuddered. "The one who gave me his message."

"Who is she?" he demanded.

"I don't know. I didn't pay attention at the time."

"But surely you'd recognize her?"

She shook her head. "It was dark and there are so many of them."

A traitor within the palace. Not the first time nor, unfortunately, would it be the last.

"She'll be found," he promised grimly. "And dealt with. I won't leave you until I'm certain you're all right. I'll have to go soon, but Grandmother Noorah will take my place. You won't be alone."

When the bath was ready, he dismissed the two hov-

ering servants. With gentle hands he unbuttoned the top
of Linnea's belly dancer's costume and eased it from
her. She wore nothing underneath, and he did his best
to ignore his flicker of desire at the sight of her rounded
breasts. He tugged off the lower part of the costume,
revealing white silk bikini panties that barely covered
her dark mound.

Blood pounding in his ears, he slid off the panties,
his arousal now impossible to control. Taking a deep
breath, he lifted her, snuggling her nakedness against
him as he carried her into the bathroom and lowered
her into the oversized tub.

"I can wash myself," she protested as he knelt and
picked up a sponge.

"Let me," he said, sliding a rose-scented cake of
soap gently over first one breast, then the other, feeling
her nipples peak under his fingers. Desire waged a battle
with his determination to cleanse her, as if washing her
would free her of the memory of what she'd endured.

"Not fair," she murmured as he continued to half
wash, half caress her. "I'm naked and you're fully
dressed." The huskiness in her voice revealed her own
need.

He grinned. "No problem." Setting sponge and soap
aside, he removed his headdress and sandals, threw off
his robe and undershorts and climbed into the tub with
her, the warm and scented water lapping softly around
his body, caressing him as he longed to caress her. Before he could claim the soap again, Linnea was lathering
his chest with it.

The feel of her fingers against his skin was both en-
dearing and erotic, and the sweet scent of roses bemused
him. He'd allowed no woman to wash him since he was
old enough to protest. Linnea was different. She was

his wife, of course, but that had little to do with the emotions rocketing through him.

Each new day with Linnea would be rose-filled, he would never tire of her touch, of touching her, of having her near him. He wanted no one else.

Remembering her poor, bruised feet, he felt his smoldering anger threaten to erupt. Damping it down firmly—now was not the time—he captured the soap and groped underwater for a foot. After raising one of her feet free of the water, he stared in dismay at the scratches and cuts on her sole and instep. The other foot was little better. As gently as he could, he lathered them, her muffled gasp of pain striking to his heart.

No one would ever hurt her again!

"I'm sorry I didn't bring Basheem's message to the king," she said, biting her lip. "I didn't intend to betray anyone. I didn't really trust him, but he claimed he'd kill Yasmin if I told anyone and I was afraid to take the risk. I should have had the sense to realize he needed a hostage to escape Kholi and had no intention of bringing my daughter to me. Unfortunately, I didn't. If you hadn't found me when you did—" She broke off.

Talal didn't dare dwell on what Basheem had intended to do or his rage would erupt. "Did he tell you where Yasmin was?" he asked.

Linnea shook her head. "He laughed at me but he claimed he knew."

Much as he longed to prolong their time together in the tub, he knew he must leave Linnea and get to the hospital to question Basheem Khaldun—if the man was capable of being questioned. He had some of the answers but not all, not enough. He now had a fair idea of why Basheem had begun this charade, but he still didn't know where Malik's daughter was nor where the changeling Yasmin had come from. Nor did he understand why Basheem had set up his web of deception in the first place. He also had to report to his great-uncle.

He leaned to Linnea and brushed her lips with his, not daring to make the kiss lingering because then he'd never leave her. "I can't stay," he murmured against her mouth.

"I know," she whispered. "Go. I'll be fine with Grandmother Noorah."

After his grandmother arrived, Linnea reluctantly watched Talal leave, trying not to show how she longed to have him stay. Never had she thought she'd find herself praying for Basheem Khaldun's survival, but she did now. He mustn't die, because he might well be the only person who knew where her daughter was.

"In *hareem*, rumors fly," Grandmother Noorah said as she seated herself in the upholstered rocker beside the bed where Linnea lay propped on pillows. "Dying, the evil one?"

"He's unconscious. Talal's gone to the hospital in the hope Basheem will have improved enough to answer questions, but..." Her words trailed off and she sighed.

"Sleep, you," the older woman said.

"I can't. What if I never find Yasmin?" She sat up, clutching the coverlet with tense fingers. "I couldn't bear that."

Grandmother Noorah reached over and patted her hand. She'd started to speak when a tap at the door alerted them both.

"Who is it?" Linnea cried, at the same time the older woman spoke in Arabic.

"Sahar and Huda. May we speak with you?"

Linnea nodded to Grandmother Noorah, who rose and unlocked the door. Both women slipped in and the older woman relocked the door behind them.

"We've come about Widad," Sahar said.

Linnea drew a blank. Grandmother Noorah asked, "Servant, Widad?"

"One of the recently hired ones," Huda said. "Another servant identified her as the one who passed Basheem Khaldun's message to Linnea. Widad admits this but refuses to speak to anyone except Linnea."

"We've locked her in a small room no one uses," Sahar said.

"Must be told, king," Grandmother Noorah advised.

"We will," Sahar told her. "But Widad threatens to kill herself if she can't speak to Linnea. What use is a dead woman who can answer no questions?"

Linnea swung her bandaged feet over the side of the bed. "I want to speak with her. I insist."

Staring at her feet, Sahar said, "Can you walk?"

"Not walk, Linnea." Grandmother Noorah's voice was firm. "Must come here, Widad. Fetch, you and you. Then stand guard."

"We'll bring her," Sahar said.

As the two women hurried away Grandmother Noorah warned, "Careful, Linnea."

When Sahar and Huba returned, they more or less dragged a limp young woman in servant's garb between them. As soon as they released her, Widad fell prostrate, her arms reaching toward Linnea as she jabbered in Arabic.

"She begs for mercy," Sahar said.

"I can promise her nothing, but if she answers all my questions, I'll try to intervene for her with the king," Linnea said, struggling not to be influenced by the desperate sobs of the woman. "Ask her what her relationship with Basheem Khaldun is."

Widad raised herself onto her knees when Sahar began questioning her, keeping her gaze fixed on Linnea as she answered. "She says Basheem knew what she was—I think because he used her—and threatened to tell the king if she didn't obey him." Sahar frowned. "It seems she was—maybe still is—a loose woman and would have lost her place here in the palace if it became known and, perhaps, even faced death."

Was it possible this woman knew where Yasmin was? Linnea told Sahar to ask that question.

"I'm not certain she understood," Sahar said, "because her answer seems to concern a child she once bore but rid herself of as an infant. Apparently she'd done this more than once—she had several children no man would admit to having fathered. All were boys except one. Basheem found this girl in an orphanage and tracked Widad down, forcing her to do as he asked or be exposed as one who lent herself to men for money and abandoned babies. This is no light matter in Kholi."

"Obviously Widad is no friend of Basheem," Linnea said. "But she must know about my daughter, Yasmin Khaldun. Did Basheem tell her where Yasmin is?"

Linnea watched Sahar frown as she listened to Widad's response. "She has never heard of your daughter," Sahar reported. "I asked her about the daughter she bore and she says she thinks the father was a foreign worker from Europe who left the country before the child was born. Because the child was a girl she was unable to sell her as she did the boys so she left her in an orphanage. This was about three years ago and she's never seen the girl since then but she knows Basheem removed her from the orphanage.''

Dread washed over Linnea in a dark tide. ''Ask her what Basheem did with the girl,'' she managed to say.

Widad hung her head and had to be persuaded to speak. While waiting, Linnea felt as though she was groping through an increasingly dense fog of misery and fear.

''Widad believes Basheem took the girl from the orphanage to bring to the king,'' Sahar said finally. ''She had no idea why.'' Shaking her head, she added, ''This woman doesn't seem to care what may have happened to her child. Or any of her children.''

Widad suddenly burst into impassioned Arabic.

''She hopes Basheem Khaldun will be beheaded by the king so she'll be rid of him once and for all,'' Sahar translated. ''She asked where he is.''

''In the hospital.'' Stunned by what Widad had revealed, Linnea spoke automatically without truly being aware of what she said.

A moment later, after Sahar told her, Widad smiled. Through her own numb despair Linnea shuddered at the hate revealed in that smile. She hugged herself, her body trembling.

Grandmother Noorah rose and rattled off orders in Arabic. Linnea heard the click of the door lock, then the older woman sat on the bed next to her, drawing her close, murmuring soothingly in Arabic. In some dim corner of her consciousness she understood the two of them were now alone in the room.

When she finally was able to stop crying, she found one of Grandmother Noorah's lace-edged handkerchiefs in her hand and mopped at her wet face. The older woman urged her back against the pillows and pulled the light coverlet over her. "Sleep, Linnea," she said softly.

Linnea tried to protest, to explain why she couldn't, but exhaustion overtook her and her eyes fluttered closed.

She woke to a sunlit room and Talal asleep in the rocker where Grandmother Noorah had been. For a moment she relished the sight of him, and then what she'd heard from Widad rushed back into her mind and she moaned in protest.

Talal sat up abruptly, sprang to his feet and leaned over her. "Are you in pain? Where does it hurt?"

"In my heart," she said sadly.

"My grandmother told me about Widad," he said, sitting on the bed and taking her hand in both of his.

Linnea bit her lip. "I'm sure our changeling Yasmin is her child," she said hopelessly. "Widad knows nothing about my daughter. I fear—" She swallowed and, with obvious effort, fought back tears. "What about Basheem?" she asked. "Were you able to talk to him?"

The desperate plea in her eyes stabbed like a knife into Talal's heart. "Basheem is in a coma," he told her. Which was the truth, if not all of it.

She sighed, but he sensed she was relieved to have a shred of hope to cling to. "I asked one of the doctors about your feet," he told her. "He said we should soak them in warm saltwater today, then leave the wounds open to the air. He suggested you keep off them as much as possible."

"My feet aren't that bad," she protested. "They're already healing. I have no intention of lying around."

"Not even with me?" he teased, hoping to distract

her, at least for a while, from what they both had to face.

Someone tapped on the door before she could answer and he gave permission to enter, aware it must be the food he'd ordered. A female servant wheeled in a cart and, under Talal's direction, pushed a table over to the bed and set out the food.

Once the servant was gone, Linnea shook her head. "I don't know why there isn't a clock in this room," she complained. "The palace seems to have practically no clocks anywhere. When I forget to wear my watch, I never know what time it is."

"Time doesn't matter in Kholi. We have a saying that translates to *same-same,* meaning that it's all the same whether things get done today or tomorrow or next week."

She rolled her eyes, slid from the bed, wincing when her feet touched the floor, and limped toward the bathroom. He stifled an impulse to scoop her up and carry her. Best to allow her a little independence—she was one determined woman.

While she was gone, he disrobed and sat back down on the bed. When she returned she was wearing a loose, translucent white robe. Though the silk didn't cling to her curves, the thin fabric hinted at what couldn't quite be seen. His groin tightened and he reached for her. She melted into his arms, clinging to him.

He stroked her back, keeping his desire tamped down, aching for her but aware she needed comforting. Whatever she wanted, he meant to try to give her.

Linnea sighed, relaxing against Talal's warmth, relishing the feel of his soothing hand. Here in his embrace she could put away her fears for a time and be safe. While he caressed her, he slipped the robe from her arms and off. A thrill shot through her as her bare breasts pressed against his naked chest. A longing to become a part of him infused her. Nothing mattered, only Talal. Always Talal, no other.

He eased them both down onto the bed and pulled her on top of him, holding her there while he touched her in all the right places. She pressed her lips to his, losing herself in their kiss.

She wanted, she needed to feel him fill her but he held off, his intimate caresses driving her up and up. When she could bear the waiting no longer, she raised herself and took him inside, almost immediately feeling the incomparable throbbing of completion.

With a growl, not releasing her, he rolled her over onto her back and thrust deeply, again and again until she gasped for breath, crying his name over and over as the waves of pleasure crested.

His shudder of release throbbed through her, increasing her own pleasure, making her believe they were truly one.

Afterward, while still holding her next to him, he fell asleep. She eased away far enough to look at him, resisting her urge to trace his profile with her finger—the proud angle of his nose, the enticing curve of his lips, then over the no-nonsense chin with its incipient cleft.

She loved the way he looked, loved his firm body, his strength, the tenderness he was capable of. She loved him. Linnea caught her breath. Even if she did, what about the dichotomy separating them? Kholi was his country—he wouldn't be likely to give it up—while she already knew she could never live here.

To hell with that problem, she decided, and snuggled against him again, closing her eyes. They were together and that's what mattered right now. She didn't want to think about anything else.

Talal woke, finding himself pleasurably entwined with Linnea, who still slept. How beautiful she was, her body made for pleasure and her personality lending character to what might otherwise have been merely a pretty face. Deep within him, he knew he'd never want any other woman. He'd need her with him forever. Somehow he had to find a way for this marriage of theirs to last.

The burden he carried troubled him. Would he lose her when he admitted the truth? After the ritual sword dance tomorrow, he must, he decided, take her from the palace, must bring her home, to the house he'd had built after the death of his first wife, the house he'd never brought a woman to. Linnea would be the first, the only woman he'd ever bring home.

There, on the edge of the desert, they would find a way to face the future together. They had to, he couldn't bear to lose her.

Chapter Fifteen

Linnea watched while Grandmother Noorah looked at the packed luggage. Nodding in satisfaction, she ordered the hovering servant to see it was taken to the proper place. She gestured at Linnea, already wearing the long-sleeved silk jacket, to pull the white silk scarf over her head, then opened the door to the main part of the palace.

In the corridor, the grand-nephew, young Ameen, waited in his palace guard uniform to escort them to the expanse of lawn in the front of the palace where, Linnea knew, the princes, Talal among them, were to gather.

Ameen led them not to the open pavilion where the other palace women were sequestered, but to where the palace guard ringed a wooden platform under the shade of a huge date palm. The uniformed men opened rank to allow the women to pass inside the ring. Before leaving them, Ameen assisted Grandmother Noorah onto the platform where the king's wife waited with one of her grandsons, a boy in his early teens. Linnea followed.

Wajeeh greeted them graciously. Before they had time to do more than exchange pleasantries with the king's wife, the white-clad princes marched onto the lawn in front of the platform. The palace guard then rearranged their ranks so the view from the platform was not obscured. Two of the guards peeled away to join the four guards escorting the king from the palace to the platform. As he joined them he greeted Linnea and Grandmother Noorah and gave his wife's arm an affectionate pat. After ordering his grandson to stand straighter, he faced ahead, his gaze on the princes.

As one they shouted and raised their swords. A hand drum rat-a-tatted and the princes began to chant, their voices rising and falling as, with a peculiar gait that resembled a dance—Linnea was reminded of Native American war dances—they formed circles within circles. At varying intervals they waved their raised swords and shouted, every face turned toward King Hakeem.

She'd picked out Talal from the other princes in their robes and headdresses but lost track of him in the concentric circles that kept forming and reforming. Stirred by the spectacle, she imagined Bedouin men performing this ritual over the years to show their loyalty to their tribal leader, for surely this sword dance had ancient roots.

After a time, the chanting ceased. With a final shout, the men waved their swords once more. The drum stopped, swords were sheathed and the princes marched away.

She'd expected to return to the palace with Grand-

mother Noorah, escorted by Ameen, but when King
Hakeem stepped to her side, she realized she was to be
honored by his escort. The two of them were flanked
by four of his guards. Instead of heading for the palace,
though, he led her toward the drive where she saw a
limo waiting.

Talal approached. The king hugged him, kissing him
on both cheeks in the ritual Kholi greeting or farewell.
He turned to Linnea, raised her hand and bowed over
it.

"Try to be a dutiful wife to this man I treasure above
all others for his loyalty," he said to her.

Escorted by his guards, he turned back toward the
platform. She stood staring after him until Talal took
her arm and urged her gently but firmly into the rear
seat of the limo.

"Wait," she protested. "I haven't said goodbye to
anyone, not even your grandmother. I didn't think
we—" He slid in next to her and shut the door, leaving
her sputtering, effectively ending any protest.

The driver put the limo into gear and sped off.

Linnea gazed from the helicopter at the land they
were passing over. They'd left Akrim with its sparsely
forested mountains behind—if *forested* was the right
word. The few trees she'd seen were stunted and the
growth resembled what she'd seen in the Nevada high
desert—sagebrush-like.

She was glad to be leaving the ruined white buildings
and towers of the ancient Turks behind, but she would
miss Grandmother Noorah. Sahar, too. Between them,
the king and Talal had given her no time to make a
proper farewell, which she resented.

When she'd asked why such a hurry, Talal's reply had been curt. "King Hakeem fears for your safety."

She'd asked why but he hadn't told her. Certainly Basheem was no threat to anyone, lying comatose, under guard, in the hospital. Did they suspect he had cohorts? She'd realized, though, if the get-out-of-town-in-a-hurry order came from King Hakeem, there was no point in being miffed at Talal.

"The desert begins," Talal said, pointing to an expanse of tannish brown just ahead. "See how the wind sculpts the dunes."

She noticed ridges in the brown, but from the copter nothing looked impressive.

"Your grandmother told me Kholi is the desert and the desert is Kholi," she said.

"We try to keep the desert in our blood, but today, only the Bedouins are successful. And fewer of them every year." He shook his head. "I fear the day we all become city dwellers with no tribal unity."

Linnea thought this over. "Are the Bedouins one large tribe?" she asked.

He shook his head. "More than one. Each Kholi family is blood-bonded to one or another of the tribes. The three men who answered my call at the ruins were my blood brothers."

"The various tribes are friendly with one another, aren't they?"

"I'd like to say yes. The truth is most of the time a truce exists, just as in the cities families who have, in the past, been at odds with one another try to keep the peace. Sometimes that becomes impossible."

"Like the Zohirs and the Khalduns?"

"The Khalduns once governed a part of what is now our united country. They never forgave my great-grandfather Zohir for bringing the various small kingdoms together under a single ruler—himself. They went to war against the Zohirs—and lost. Kholi now includes their former kingdom. Old hatreds die slowly.''

''If ever,'' she said, hugging herself.

He touched her hand lightly. ''You'll like my house—our house. I had it built to blend into the desert.''

Our house? The words seemed to hang in the air in front of her. Did Talal expect their marriage to be permanent? Expect her to live with him in Kholi? She thrust the disturbing questions from her mind for the moment and asked, ''Is your house right in Rabbul?''

''No, I'm a few miles beyond the city outskirts, at the edge of the open desert.''

Isolated. But possibly no more so than Zed and Karen's ranch in Carson Valley. Their nearest neighbor was more than a mile down the road. Yet, to her, what a difference between being isolated in Nevada as contrasted to Kholi. Still, until she actually arrived at Talal's house, it was only fair to reserve judgment.

''You're sure the man you left with Basheem will know exactly what to ask him when he comes out of the coma?'' she said, a variation of the same question she'd asked more than once since they'd been aboard the copter.

''He's been thoroughly briefed.'' Talal's terse response meant his patience had begun to erode, but she plunged on.

''What about Widad?''

''I told you she remains safely locked in a room at the palace until the king decides her fate.''

''She begged me for mercy. Whatever she's guilty of surely doesn't mean she should be put to death.''

"Linnea." Something in his tone dried up her words. "Enough. We are not going over these details again. I'm as eager as you to have everything over and done with. At the moment, we can do nothing more."

She supposed he was right—knew he was, actually. But she was unhappy about being forced to leave Akrim. In the palace *hareem* the women always seemed to know the details of what was going on and were happy to share any news with her. In contrast, Talal handed out mere tidbits, and she'd have only him for a companion until King Hakeem decided it was safe for her to return.

"You seem less than happy for a bride setting off on a delayed honeymoon," Talal said.

"Honeymoon!"

He smiled, that damned disarming smile of his that had charmed her from the first, and she melted like butter on a hot day. Companion and lover, she amended. Abandoning her resentment at the way everyone seemed to have combined to rush her away from the palace, she smiled back at Talal.

His dark gaze caught hers, the gleam in his eyes telling her how impatient he was to be alone with her. She had to admit how much she was looking forward to that moment, too.

Loyal, the king had called him. Which meant Talal was a man to be trusted. Since they'd boarded the copter, she'd done nothing but question his judgment. Shouldn't she make some effort to offer this man who was her husband—at least temporarily—her trust?

Maybe she'd never be the dutiful wife King Hakeem had urged her to be, but she could at least try to behave more like a wife than she'd been doing. Beginning when they arrived at his house. Our house, she corrected herself under her breath, trying out the feel of the words.

Talal turned toward her, eyebrows raised inquiringly.

"I'm looking forward to getting acquainted with the house you built at the desert's edge," she told him, meaning every word.

His pleased expression warmed her, making her vow to do her best to place her anxiety over the two little Yasmins on hold. Incessantly going over and over the same ground didn't bring her birth daughter any closer to her. She hoped she'd be able to keep her chosen daughter. Whatever might happen to Wadid, it was obvious the woman did not want any of her children. As for her birth daughter, she'd been waiting for news of her for almost three years, couldn't she manage to control her fear, to wait a few more days, perhaps a week?

When the capital city of Rabbul came into view, she expected they'd soon set down at the airport. To her surprise, the copter flew over the city and beyond. Maybe she was wrong about where they were.

"Wasn't that Rabbul?" she asked.

"I have a helicopter pad at the house," Talal said. "We'll set down there."

Would she ever grow accustomed to being married to a prince? Of course Talal would have more than the ordinary conveniences—he'd have everything.

"We'll have time to talk," she said.

"Among other things." The warmth in his voice told her exactly what he meant.

The anticipation thrilled her. Suddenly she could hardly wait to be in his arms.

As the copter lowered, quick impressions flashed one after the other, tan brown desert-colored walls, a rambling house with a tiled roof, greenery and cascading water within a courtyard, a vast nothing of desert beyond.

Nearer the ground, she noticed people running toward the copter, servants, no doubt. By the time the pilot stopped the whirling vanes, the servants were at the door. Talal slid out first and helped her to the ground. After a quick greeting to them, he paid no attention to the servants unloading the luggage from the copter. She stepped into stifling heat that took her breath away.

Taking her hand, Talal led her from the pad, through a gate and into the oasis he'd created outside his house. Flowering bushes with pink and red blossoms lined the drive and palms spread their fronds, creating shade pools. The elaborately carved front door, tall and arched, opened into a high-ceilinged entry that she was pleased to note was as sparsely furnished as anything in Grandmother Noorah's house. Cool air welcomed her, wrapping her in comfort.

She took a deep breath and felt her tension ebb away. Women servants in long but sleeveless cotton dresses appeared.

"This is my wife, Princess Linnea," he told them in English. "She will choose one of you to attend her." He spoke in Arabic, no doubt repeating the words.

Aware she had no choice but to choose, Linnea asked, "Which of you speaks English fluently?"

No one moved or spoke for a long moment, then a dark-skinned young woman stepped forward. "I'm Shadi, Princess," she said hesitantly. "I speak English good."

About to tell the woman she'd picked her, Linnea hesitated. Wouldn't a dutiful wife, at this point, defer to her husband? As a small concession, she turned to him, saying, "Shadi's my choice."

He nodded. "Shadi, you'll see to the luggage."

"Yes, Prince." She turned and left.

Talal issued orders in Arabic and the rest of them dispersed. "We'll have lunch in our rooms," he told Linnea.

"Rooms?" she echoed.

"A suite of three with but one bed. The two of us will initiate its use."

"You've never slept there?"

He shook his head. "I had my bachelor quarters."

"Which, I imagine, you never expected to leave," she teased.

"I should have known my life would never be the same after I rang your doorbell in New York," he said with a rueful grin.

"Nor mine," she agreed. How many times since then she'd wished she'd never met him. And now? She looked at the man before her, a Kholi prince, impressive in the clothes of his country, and her breath caught.

It didn't matter who he was or what country he came from, he was Talal. He was the man she wanted.

He led the way to their suite and, when they reached the open door, lifted her into his arms and carried her into the room, depositing her on the bed.

"Is this going to become a habit?" she asked. "Carrying me from one bed to another?"

"It's one way to get you there quickly. Besides, I was honoring what I thought was an American custom, carrying the bride across the threshold."

She stretched out on the bed, flinging her arms out, and gazed up at him. "*Ya*, Talal," she said, "*Yallah!*"

He threw back his head and laughed. Moments later he'd slammed the door shut, peeled off his headdress and the rest of his clothes. "Your wish is my command," he said, looming over her.

While *yallah* meant *let's go* or *hurry up,* she hadn't expected him to take her quite so literally. It was highly evident he was ready to go in more ways than one. Gazing at his splendid nakedness brought an urgent need to be in his arms, flesh to flesh. She sat up and began flinging off her clothes.

He reached for her, but only to take her hand and urge her to her feet, leading her across the room and through a door into what she could only think of as a bathroom suite, with separate rooms for tub and shower, toilets and two dressing areas complete with sinks.

"Because this is my house, now ours," he said, "and I've brought you here as my wife, we will shower together first and come to one another as though for the first time."

His words took her breath away, making her feel that, in a way, what he meant was a reenactment of the wedding ceremony, this time for real. Though the idea unnerved her, she had no desire to refuse.

A few minutes later they stood under the flow of water, at first scrubbing each other with sponges. Then the sponges got tossed aside and the scrubbing turned to caresses.

Sheer determination to carry out his ritual cleansing was all that kept Talal from making love to Linnea under the shower. Using all the willpower he possessed, he shut off the water, opened the shower door and reached for the towels. He meant to make their first lovemaking in this house as perfect as possible. He'd make Linnea as happy and fulfilled as a man could. He would not allow what he'd have to tell her later to interfere with what he meant to be the true consummation of their marriage.

He watched her towel herself, admiring her grace of movement as well as the beauty of her body. She was, as he'd realized from the first moment he set eyes on her, a woman made for keeping. Then, that knowledge had scared him off. The king's edict had forced his hand; he hadn't wanted to marry her—or anyone. But the shock of almost losing her had woken him to his own blindness and rearranged his thinking, not only about his true feeling for Linnea but about his own selfishness.

He'd finally understood that no woman had ever deliberately betrayed him. Not his mother, nor his grandmother, nor his poor, misguided first wife. And not Linnea, either. They'd all been driven by circumstances they couldn't control to act as they did. He regretted his hasty words to Linnea and he'd tell her so. But not at this moment. Later.

"My beautiful princess," he murmured to her as he flung his towel aside and took her hand to lead her to their marriage bed.

"Even though blue eyes and golden hair didn't come with the title?" she asked, smiling at him.

"Your amber eyes trapped me from the beginning," he said, pausing to take her in his arms and kiss her. A mistake. As soon as he felt her soft sweetness against him and her fervent response to his kiss, his control slipped.

He couldn't let her go, couldn't move, could only deepen their kiss and caress her enticing body, her soft moans further eroding what fragments of control he still clung to. Her scent, her taste, the silken wonder of her body, intoxicated him in a way alcohol never had.

Gripped by such intense passion, he lost all contact with his surroundings. Talal felt himself swaying on his feet, felt them both swaying. In a moment they'd be on the floor, locked together, and he didn't want that. Still holding her, he staggered toward the bed and they fell across it.

Then, somehow, he was inside her, enclosed in her warmth, and traveling again, like Omar, to Saturn's throne.

Linnea threw her head back, gasping, her body arched against Talal's as they joined in the most ancient dance of all, the mating dance, the one that celebrated life itself. She gave herself up to pure feeling as her pleasure spasms of completion triggered his release.

Wonderful as making love with him was, she enjoyed the snuggling together afterward almost as much. He made her feel she was still a part of him, that, though apart, they were one in a way that would last far beyond the physical act of lovemaking. Last forever.

A stray thought made her smile. "Was that another variation of the Kholi sword dance?" she murmured.

He chuckled. "Irreverent woman. Have you no respect for custom?"

"I think I might be able to get accustomed to your particular variation," she said, sliding her hand along his abdomen until she reached the sword in question.

Someone tapped at the door.

"Later!" Talal called.

"Don't you think whoever that might have been was bringing us food?" she said.

"I plan to starve you into submission," he growled, nuzzling her breast.

The knocking came again. A man's voice spoke urgently in Arabic. The only word Linnea could clearly identify was Hakeem. The king.

Alarm shot through her. She watched apprehensively as Talal called back a few curt words, slid from the bed, strode to the door, eased it open and plucked a portable phone from whoever stood outside. He began talking into the phone even before closing the door. In Arabic.

Linnea sat up, clutching a pillow to her, her gaze fixed on Talal's face. If the king had called him, it was sure to be with bad news. During the conversation, no smile crossed his face, confirming her impression. An eternity passed before he hung up.

"We must dress," he said, without looking at her. He grabbed his clothes and made for one of the dressing rooms.

Linnea released a pent-up breath, her anxiety all but overwhelming her. Her hands trembled as she gathered her things together and walked slowly toward the other dressing room.

When she returned to the bedroom, Talal wasn't there, he'd gone into the sitting room. She joined him. Food had been set out on a table, but he wasn't eating or even drinking tea. He stood in a bay window, his back to her. She crossed to join him and looked out into the desert's sandy expanse, drifting clouds casting dark patterns on the tan surface. The lowering sun told her it was late afternoon.

"Talal?" she said. "Talal, what is it?"

He took so long to answer she'd almost given up before he turned to her. She wanted to flinch from the sadness in his dark eyes, afraid of what he might be about to tell her.

"King Hakeem's call was to let us know we'll have

to leave Kholi as soon as possible. He suggested tomorrow and he's offered his private jet."

Taken aback, she asked, "Why? What's happened?"

"I told him we'd be on our way before noon tomorrow."

"You haven't said why."

"Basheem Khaldun is dead. Though he's the last of his immediate family, others are related to the Khalduns. I'll be held responsible for Basheem's death and the king fears they may target me for a retaliation assassination. He believes I'll be safer in America for the time being, until tempers cool."

She put a hand to her heart. "You mean you're in danger of being killed?"

His attempt at a smile didn't reach his eyes. "Maybe in Kholi. Not in America."

She tried to feel relieved, but it was clear he hadn't yet told her everything and the heaviness in her chest remained. "Did Basheem wake enough to talk before he died?" she asked.

The muscles tensed in Talal's face as though he was gritting his teeth. "Not after we left." He put an arm around her shoulders and led her to a white wicker settee where he pulled her down beside him.

"I was able to speak to Basheem before we left," he said.

"Why didn't you tell me!" she cried. "Did he say where my daughter is?"

"He told me a story I couldn't bring myself to repeat to you immediately. I wanted to bring you here, where we could be alone together, first. I planned to tell you in the morning, but Basheem's death means you'll have to hear everything now."

Her urge to demand he hurry faded with each word

he said as she began to realize Basheem's story might
be one she'd rather not hear.

Talal took a deep breath. "Basheem was not a party
to the abduction of your daughter. As you know, another cousin was with Malik. But Basheem was waiting
for them at the airport when they returned from America. Linnea—" He paused and took her hand.

She gripped his hand hard, her entire body tense with
dread.

"Malik came off the plane with the baby completely
swathed in a blanket despite the heat. Basheem soon
realized the swathing was so those on the plane
wouldn't realize the truth. Somewhere en route to Kholi,
your daughter died—possibly from her heart condition.
She was dead when Malik carried her off the plane."

Linnea heard herself whimpering, but it was as
though the sound came from another woman because at
first she couldn't control it. She clung to Talal's hand
so frantically that hers began to ache. At last she was
able to swallow her grief so it stuck in her throat instead
of emerging in whimpers. "What—what did Malik do
then?" she asked.

"After he swore his two cousins to secrecy, they took
the baby into the desert that same night and buried her.
No one ever asked what became of the child."

Tears rolled down Linnea's face. "My baby's been
dead all these years. All these years I've searched for
her and she's been dead. I'll never even know where
her grave is. Why didn't he tell me?" Her voice broke
on the last few words.

Talal tried to put his arm around her but she resisted,
saying, "There's more to the story."

He nodded. "Three years later, when the king demanded Malik's daughter be brought to him, Basheem

panicked. With Malik and the other cousin both dead, he feared the king's wrath would fall on him if Malik's daughter couldn't be produced. King Hakeem wouldn't take kindly to the truth, and there was no one left to punish except Basheem. So he searched orphanages until he found a child of the right age whose eyes matched Malik's description of his daughter's eye color. With the real birth certificate and the baby ring that had been among Malik's belongings inherited by him when Malik was killed, he arranged to have the child sent to the king. You know the rest.''

''Widad's daughter,'' she said brokenly. ''He hunted Widad down and forced her to do his bidding. How could he be so cruel?''

''When you arrived in Kholi and Basheem heard the rumor that the king had sent me to find the man who was guilty of the hoax, he lost his head completely. That's why he tried to get rid of you.''

''Involving Widad in his schemes. I feel so sorry for her.'' She laid a hand on his arm. ''Please intercede—''

''I can't. Widad is dead.''

Linnea gaped at him. ''The king?'' she cried in dismay. ''Did he have her killed?''

''Widad escaped from the palace and found her way to the hospital, bursting into Basheem's room and stabbed him even as he lay dying. She was killed by the men guarding him.''

Remembering Widad's sinister smile, Linnea said sadly, ''How she hated him, that poor abused woman. Oh, Talal…'' She flung herself into his arms, sobbing.

In bed that night Talal held his wife close, experiencing her sorrow as his own. Linnea was inconsolable, feeling bad about Widad's death as well as trying to cope with the grief of knowing she'd never hold her daughter in her arms again.

He understood. Hadn't he lost his own newborn son? But he realized there was nothing he could say now that would ease her suffering, so he tried to show how he felt by holding her in his arms, offering her the dubious comfort of his presence. Or maybe not so dubious. By the way she nestled against him, he knew she needed him there and that meant more to him than anything else in the world.

Love was more than the fondness he'd felt for his first wife, more than the lust a pretty woman evoked. Lust could be a part of love, but love, he was learning, involved so much more. Among other things, love meant the beloved was so important to you that you put her before yourself.

He loved Linnea. And he meant to keep her with him no matter how many problems remained to be solved.

Chapter Sixteen

The room was still dark when Linnea awoke. For a moment or two she relished Talal's warmth next to her, then she remembered. Her daughter, her baby Yasmin was dead. Though grief rose to clog her throat, she'd gone beyond tears.

She tried to ease away from Talal without waking him but failed as his arms tightened around her. "Linnea," he murmured.

Comfort lay in his embrace but she didn't want to be comforted. The ache in her throat eased as she remembered her chosen daughter waiting for her in Nevada. She pictured her changeling's smiling face, her sweet voice saying "Mama." She was Yasmin's mother, the only mother the girl had really ever had. And Talal—Linnea blinked at the realization their marriage made Talal Yasmin's father. They'd care for her together.

"Dawn comes swiftly in the desert," he said. "We

will dress and meet the sunrise." He kissed her forehead, released her and slid from the bed.

Linnea rose, belatedly remembering they'd be leaving
Kholi today. She was going home to America. With
Talal. But the elation she'd expected to feel at leaving
this country that had brought her such grief was muted.
Though she looked forward to being in her own country
again, how did Talal feel about being exiled from his?
She knew he loved Kholi.

In the relative cool before the sun rose, they walked
hand in hand away from the oasis of the house into the
barren sands on the other side of the walls. The sky had
lightened enough so Linnea could see the vastness
stretching before her, seemingly endless, majestic in its
own way but frightening, too.

When the first streak of rose tinted the eastern sky,
Talal stopped and put his arm around her shoulders
while they both stared up at the first sign of the coming
day.

"Because of the stars, my favorite time is night," he
said. "Dawn is a close second."

The pink intensified, joined by reds and oranges, colors across the entire red spectrum. The sand beneath
their feet no longer seemed inert, lifeless, as the increasing light picked out different shades of warm browns
and tans.

When the red edge of the sun moved above the horizon, scattering light over this desert world, Linnea
drew in her breath, awed, understanding at this moment
why primitive people had greeted each sunrise with in-
cantations. In modern times it was easy to forget that
the sun brought life to every living creature on earth.

Talal drew her closer, gesturing toward the vast desert with his free hand. "My son was born and died out there in the midst of the sandstorm that killed his mother as she tried to flee to her people because she misconstrued my actions. I was never unfaithful to her but she couldn't believe that.

"I've been a long time in forgiving her, but now, I see, she did what she had to do, misguided though it might have been."

He turned to look at her, his dark eyes luminous with love. "Omar's lines remind us we're not the first to suffer loss. 'For some we loved, the loveliest and the best…one by one crept silently to rest.'

"My son, like your baby daughter, lies underneath these sands, at peace, a part of the earth as we all are."

She heard his love for her in his voice as well as seeing it in his eyes. She felt his love in the tender way he held her. The ache in her throat vanished as did her resentment of his country. Kholi had taken her baby but had also given her Talal to love, as well as one of its own children, little Yasmin, to nurture and cherish. Talal, she'd come to realize, needed her love as much as Yasmin.

She'd never forget her baby daughter, but the past was beyond change. Ahead lay a future full of love and happiness. Without pausing to realize what she meant to do, Linnea freed herself from Talal and raised her arms to the sun, embracing life.

And then she turned and flung her arms around the man she'd married, the man she'd love forever. "Did I ever tell you how much I love you?" she whispered.

He bent his head to kiss her, and as their lips met, the sun rose completely above the horizon, flooding the desert, flooding them with light.

Epilogue

"And so the brave mother faced the Ghoul." Bemusedly, Linnea listened to Talal's deep voice telling Yasmin the rest of the story he'd begun before they left her in Nevada. How happy she was to be back here again!

"'You can't have my daughter,' the mother said," Talal continued. "'I love her and will never give her up. Begone! Go back to your evil dwelling and don't bother us again.' The Ghoul howled in rage, but he was no match for her bravery and her love. So he disappeared in a puff of smoke, and the mother and the daughter lived happily ever after."

"With a father," Linnea added. "With the daddy."

Yasmin, sitting between them on the couch in Zed's living room, looked at Linnea, then at Talal for confirmation. "Daddy?" she said tentatively.

He picked her up and hugged her. "Daddy," he repeated.

"My daddy?"

"Yours. Otherwise how can we three live happily ever after?" He gazed over Yasmin's head at Linnea, his eyes promising her all the happiness he could give.

Danny squirmed down from Zed's knee and walked to the couch. "*My* Daddy T," he exclaimed, laying a possessive hand on Talal's knee.

Karen sighed but Zed chuckled. "Let's see you get out of this one," he said to his twin.

"I'm Yasmin's daddy, too," Talal said, tousling Danny's hair. "Just like Zed is your Daddy Z and Erin's daddy at the same time."

Linnea smiled, admiring Talal's explanation. Eventually Danny would be old enough to understand the complicated relationships but, for now, this was a happy solution.

Danny's scowl lightened. He reached up and tugged at Yasmin's shirt. "*My* Yasmin," he said, looking around as if daring anyone to oppose him.

"*Aiwa,*" Yasmin said, wriggling down from Talal's lap until she stood on the floor beside the boy. "*My* Danny," she said, taking his hand.

Listening to the grown-up's laughter, both children smiled and Linnea's heart overflowed with her sense of belonging. Like the mother in Talal's story, she'd banished the Ghoul. The bad times were behind her, now she was part of this wonderful family, she had her beloved chosen daughter and she was loved by the only man she could ever want. Maybe living happily ever after wasn't a fairy tale, after all.

* * * * *

MARILYN PAPPANO

**Concludes the
twelve-book series—
36 Hours—in June 1998
with the final installment**

YOU MUST REMEMBER THIS

Who was "Martin Smith"? The sexy stranger had swept into town in the midst of catastrophe, with no name and no clue to his past. Shy, innocent Julie Crandall found herself fascinated—and willing to risk everything to be by his side. But as the shocking truth regarding his identity began to emerge, Julie couldn't help but wonder if the *real* man would prove simply too hot to handle.

For Martin and Julie and *all* the residents of Grand Springs, Colorado, the storm-induced blackout had been just the beginning of 36 Hours that changed *everything*—and guaranteed a lifetime forecast of happiness for twelve very special couples.

Available at your favorite retail outlet.

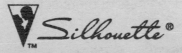

MATERNITY LEAVE

Coming September 1998

Three delightful stories about the blessings
and surprises of "Labor" Day.

TABLOID BABY by Candace Camp

She was whisked to the hospital in the nick of time....

THE NINE-MONTH KNIGHT
by Cait London

A down-on-her-luck secretary is experiencing
odd little midnight cravings....

THE PATERNITY TEST by Sherryl Woods

The stick turned blue before her
biological clock struck twelve....

*These three special women are very pregnant...and very
single, although they won't be either for too much longer,
because baby—and Daddy—are on their way!*

Available at your favorite retail outlet.

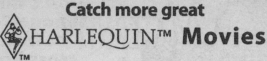

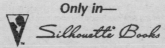

In **July 1998** comes

THE MACKENZIE FAMILY

by *New York Times* bestselling author

LINDA HOWARD

The dynasty continues with:

Mackenzie's Pleasure: Rescuing a pampered ambassador's daughter from her terrorist kidnappers was a piece of cake for navy SEAL Zane Mackenzie. It was only afterward, when they were alone together, that the real danger began....

Mackenzie's Magic: Talented trainer Maris Mackenzie was wanted for horse theft, but with no memory, she had little chance of proving her innocence or eluding the real villains. Her only hope for salvation? The stranger in her bed.

Available this July for the first time ever in a two-in-one trade-size edition. Fall in love with the Mackenzies for the first time—or all over again!

Available at your favorite retail outlet.

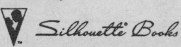

Silhouette Books